Unobserved, Is[...] could.

His tunic was finely woven, his attire of the old-fashioned longer sort, rather than the ridiculously short doublets men of rank were wearing lately. His hair was not as dark as she'd first thought, but a sort of tawny chestnut, and that, too, was not of a fashionable cut but lay close to his skull, falling just short of his collar.

It was as she wondered yet again why someone so young should be so serious that his head turned and his eyes locked on hers. And for the life of her, this time, she couldn't snatch her gaze away. Her surroundings all faded to nothing as a strange sort of excitement billowed at the bottom of her stomach.

And in its wake, a sense of awareness oozed along her nerves that had nothing to do with their encounter in the lane, for she'd had the same feelings when they'd stared at each other in the square. It was as if she'd always known him, this man who she didn't know at all. And worse, he looked back at her as if he, too, felt the same.

Author Note

I've always been fascinated by the Wars of the Roses and the turbulent period of English history that spanned the deposition of Richard II in 1399 and the usurpation of Richard III in 1485. Until recently, much of what was written about this time focused on the fate of kings and the ambitions of the nobility but ignored the lives of ordinary people, whose existence was rarely documented by the chroniclers of the age. However, in between the sporadic and brutal battles, daily life went on as usual, and it is during one of these uneasy lulls that Hal and Isolda's story takes place. The setting is my favorite Shropshire town of Ludlow, which witnessed one of the early confrontations between the houses of Lancaster and York, and while doing my research, to my unexpected delight, I discovered the medieval ancestors of our modern "piggy banks"—look out for them!

ALLIANCE WITH HER RENEGADE KNIGHT

LISSA MORGAN

Harlequin
HISTORICAL

If you purchased this book without a cover you should be aware that this book is stolen property. It was reported as "unsold and destroyed" to the publisher, and neither the author nor the publisher has received any payment for this "stripped book."

ISBN-13: 978-1-335-54022-5

Alliance with Her Renegade Knight

Copyright © 2025 by Lissa Morgan

All rights reserved. No part of this book may be used or reproduced in any manner whatsoever without written permission.

Without limiting the author's and publisher's exclusive rights, any unauthorized use of this publication to train generative artificial intelligence (AI) technologies is expressly prohibited.

This is a work of fiction. Names, characters, places and incidents are either the product of the author's imagination or are used fictitiously. Any resemblance to actual persons, living or dead, businesses, companies, events or locales is entirely coincidental.

For questions and comments about the quality of this book, please contact us at CustomerService@Harlequin.com.

TM and ® are trademarks of Harlequin Enterprises ULC.

 Harlequin Enterprises ULC
22 Adelaide St. West, 41st Floor
Toronto, Ontario M5H 4E3, Canada
www.Harlequin.com

Recycling programs for this product may not exist in your area.

Printed in U.S.A.

Lissa Morgan hails from Wales but has traveled far and wide over the years, usually in search of the next new job, and always pursuing her love of the past along the way. A history graduate and former archivist, she now works in website design and academia. Lissa lives between the mountains and the sea in rugged North West Wales, surrounded by medieval castles that provide the perfect inspiration for her writing—the best job of all! Visit her at lissamorgan.com, Facebook.com/lissamorganhistoricalromance and X @lissamorganauth.

Books by Lissa Morgan

Harlequin Historical

The Welsh Lord's Convenient Bride
An Alliance with His Enemy Princess

The Warriors of Wales

The Warrior's Reluctant Wife
The Warrior's Forbidden Maiden

Visit the Author Profile page at Harlequin.com.

To Kate Walker

For her friendship and fabulous writing courses

Chapter One

Ludlow, October 1459

'Who would have thought to see Proud Cis brought so low? How shaming for her!'

Isolda, standing at the window and looking down onto the town square, nodded in response to her mother's remark. 'Yes, but how brave she is.' She pressed her nose closer to the glass. 'She has more courage than her husband, at any rate!'

All of Ludlow knew by now that Richard, Duke of York, had fled during the night, reluctant to take up arms against his sovereign, abandoning his men, his castle and his town to the mercy of the Lancastrian army. His two eldest sons had flown with him, leaving his Duchess, Cecily Neville, to face the King alone on this bleak October morning.

King Henry entered the square, flanked by his captains, the Dukes of Buckingham and Exeter. The pious monarch was almost insignificant in comparison to the two Lancastrian lords, with their scarlet cloaks billowing and golden armour gleaming. Cecily, on the other hand, with her daughter and two youngest sons beside her, stood like a bastion of all that was left of Yorkist honour.

York's flight had shocked the whole town. Ludlow was the Duke's holding and as such would suffer for his challenge to the Crown. Their punishment had already begun, for as soon as the Yorkist forces had scattered, the Lancastrian soldiery had swarmed across Ludford Bridge and into the town to plunder, pillage and despoil.

Here in the square, however, all was calm as the Duchess awaited the King, looking like an ice queen, too proud and disdainful to walk towards him.

'Surely she'll lose her freedom, even her life, for this.' Isolda's mother's voice was filled with awe. 'If for no other reason but as a scapegoat for her husband's treachery.'

Isolda shook her head. 'I think the King will consider her of more value alive than dead. Besides which, they are cousins.' Not that that meant Cecily would be safe, since it seemed kin fought against kin more fiercely than ever since Harry Bolingbroke of Lancaster had deposed King Richard and claimed the throne, half a century ago.

But nevertheless she was proved right. The King approached and the Duchess curtseyed and awaited his pleasure, or otherwise. There was a moment's pause and then Henry took Cecily's hands and drew her courteously upwards. Weak, indecisive, and some said feeble of mind, he was not the man to take out his wrath on a woman, especially one so imperious.

Isolda opened the window, eager to hear what words would pass between them, but the pane swung wide, whipped by the wind, and banged on the wall. In the excitement the noise went unnoticed by those below, and she leaned out to draw it to again, balancing precariously on the sill, for the upper storey of their house jutted out into the square. A head lifted in the crowd below and a face turned skywards.

It was a young face, though the brow was furrowed and the mouth set so sternly it seemed it had never smiled, while his eyes were equally sober, though arresting. Time seemed to slow, the noise from the square and the streets faded and the air grew still, yet taut with something other than the excitement below. Isolda felt her heart start to thud and her breath got stuck in her throat.

They stared at each other for an eternity it seemed and although she knew she'd never met nor seen this man before, yet…she felt she'd known him all her life.

And then the moment was shattered as trumpets blared and the crowd began to disperse, boots and hooves drumming on the cobbles. The square emptied slowly, the nobles going to find accommodation in gentle houses for the coming nights, while the Duchess of York, accompanied by the royal party and the major lords of the realm, went through the gated arch of Ludlow's great castle and disappeared from view.

The young knight moved off too and Isolda watched him go, her mind awhirl and her heart still fluttering. It was a long time since a man had looked at her so frankly. There had been no scorn or dislike on his face, which was the usual way a man surveyed her, if he met her eyes at all. She was an unmarried woman in the largely male world of the wool trade and to her fellow merchants she was outspoken, an anomaly and a threat.

If her mother had taken over the business after the death of her husband, lost at sea en route to Bruges on a stormy January sailing three years previously, that would have been acceptable. But Agnes Breydon had gone to live with her ailing sister in Tewkesbury, only returning to visit her daughter from time to time.

It was Isolda who had the zest and the head for trade,

inherited from her father, Jacob. And although her mother had begged her to give it up, leave this town on the turbulent Welsh Marches and go to the gentler and kinder landscape of Tewkesbury, she refused. Even if she hadn't loved the town and the wool trade she would have carried on the business because, after the death of her brother, Dieric, she liked to think her father would have finally recognised her abilities, perhaps even have approved.

The church bell rang the hour and the daylight began to creep away, casting shadows over the square below. Moving away from the window, Isolda listened to her mother's footsteps descending the wooden stairs to the ground floor.

'I'll get supper going early.' Agnes's voice drifted upwards. 'Lord only knows what this night will bring.'

Her mother had aged these last years, the change made more startling as Agnes visited less and less lately. Isolda sighed. Should she have gone to Tewkesbury after all? Had she done the right thing by taking over the business and trying to make her own living as the wool trade declined year by year? Should she have married and been content to keep house, help her husband, look after her mother?

So many 'shoulds', but she'd made her choices and she would see them through. If Agnes's health deteriorated, perhaps she would have to give up the business one day, go to Tewkesbury and care for her. But she would never take a husband, come what may. She'd considered marriage once and that had been lesson enough never to consider it again!

Robert, her former betrothed, had taught her well that not only could men not be trusted, but one's own feelings could be just as deceptive, even more so in her case. Because she'd not been sure of her feelings towards him, she'd considered other, more practical, reasons for marriage, all of which had gone against everything she believed in.

And now, looking back, she knew if she *had* married him she'd have lost her pride, her freedom, even her soul, and become a laughing stock in the bargain, since he was already married!

Shaking away the angry indignation that still rankled even now, three years later, Isolda took up a candle from the table and made her way downstairs. Turning into the shop at the bottom, she checked the bolts were secure on the front door before passing through into the hall and from there into the kitchen.

Her mother was at the hearth, her back bowed as she busied herself over pots and pans. 'I'll get the hens into the hutch for the night,' Isolda said, putting the candle down and crossing to the back door. 'Lest they be filched by some thieving Lancastrian.'

Stepping out into the garden, she called to the hens. They came willingly, for the nights encroached quickly now. But as she tied the door of the hutch securely she noticed a pall of smoke against the sky, rising from the direction of the Linney Gate.

Isolda stared, the acrid sting of smoke reaching her nose, the sound of crackling timber growing louder and louder. From somewhere to the east of the town a gun sounded, making her heart turn over, and all at once the autumn afternoon sank into twilight.

The smoke was billowing upwards fiercely now, some unlucky merchant or vintner's house being robbed of its riches no doubt. Or even the church itself, for soldiers drunk with victory had no thought for man or God. A cold dread slipped down her spine Would their house be next? At least they lived on the western edge of the square, very near the castle, and hopefully that would be deterrent enough.

But fire or guns or looting, it made no difference. She would have to venture out that night, come what may.

Henry Wevere left the Rose and Crown, hoping that that was the last of them. This was the third tavern he and his squire had cleared of errant Lancastrian soldiers, and this one had been dangerously near to violence.

He leaned against the side of a wall for a moment and cast his eyes around the dark square. It frequently happened after battles, to greater or lesser extent, the looting that got out of hand the freer the ale from broken barrels flowed. The soldiers, especially those pressed reluctantly into fighting, felt it was their due to plunder and rape in the towns and villages. Unchecked, they molested and even destroyed those unlucky souls that got in their way—as his family had got in the way of the Yorkists at St Albans...

Swallowing down the familiar surge of guilt, Hal roused himself and walked on, his squire following behind him with the lantern. Thankfully, none of the men under his rule were still in the town now curfew approached, but were encamped with the main army in the meadows outside the walls.

Most of the victorious Lancastrian lords had turned a blind eye to the looting and even encouraged it, to replenish royal coffers as much as retribution for York's heinous crime against the King. He, however, wasn't that sort of commander.

But it was more than duty that brought him onto the streets of Ludlow. He couldn't bring his parents and siblings back, but he could at least try to ensure that others didn't suffer a like fate at the hands of soldiery out of all control.

It had been a sunny morning in May four years ago that his life had changed. The battle at St Albans, an overwhelming victory for York, hadn't lasted more than an hour. But Hal had relived that hour over and over since then. Every burning brazier, every camp fire, every flicker of a flame in the hearth or in a sconce on a wall brought it vividly, terribly, back to him.

Fire had taken his family away in a tragedy that should never have been, but he had escaped because he wasn't at home when he ought to have been, when he'd *promised* to be.

Swallowing down the bile of remorse that filled his throat, Hal strode on through the October evening, the streets quieter now as the darkness thickened. Several houses belonging to rich wool merchants and clothiers, silversmiths and vintners had been looted, and in one instance a servant had been killed trying to protect his master's goods, the culprits getting clean away.

'If whoever murdered that poor wretch knows what's good for him, Hal,' his squire muttered from behind, 'he'll make tracks as quick as he can.'

Hal concurred, pulling his hood up as a light rain began to fall and the evening turned colder. 'He's deserted, no doubt, and slunk back to whatever cesspit he hails from.'

They crossed the square, the cobbles shining in the lights from the houses that flanked it and the glow of torchlight from the castle gatehouse. The marketplace was almost empty now, where it had been full to bursting earlier that afternoon. The townsfolk, apart from one or two braver souls, were staying wisely behind bolted doors until the rampaging was over, saving their lives at least, if not their goods.

Hal glanced towards the house on the far corner of the row nearest the castle, where the woman had leaned out to shut the window. It had only been a moment but in that short time he'd seen everything—the long, thick plait of golden hair that hung over one shoulder, the full mouth that had scowled at him, the wide eyes set in a pretty and determined face.

For a mad instant he'd thought of asking one of the townspeople gathered around who she was, but to what point? Likely he'd be gone in a day or two and, from the sack that hung over the door, she was clearly wed to one of the town's wool merchants. He wasn't the sort of man to wed anyone, let alone steal another man's wife—although once upon a time he'd evaded many an outraged husband. But yet...as their eyes had locked and held, he'd almost wished that he was.

Her beauty had reached down to him, as if she'd stretched out a hand, though she hadn't, of course. And even if she had, playing the coquette like so many did, he wouldn't have taken it—though he'd have been sorely tempted. But with love, even the lightest and most fleeting kind, came an end eventually, be it the wounding of a heart or merely a prickle to the pride.

He'd felt that prickle many times but his heart had never been wounded by a woman, because he had never given it to anyone. The death of his entire family had taught him how unbearable loss was when people you loved were taken away from you and he never wanted to experience that loss ever again.

Suddenly a scream rent the air, coming from one of the nearby streets, followed by ugly laughter. Hal gestured to Simon and set off in the direction of the disturbance. The cause of it wasn't long in the finding. Halfway down a narrow lane, two figures were locked in a monumental but ill-matched struggle.

One was a man, bareheaded but wearing the hauberk and long boots of a bowman. The other was the tall but slight figure of a woman, her hair flying about her shoulders as her assailant bent her this way and that. As he heard their running feet the man turned and, still holding his victim fast, issued a growling warning.

'Gerrowt o' 'ere! Find yer own piece o' skirt!'

Hal slowed as caution tempered urgency. The fellow was tough-looking, more wiry than muscular, and the last thing he wanted was to draw his sword. Equally, he had no idea of what weapon the man carried, or whether he would be quick to use it.

And then, taking advantage of the moment of distraction, the woman squirmed free, writhing and hissing like an enraged serpent. But, instead of taking to her heels, she swung her arm and dealt the archer a punch in the face. He tottered for a moment and then fell backwards like a tree before an axe.

Hal, dashing forward, was forced to duck as the woman's arm swung again, this time at him, blindly and in panic. 'Hold hard!' he cried, raising his palms. 'You have nothing to fear from me, mistress.'

Two wide eyes glared at him through a mane of dishevelled hair. 'Don't come any closer!'

Simon, keeping a cautious distance too, stooped to the man on the ground. 'Senseless and dead drunk, from the stench of him,' he said. 'And wearing the livery of FitzAlan.'

'Can you get him back to his camp by yourself?' Hal asked, his eyes not on the prone figure on the ground but on the woman, poised like a hart about to leap. 'Better that than the town gaol.'

His squire nodded. 'I suspect he's heavier than he looks, but I reckon I can carry him over my shoulder.'

Simon, a strong lad of nineteen from Evesham, had been his squire for only two months, since he himself had been knighted, but in that time they'd become firm friends.

'Right,' decided Hal. 'Let's get him up.'

Together they got the archer over Simon's shoulder and his man lumbered away, leaving him with the lantern. Hal turned back to the woman and held the light aloft.

She'd composed herself somewhat. Her hood was pulled up over her head and her cloak was wrapped tightly around her. She still hadn't run but she stood firm, proud even, as if daring him to do his worst. He wondered why—and then he realised that the alley behind her was blocked by a cart that had lost a wheel and some broken barrels. Some poor vintner's cellar was being ransacked no doubt, the looters drinking as much wine as they stole. There was no sound or sight of anyone there now, but that didn't mean the looters had left.

'What's your name, mistress?' he asked, taking a cautious step towards her, to avoid another swing of that useful right fist as much as not to alarm her further. 'Are you injured in any way?'

There was no reply but she granted him a small shake of her head.

'Very well,' he conceded. 'There's no reason you should tell me your name, of course, but for God's sake come forward and I'll escort you home.'

This time she replied, her voice without a tremor, despite the rough handling she'd received at the hands of the bowman. 'No.'

'No?' he echoed.

'Why would I go anywhere with you, when I do not know who you are, except that you are a Lancastrian.'

The last word was spat out with venom, but at least it was a response.

'The extremity of the situation made me forget my manners.' He bowed. 'My name is Henry Wevere and I am indeed a Lancastrian, a knight in the service of John Talbot, Earl of Shrewsbury.'

'Given the behaviour of your comrades in this town this day...' she tossed her head '...the last thing I require is assistance from you, Sir Henry.'

Hal moved the lantern nearer and peered closer and recognised, with a vividness that went beyond sight, the full mouth, the high cheekbones, the wide-set eyes that he'd glimpsed as she'd leaned out of the window of the wool merchant's house that afternoon.

He'd never thought to see her again, and certainly not out alone at night, nor so hostile—although that was perhaps understandable under the circumstances.

'Either way, mistress—' he beckoned to her '—let us make haste out of this alleyway, if you please.'

Hal got no further. A door banged to his left and he spun around towards the sound, just as the lantern was knocked from his hand. Something thick and heavy came down over his head and suddenly everything was utter darkness. His heart started to pound hard against his ribs and stark fear chilled his blood.

He struggled with all his might against whatever giant seemed bent on crushing the life out of him, but his arms were pinioned tightly to his sides and he fell to his knees.

A vicious kick in the small of his back sent him sprawling and, gritting his teeth and tasting blood, Hal braced himself for the knifing that would surely follow.

But, in place of a blade, the woman's voice came instead. 'No, Jac! Don't harm him further. He came to my assistance so... I owe him that, if nothing else.'

There was an answering and unintelligible grunt and, as a farewell gift, his assailant gave him another kick, this time in his gut. Hal gasped and doubled in pain as the sound of feet running fast and away filled his ears.

He lay still for a moment, fighting for breath and calming his nerves. There was only silence now and, wriggling up onto his knees, he dragged the covering off his head and gulped gratefully of cool fresh air. He leapt to his feet but the lane was empty now, apart from the cart and barrels further down. The woman was gone and so was his attacker, as completely as if they'd never been there.

Hal stared down at the thing in his hand, but he needed no lantern light to tell him what it was, since the distinctive cloth and pungent smell was enough.

It was a wool sack.

Chapter Two

All Saints' Day, three weeks later

Isolda made sure that she was the last to enter the church and then slipped in through the inner doors of the porch, shutting them softly behind her. The mass had already started when, a few moments later, she joined her mother in the southern aisle. There she bowed her head, a little out of breath, a smile hovering about her mouth.

Unlike everyone else, however, her head wasn't bowed in memory of the lives of the saints in heaven—far from it!

Gradually, her heart began to slow from its frantic pounding, when she sensed with a jolt that perhaps her entrance hadn't gone unnoticed after all, for her face tingled with the awareness of someone's scrutinising eyes. Isolda glanced around from person to person, but all of them had their heads bowed too. Then, looking across the nave to the northern aisle, she found the Lancastrian knight of three weeks earlier looking straight back at her.

A thrill ran through her and quickly she snatched her eyes away. Had he seen her come in? And, if so, had he recognised her? And, if he had, was he here to demand why her companion, Jac, had put a sack over his head, bundled him to the ground, kicked him in the midriff and left him helpless in the lane?

But what else could they have done? Even if he had come to her aid when that oaf of an archer had accosted her, her rescuer, for all his apparent good intent, would have upset their plans that night.

Under her lashes, she glanced across at him again. He seemed none the worse for the rough treatment her apprentice had dealt him. In fact, now in the light of day, bareheaded and dressed in a soft woollen cloak of grey with a darker tunic below, instead of armour and doublet, he was even more comely than when she'd stared blatantly down at him from her window.

What had his name been—Wevere? That was it. Sir Henry Wevere, a knight in the service of the Earl of Shrewsbury, to whom the town had been given following the Yorkist flight three weeks earlier. The King and his nobles had long gone, leaving the castle in the care of Edmund de la Mare, a loyal Lancastrian.

Isolda moved her lips absently as a prayer began. The knight's head was bowed too now, his arms folded over his chest, but his lips weren't moving. Perhaps he wasn't a godly man—or perhaps he wasn't here to pray at all!

Unobserved, Isolda studied him as best she could. His tunic was finely woven, his attire of the old-fashioned longer sort, rather than the ridiculously short doublets men of rank were wearing lately. His hair was not as dark as she'd first thought, but a tawny chestnut, falling just short of his collar.

It was as she wondered yet again why someone so young should be so serious that his head turned and his eyes locked on hers. And for the life of her, this time she couldn't snatch her gaze away. The voice of the priest, the hissing of the candles, the stench of the people packed in the church faded to nothing as a strange sort of excitement billowed at the bottom of her stomach.

And in its wake a sense of awareness rippled along her nerves that had nothing to do with their encounter in the lane, for she'd had the same feeling when they'd stared at each other in the square. It was as if she'd always known him, this man who she didn't know at all. And worse, he looked back at her as if he too felt the same.

Isolda jumped as her mother touched her arm. 'Mass has ended, daughter.'

She bowed with everyone else as the priest and his choir passed into the vestry, the organ accompanying their departure. Then people began to file towards the south door, the great ones among them going first, leaving the lesser folk to follow.

The knight had already gone before, according to his status, his head and shoulders visible above almost all the congregation, which had come to an abrupt halt, the foremost of them already in the south porch. And then a loud bellowing rolled down the nave and echoed up to the domed roof.

'God's wounds! Here's another one! Pinned up *inside* the porch door this time! And on this day of all days! Devil take the rascal!'

Isolda fought down a bubble of laughter and, taking her mother's hand, began to edge towards the west door, not used by the congregation nowadays since the building of the new bell tower had begun. She had no intention of lingering, as the rest of the merchants would do, tutting and shaking their heads at this latest audacity, but would instead slip out unnoticed.

However, even as they navigated the crush in the nave,

a figure stepped into her path and Isolda found herself staring once more into the sombre eyes of Henry Wevere. She was startled to discover their colour was somewhere between green and hazel, with flecks of gold around the iris. They were beautiful—and compelling—but the parchment he held in his hand sent a shiver down her spine.

'No one is allowed to leave the church just yet...so if you'll bide awhile, ladies.'

Hal had to suppress a smile as the look of shock on her face disappeared behind a mask of demure compliance. She inclined her head and backed away, drawing herself and the older woman who accompanied her into the crowd. But if she thought he couldn't see her any longer she was wrong.

At his shoulder the priest appeared, and at the other stood Ralph Shearman, the town bailiff and one of the most powerful and vocal of Ludlow's wool merchants. With an exquisitely gloved hand, the bailiff pointed at the paper that had been discovered on the church door.

'By the Rood, the fellow will hang for this!'

Hal made no reply but looked down at the poem in his hand. It was a scurrilous and eloquent attack, written in an educated but irreverent hand, on the merchants and wealthy folk of the town. It wasn't the first time he'd read such a tirade, for copies of previous ones had been sent to Lord John Talbot, since the Earl had taken over jurisdiction of the town.

And so his overlord had sent him to investigate in his stead, due to his background in trade and his self-taught knowledge of law, more than any military skill. But Hal didn't fool himself for a moment that his nocturnal encounter with the woman of the window hadn't been a factor in his acceptance of the task.

And now here she was, doing her best to appear as meek as any pious parishioner, and looking nothing like the slippery wench he'd tried to rescue in Narrow Lane, where he'd got a kick in the ribs for his trouble. The words she'd hissed to his attacker had niggled at him ever since. Who was he, that man who had come out of nowhere and might well have slit his throat if it hadn't been for her? And who was *she*?

Hal turned away from that conundrum and, requesting quiet in the church, was granted it. Then he began to read the rhyme aloud, one eye on the parchment, the other scanning the faces of the listeners for any sign of recognition and guilt, coming back time and again to one face in particular.

Wappys and bees though small do be free.
Fly high as they might, they sting where they 'light.
Lest ye be the next to be bit and sore vexed,
Hark this their just song, and make right a great wrong.

The poem ran on for another three verses, becoming more ribald and accusing with every line. Sniggers and hoots began to break out from some of the listeners but from the rich and the prosperous came a torrent of curses and more than one fist shook furiously in the air.

As the reading finished and the priest addressed his wayward flock, begging for silence and decorum, Hal didn't know which camp he belonged in, the accused or the accusers. But the urge to join in the merriment should have told him plain enough where his preference lay.

He looked to where the woman stood. She was laughing too and her eyes twinkled with something akin to triumph. No need to guess which camp *she* was in then, although, from her dress, she belonged to the higher classes of the town not the lower. A sympathiser—or a defector?

Sensing his stare, her head turned and the gleam in her eyes became a blaze of defiance. The sunlight that came in through the great window over the west door caught the wisps of golden hair that peeped out from under her coif. The clear brow and delicate cheekbones were illuminated with a sort of brilliance as she tilted her chin higher.

Intrigued by that rebellious gesture, Hal let his gaze linger. The colour of her eyes might have matched any of the glorious hues reflecting from the glass behind him, and he found himself wanting to know their exact shade, like a final detail in that perfect picture before him.

He was almost tempted to step closer and do exactly that but a voice at his elbow dragged him back to the matter of the poem. Turning to the bailiff, and the group of merchants who'd assembled around him, Hal held up a hand and the whole church fell silent.

'My lord John Talbot, Earl of Shrewsbury, has given this matter his attention and has appointed me to act as his inquirer here. You can be assured that whomsoever person or persons that are penning these attacks will soon be apprehended and brought to justice. And now, I advise you to return to your homes.'

'No, by God! I'm not going anywhere until I hear how exactly you mean to go about it.'

Hal looked at Ralph Shearman and disliked him at once. The man was arrogance personified, and his clothing alone would have fed a poor family for a year.

'If I am to catch the fellow,' he replied, 'announcing my methods to the whole town here would hardly be wise.'

The bailiff's mouth dropped open but Hal dismissed him from his mind. Instead, over Shearman's shoulder, he watched the woman of the window filing out with the rest of the common folk, even though she was clearly of a higher station. And, remembering the wool sack over her door, he wondered...where was her husband?

Storing that curiosity for later, he addressed Shearman again. 'But by all means,' he said with all the patience he could muster, 'come to the castle this afternoon at the hour of None and we will discuss the solution to this problem.'

There was a muttering of disgruntled acquiescence and the great and the good began to disperse too. Hal followed in their wake and outside, halting at the market cross in front of the church, he noted the different directions people took as they returned to their shops and houses.

Later he and Simon would go to those houses and get names and other information, but there was something that couldn't wait for later. Slipping the rolled-up parchment into the pouch at his belt, he strode purposefully in the direction of the wool merchant's house.

Isolda knew, without knowing how she knew, that Henry Wevere would appear at her door, but she didn't expect it to be within the half hour of arriving home! When the knock came she was in the hall, pouring a cup of warm ale for her mother. Her hand paused a moment and then she calmly resumed.

Jac was in the shop but the shutters were closed. It was a feast day so there would be no trade, but doubtless the boy would open the door. She handed the ale to her mother and, taking up a shawl, placed it around the older woman's shoulders. Agnes took cold easily these days and the interior of the church had been chilly.

The sound of a man's voice drifted across the passageway that separated hall from shop, and then her apprentice appeared in the doorway.

'Mistress...there be a gentleman asking to speak with you.'

Behind Jac, and directly in her eyeline, Henry Wevere filled her vision. He was bareheaded, as he'd been in the church, and though not a thickset man, but instead as lean as a whip, his presence seemed to reach into every corner of the house.

She nodded to Jac and closed the hall door. The boy followed her into the shop and returned to the task of taking samples of wool out of sacks and arranging them on the long table next to the window.

'You wish to purchase some wool?' Isolda inclined her head to the Lancastrian, pretending that she'd never seen him before in her life. 'I'm afraid my shop is closed, since it is a holy day, but return tomorrow and I will show you some of the best Shropshire fleece.'

The knight shook his head and the swift gleam of amusement in his gaze told her he knew full well she recognised him, and that he recognised her too. 'I am not here to buy wool.'

She'd already guessed that!

'Then what do you wish to speak to me about?'

He drew from the pouch at his hip the parchment he'd removed from the church door. 'This...among other matters.'

His voice carried the same unfamiliar lilt she'd noticed three weeks ago. Not a local man then, nor even a Shropshire one.

Isolda looked from the parchment to his face. 'Yes, I heard it was pinned up in the porch of the church. What of it?'

'I found it strange that you were the only one among the merchants and town leaders who saw no insult or injury in it, but only amusement.' In the light from the window his eyes glinted like bronze when it came out of the fire and was cooled in water. 'Why is that, I wonder?'

Isolda paused, her mind racing. He was different, more aloof, since the night she'd encountered him in Narrow Lane, and she couldn't really blame him. After all, he'd come to her aid, and had ended up with a sack over his head and a kick in his vitals for his trouble. And, although he'd not alluded to that night yet, she sensed it was there, waiting in line until the official matter had been dealt with.

'I happen to agree with the sentiments of the verse,' she said at last, and with passion. 'Not every merchant thinks only of profit and wealth, while watching the poorer grow ever more poor. Some of us care about justice and the rights of the common people.'

'The wasps and the bees being the poor folk hereabouts?'

She nodded. 'The commoners might be lowly but, as the song says, they have a sting in their tails, and will use it if pushed too far.'

'Evidently some of the commons are well educated in these parts, if this poem is anything to judge by.'

'And what would a knight know about the education of poor folk?'

Jac's hands paused in their work as Wevere walked over to the table and examined the samples. After a little silence he spoke again, but he didn't answer her question.

'A fine wool,' he said. 'As fine as any in Ludlow, I'd wager.'

'Yes, it is.' Isolda recognised the diversion, like the changing current of a river, unseen but perilous. 'But if you are not here to discuss buying any, I'll bid you good day. I am too busy to talk about poetry, Sir Henry.'

His head turned and his eyes met hers. 'You remember my name, then?'

She smiled, none too sweetly. There was no point in continuing to pretend. 'How could I forget it?'

'How indeed.' His gaze swept her face. 'I am glad to see you suffered no harm that night, after you and your accomplice ran away.'

'Jac—' Isolda gestured to her apprentice '—please go to tend to the animals, and collect any eggs the hens have laid today. Look spry, now.'

Jac, not yet sixteen, was strongly built but slow of wit. An orphan and petty thief in the making that her father had rescued from the backstreets of Bruges six years ago, he would be best out of the way lest he let something slip.

When he'd gone, Isolda walked over to Henry Wevere and, despite a flutter of nerves, looked calmly up into his face.

'I told you I was perfectly safe that night.'

'So it transpired.' A smile almost hovered around his mouth. 'Even if your man did come tardy onto the scene.'

'My man?' Isolda shook her head and lied to him. 'He was a stranger to me but naturally thought that you meant me harm.'

'A stranger?' His tone was smooth, disarming. 'Even though you called him by name—by coincidence the same name as your boy—and told him I'd come to your assistance?'

Damn! He *had* heard her plea to Jac after all, even with his ears muffled by the sacking.

'Whoever it was, he fled, and Jac appeared at the same time, and naturally assumed you were up to mischief. An easy mistake to make in the dark, on a night when your soldiers were ransacking the town, stealing our possessions and raping our womenfolk!'

His lashes flickered and a shadow darkened his eyes, as if her words had plucked at a shred of conscience. 'You do not need to remind me of that night's atrocities, Mistress Breydon.'

Isolda felt her face flame. How had he found out the name she'd been careful not to give him that night? She reached out to tidy the samples he'd disarranged, her hand not as steady as she would have liked.

'How do you know my name?' she asked.

'It is over the door.' There was a weighted pause before he went on, his gaze scouring her cheek. 'Who was the woman in church with you?'

'My mother, Agnes.'

'And your father?'

'Lost at sea, along with my brother,' she added, the pang of sorrow just as deep as it had been three years ago when their ship had sunk in a storm. 'En route to the wool market in Bruges.'

'You are not married?'

The question caught Isolda unawares, though perhaps it shouldn't have. She was long past marrying age after all and, but for the grace of God, might have fallen into that trap after her father died, and there was no man in the house. When Robert of Bristol, a prosperous and charming wool merchant, had visited Ludlow on business and began to woo her, her mother, still grieving her husband, was beside herself with joy. Talk of Isolda's marriage was abroad in the town even before she herself had said yes!

'No,' she said shortly, since she had no intention of elaborating further, least of all to this Lancastrian. 'I live here with Jac, and my mother lives with her sister in Tewkesbury.'

These days, she tried not to dwell on her one and only experience of men but now, inexplicably, the indignity of it stung her sharply. Finding out, just in time, that Robert was a bigamist was a shame she would never live down. Even worse, the disapproval of her mother as she spurned other suitors had shown Isolda that Agnes Breydon had never understood her, and that their social position in Ludlow was more important to her than her daughter's happiness.

'And how does your wool business do?'

It was both unsettling and ironic that the question should so closely align with the hard journey she'd embarked on following Robert's departure from her life. It had partly been the criticism, the disapproving looks, not just from her mother but also their friends and neighbours, that had made her determined to carry on her father's trade when Agnes would have sold up. That, and the desire to show Jacob Breydon, even though he be in his watery grave, that a woman could succeed in wool as well as a man, and that his daughter would be that woman.

'The trade is not what it once was,' Isolda replied. 'Exports have dropped since cloth is being made up in England nowadays instead of overseas.' She fingered the strands of wool on the table, making them untidy all over again. 'Times are harsh too, with high taxes and the common land being gobbled up by greedy men who have more than enough land already.'

'Hence these verses...' The parchment danced before her eyes. 'Do you recognise this writing?'

Isolda glanced askance at the lines of verse, while the echo of his rich voice with its lilting accent as he'd read them out in the church came again to her ears. 'No.'

'Did you see who placed this on the inner door of the porch?'

'No. How could I?'

'You were the last to enter, so must have closed the outer door behind you. Was the parchment there then?'

Isolda hesitated, considered her reply and tried to ignore the scent of leather and cold air about him that vied with the thick aroma of washed wool. 'The fellow—whomever he was—must have entered after I did, if he entered at all.'

'No one entered after you did.'

'Then it is a mystery,' she said.

'Is it?'

He placed his free hand over hers, stilling her restless fingers, and though his touch was light, the shock of it made her breath catch. His fingers were long and slender, and despite the fine shape of his palm she felt old calluses beneath the skin. The sunlight through the window caught his tawny hair, his sharp cheekbone and the bridge of his nose, and a warmth began to seep into the back of her hand, mirrored by the heating of her face.

'To return to that night...' he said, his eyes boring into hers.

Isolda's heart began to beat fast. Robert had never made her breath shake nor her pulse quicken, but instead had repelled, even annoyed her sometimes, with his grabbing and squeezing and lecherous kisses. So why did *this* man have such a different effect on her? Why did her eyes want to look at him when they should not? Her ears prick to listen when they should shut him out? Her hand remain where it was instead of pulling out from under his?

'Wh-what about it?' she stammered, reeling from this unexpected confusion of feeling. 'No real hurt was done you.'

'No, and that is what puzzled me. I expected to get much more than a kick in the ribs when I was on the ground and helpless.' He paused and his fingers seemed to tighten on hers. 'Why didn't I?'

Isolda shrugged. 'Who can tell?'

'The sack over my head was pungent...like a wool sack...'

She resisted the urge to fidget as his questions threatened to ensnare her. 'Ludlow is a town that has grown up on the wool trade. Shropshire and the Marches are rich in sheep, and many yeoman farmers come to the town every day.'

His brows rose. 'Then the man who assailed me was a farmer?'

'I told you, I don't know who he was... I turned and ran for my life.'

An elusive smile touched his mouth. 'After entreating the man not to harm me further.'

'Yes...no. Jac appeared just then, as I said...' Isolda felt flustered, as if that wool she'd been fingering had tied her up in knots, even as the constancy of his hand on hers was doing. 'The other man had gone. I didn't recognise him.'

'You *did* know him, and there was one man only—your apprentice.' He looked at her without a blink. 'When you fled, I heard two pairs of feet go together, not just one, Mistress Breydon—yours and Jac's. There was no one else.'

Holy Virgin, sack or no, he had ears like a hare!

'Perhaps your ears were playing tricks on you?'

This time, the smile did form, full and wide and so unexpected that it was dazzling. 'Very well, we'll leave it at that—for now.'

For now? Isolda felt an icy foreboding slide down her spine and as his palm lifted and released her she snatched her hand away and curled her fingers at her side. 'Then I take it you are remaining in Ludlow?' she asked.

'You heard me say in the church, did you not, that the Earl of Shrewsbury has charged me with discovering the author of these letters.'

'Yes, I heard.'

The smile had gone, and the stern line she'd marked on the first day she saw him had reinstated itself. 'I will need the cooperation of the townspeople—all of them—to bring the fellow or fellows to justice.'

'And when you catch him... What will happen to him?'

He rolled the parchment up and returned it to his pouch. 'Prison, no doubt, and a hefty fine to boot.'

'Is it wrong then to speak the truth and make it known?' Isolda felt her blood start to boil furiously, as righteous anger replaced the unsettling confusion of a moment ago. 'Is it a crime to stand up for the rights of the oppressed?'

'No, but there are proper means by which to do it.'

'Proper means!' She laughed out loud at that. 'You come here and accuse me, accuse my apprentice—of what I know not—when far greater wrongs are being committed in this town. It is clear that *you* have never been a victim of injustice, Sir Henry!'

Chapter Three

Hal stared into the beautiful, angry face but instead he saw the charred remains of a house from which smoke still spiralled. He saw bodies burned beyond recognition so that even he couldn't tell which was his father, which his mother, his sister…while his brother…

He spun on his heel and faced the window, fisting his hands. His eyes began to smart as if that smoke had risen again, around *him* this time, and the flames consumed him too—the only one to escape on that terrible day, when he shouldn't have escaped at all.

And behind the smoke, the fire, and the death, the dismissive features of the Earl of Warwick, the hand that had waved him aside, the shoulders that had shrugged and said the words that had changed the whole course of his life thereafter.

'Accident of war.'

Hal shuddered, a roaring filling his head and every sinew in his body pulling tightly. How could he ever forget, less still atone, for his action that day? For leaving his brother in charge of the workshop while his father lay in his sickbed, abandoning his whole family to a fate Warwick had blithely dismissed as regretful but of no importance compared to the fate of kings and nobles.

'Sir Henry...?'

He started as, through the roaring, a voice came, quiet, questioning, concerned. Turning back into the room, he saw Isolda Breydon standing closer than before. So close that, in the shaft of sunlight behind him, her eyes betrayed their true colour at last. A deep and pure blue, the colour of sweet violets in spring.

'I though you said something...'

His stare dropped to her mouth as she spoke. *Had* he said anything while those visions of destruction had flashed across his soul?

'No,' he replied, pushing himself away from the table. 'I didn't say anything.'

And neither should he have reached out his hand as he had and placed it over hers a moment ago. Felt the warmth of the flesh that was so different to the coldness of her manner. And he shouldn't have allowed his hand to linger, enjoy the stirring of sensations he'd suppressed for so long that he'd thought himself devoid of them now.

But he wasn't, and not even the nightmare of the fire of St Albans that had raged again, momentarily, to engulf him could alter that truth. Because the moment he'd touched her, his heart had kicked violently in his chest. His blood had quickened in the same way it had that first time he'd seen her, leaning out of the window. He'd left the following day with Talbot's forces, never dreaming he'd ever see her again, and those reactions—unwelcome and strange—had been pushed away, but not forgotten.

And now here he was, back in Ludlow, and the reactions were stronger than ever.

'There is a delegation of merchants coming to the castle later today, to discuss these pamphlets.' He glanced around the shop, tamping down those insistent stirrings of desire. There were only a few sacks of wool, though well filled, and everything was neat and tidy. Through the door, there must be the hall and kitchen, and above, the bed chambers. It was a good house, if not a rich one. 'Will you be among them?'

She shook her head. 'I would not be welcome. I am not a member of the Merchants' Guild.'

Hal frowned. 'Yet women may engage in trade, may they not?'

'They may, and if they are wife or widow, they might even be accepted.' There was a pause and her next words were said with resentment. 'I am neither so am *not* accepted.'

'But still you are able to sell your wool within the town walls?'

'They allow me to do so only out of respect for my father's memory.'

'They do not respect you as they did him?'

'No, they do not.' Her chin lifted. 'They mistrust and dislike me because I am not afraid to speak out against their greedy, self-serving ways, and—' She stopped abruptly, as if realising she'd said more than she'd intended to say. 'And now it is nearly dinner time, and so...'

She walked across to the door and opened it, waiting, one foot tapping impatiently on the wooden floor. Hal heeded the dismissal but, halting on the threshold, he paused. Outspoken in Ludlow Guildhall matters he could well believe, but she was keeping deliberately silent where his questioning was concerned, that fact he would bet on.

'My ears didn't play tricks on me in that lane, Mistress Breydon,' he said, 'and they played no tricks on me this morning in the church.'

'Your meaning?'

'Meaning I advise you to take great care.'

'As I've told you more than once, I can take care of myself.'

Hal shook his head. 'That's not what I meant. Before, I was on the lookout for looters and drunken soldiers. Now I am here in quite a different role. I have a charge of duty and I must see that charge through, to wherever and to whomever it leads.'

With that, he walked away, his mind fixed firmly once more on that duty. Isolda Breydon knew who'd penned those verses and pinned them to the church door, he'd stake his life on that. She might even have written them herself and if so...

His footsteps faltered only for a moment and then, blinking against the sunlight that bounced off the cobbled square, he strode on to the castle.

Isolda watched until Henry Wevere disappeared beneath the castle gates. Then she shut the door and crossed through to the hall to meet the inquisitive eyes of her mother.

'Who was it, daughter?'

'The Earl of Shrewsbury's officer, the man who read the poem out in the church.' Isolda cursed the blush that rose to her cheeks. 'He came to ask if I knew anything about the writer of the poems that have been appearing around the town.'

She hadn't told her mother anything about what she was doing and why. Agnes had always been a timid woman, even when her husband was alive, and she wouldn't understand, let alone condone.

As if her mother had read her thoughts, she sighed. 'If only your father were still alive, things wouldn't be the way they are. Life was good then, people were kind, they looked after each other in times of trouble.'

'It is this conflict between York and the King that has turned people awry. Now everyone mistrusts their neighbours, and their lords too.' Isolda replaced the shawl that had fallen from about her mother's shoulders. 'But perhaps now the Duke and his sons are in exile, things will settle down again.'

The bells of St Laurence's rang the hour. Out of habit, Isolda cocked an ear to the shop, even though there would be no custom today, the Feast of All Saints. Not that there was much any day, due to the decline in wool. By thrift and common sense, she kept her business going by selling to smaller local producers instead of turning to cloth as most of the wool merchants were doing. She would never be rich, as her father had once been, but her love for the wool trade and affinity with the farming class who produced it meant more to her than riches.

Her mother put the lid on the pot of broth over the fire. 'Your brother would have been nineteen today…if he'd not been taken by the sea…'

'We will remember him well, and keep a candle burning tonight.' As she comforted her mother, Isolda felt her eyes fill. She didn't weep easily but she and Dieric, three years younger, had been close. That voyage with their father, taking wool to Bruges, had been her brother's first and last. All on board had perished, most of the bodies never recovered, Jacob's and Dieric's among them. Her brother hadn't even wanted to go, and she had begged to go in his place, longing to sail on the sea, to see the Continent, and the famous wool city.

But her father had refused. To his mind, his son would follow in his footsteps, not his daughter, even though she had the better head for business, the inherited understanding of the wool trade. The unfairness of it had hurt her at the time but it had saved her life and, ironically, allowed her to follow the dream that her father, though fond of her, had never recognised, or if he *had* seen it, had ignored because of her sex.

The door opened and shut and quickly she leapt to her feet. But it was only her apprentice come in from tending the few animals they kept, these days just the hens, a pig and the pony that pulled the cart. Jac had a basket of eggs in his hands, which he placed down upon the table.

'Has the Lancastrian gone?' he asked.

Isolda nodded and counted the eggs. Six today, a good clutch. 'And hopefully that is the last we will see of him.'

They ate a simple dinner of fish and cabbage, Jac chattering non-stop as was his wont. Isolda only half listened, her thoughts preoccupied with what Henry Wevere was about up at the castle. These last weeks, they'd succeeded in outsmarting the town catchpoles and even the constable at the castle.

But all that had changed now. York was fled, Lancaster held Ludlow, and the new constable, Edmund de la Mare, was reputed to be no fool. And from the little she'd seen of Henry Wevere, he was no fool either.

On market day a week later, Hal wandered around the stalls and booths that were crammed into the square. Every possible commodity was on display, from pies to poultry, cheese and eggs, autumn fruits and vegetables, to candles, gloves and shoes. And of course, ale booths were aplenty, around which men gathered to gossip as much as to drink, while the womenfolk shopped and doubtless also gossiped.

He glanced over to the Breydons' house. The shutters were up today and behind the counter at the window stood the young apprentice. There was no sign of Isolda. Was she inside, with a customer perhaps? Or out and about, browsing the market stalls?

Hal strolled on, looking casually around him, as would any marketgoer, but his eyes taking in every detail. He passed the market cross and walked leisurely along Drapers Row, where the shops blazed with cloth of every hue made by the weavers, fullers and dyers of the town. The cloth trade was fast displacing the wool trade, here as all over England, but he didn't look at anything, let alone stop to examine the quality of the material, the neatness of the stitching, the durability of the dyes. He'd left all that far behind him.

The stares of people followed him, some merely glances, others curious, but one or two—doubtless loyal Yorkists—openly resentful. Hal paid none of them any heed, though he nodded now and again to some of the merchants he'd met with at the castle on All Saints' Day.

Most of them were good men, he'd decided, while a handful of the most ambitious were overfull of self-importance and driven by wealth and greed. But, good or bad, they were not his sort of people. The craftsmen and artisans were his sort—or had been once—having been born within their ranks.

As he passed into the beast market a muddle of noise and stenches assailed his senses—the bleating of sheep and goats, the lowing of cattle and squealing of pigs, the squawking of fowl. Even so, above all the raucous confusion, a commotion from the toll house beyond, at the Galdeford Gate, caught his attention. He strode quickly in that direction to discover several yeomen farmers were remonstrating with the toll keeper, their hands gesturing and their ruddy faces red with anger.

'What is amiss here?' he demanded.

All heads turned but it was the keeper who answered, his tone clipped with frustration. 'They are objecting to paying to bring their wares through the gate, Sir Knight.'

One of the yeomen, a young man in a dirty smock, then gave voice. 'We are not objecting to paying, but at paying more than we did last time, that being high enough as it was.'

The gatekeeper shrugged. 'The tolls have increased.'

'By whose orders?' asked Hal. 'And by how much?'

'By the orders of the greedy persons who run this town, who else?'

The heated response came, not from the toll keeper nor the yeoman, but from behind him. Turning, he saw Isolda Breydon standing there, hands on hips, eyes blazing. 'And since you ask by how much the tolls have gone up,' she went on, 'I can tell you that, whatever amount it is, it isn't the first increase this year.'

Hal hadn't seen her since the day he'd visited her house, although he'd thought of her often, even when he didn't want to—*especially* when he didn't want to. But he'd heard much *about* her from men and women who shared a mix of envy and dislike arising, he'd soon gathered, from her haughty beauty, her tendency to speak her mind, no matter to whom, and her stubborn but excellent head for business.

Now, looking at her sparking eyes and determined stance, their opinions of her seemed apt and at the same time unjust. In their words, Isolda Breydon should be married and kept in her rightful place—running a house and bringing up babes, instead of encroaching into the wool trade, which was the realm of men and widows, not attractive young maidens.

'How much is the toll?' he asked again as Isolda moved to stand between him and the yeomen, who welcomed her like one of their own.

'Three pence per head, Sir Knight.' A man with a staff, clearly a sheep farmer, supplied the answer. 'Gone up from tuppence and a half last week.'

Isolda nodded vigorously. 'And that amount was already too high for the common folk to pay.'

Hal's mind sifted through her words as his eyes devoured her appearance. She was dressed in a blue kirtle with a soft grey surcoat over, and a fine wool cloak of russet brown flowed from her shoulders. Her hair was coiled over her ears, soft tendrils caressing her brow and cheekbones every now and then as the breeze picked up.

'But you can redeem much more than that when you sell your beasts, can you not?' He tore his gaze from her face and addressed the farmer with the staff. 'After all, that is why you are here today.'

The man opened his mouth but, once more, it was Isolda who retorted. 'Provided he can *sell* his sheep! The wool trade isn't what it was. More of the merchants are turning to home-made cloth now, not exports, and those of us who still deal in wool are struggling for markets.'

The barely controlled tremble of anger, and desperation too, behind her words eclipsed all the noise and the smells and bustle of the marketplace. Memories stirred at the back of Hal's mind—of another town, another market, another angry face and heated tones telling him of injustice.

'Unlike the merchants, farmers cannot adapt so easily, and they still have families and animals to feed. Do you not care about that, Sir Henry?' she challenged, taking a step closer and bringing a vague aroma of rose petals and lavender to his nose. 'Or are you insensible to poverty and hardship?'

His mind lurched back from that other market, so long ago, to this one. Isolda looked nothing like his sister, since Beatrice had been dark-haired and rosy-cheeked, her eyes as clear blue as sapphire, whereas Isolda was fair and pale. It was the abhorrence of injustice that linked them, the determination to uphold the rights of those who suffered, to speak out where others—or *because* others—would not.

The violet-blue eyes were stormy now as she waited his answer, mouth pursed and arms folded beneath her breasts. She had no need to colour those lips with angelica like some did, nor lighten her skin with wheat flour. No need either to scrape her hair viciously back from her brow, nor pluck her eyebrows to an almost invisible line. In fact, Isolda Breydon had no need at all to enhance the simple beauty that was perfection all on its own.

There was a shuffle of feet and Hal remembered that the yeomen still hovered and that a line of others waiting to pass through into the market had begun to form behind them.

'By whose orders has the toll been increased?' he demanded, turning to the keeper.

'By the Twelve and Twenty-Five that govern the town, Sir Knight.'

'I see. Then I will investigate the reasons for the increase at the soonest opportunity.' He took several coins from his purse. 'For today, I can see no solution but to pay the tolls for those who cannot, but I expect this money to be redeemed at the end of the day.'

'*You* will pay, Sir Henry?' The gatekeeper frowned. 'With your own money?'

Hal nodded. 'It is the most expedient way to settle the problem.'

'But if the yeomen don't sell their livestock and other produce,' the man argued, as if for all the world it was *his* money he was handing over, 'they may not be able to repay you when they leave here.'

'Then you will make a note of who the borrowers are and how much they owe me, and I will trust them to repay the debt as and when they are able.'

The man shrugged. 'As you wish, though you'll be lucky if you see half this silver again!'

Hal ignored the gloomy prophecy and, standing aside, watched the yeomen pass through. They thanked him, some with suspicion and some grudgingly but, without exception, each and every one nodded to Isolda. And although no words were spoken, he got the feeling that something was conveyed all the same.

Behind the menfolk came women and children with baskets of vegetables and fruits and small sundries. At the very end, a small, thin girl who couldn't have been more than seven, wearing a smock that was too big for her and clogs that were too heavy, carried a scrawny red hen under her arm.

A bittersweet vision rose behind his eyes as the image of another girl appeared, also dressed in smock and clogs as she came running to him with a squawking hen in her arms, tears streaming down her face.

'Hal! Hal! Come quickly! The fox has got at the hens!'

Beatrice had cried bitterly when they'd run together to the hen house to find it was too late. The fox had gone and all the hens were dead, except the one his sister clutched protectively under her arm.

'Oh, why kill the hens if he's not even hungry?'

Hal had had no answer to her wailing question then, as he'd been little more than a child himself. He hadn't even spared much of a thought for the five dead hens, only acknowledging that his family would eat well that night and several nights to come, and even exchange one or two of the carcasses for other produce that they needed.

Now, as a grown man, he could have told his sister all about the lust for blood of foxes and men alike. But he couldn't because Beatrice was dead too, as much a victim of bloodlust as those hens had been, as were the rest of his family. He should be dead too, consumed in the fire as they had been. But instead he'd lived because he'd shirked his duties that day, leaving his younger brother in charge of the workshop, excusing that negligence because Will loved the trade while he hated it, and had gone with his friends to watch the battle.

'Here be the tally of debtors, Sir Henry.'

Hal blinked as remorse stung behind his eyes and, turning to the gatekeeper, lowered his gaze to study the names listed. If only he could change the past as easily as he could lend these farmers coin. If only he'd been content with his lot, accept that he would be a weaver like his father, contain the restless urge to be something more, even if he didn't know what that *more* was.

But, in trying to find it, he'd been lured into rebellion and recklessness, idleness and waste, and death had been the result—though not his own.

'I will come to the treasury this evening to collect the repaid money,' he said, grief and guilt absent from his voice but a bitter and eternal penance in his heart. 'If there is any.'

He turned on his heel and found himself face to face with Isolda once more. She was looking at him with a puzzled expression on her lovely face as she asked him the same question the gatekeeper had asked him.

'Why did you do that? Why be so generous to men you don't even know?'

Hal shrugged and made his reply as steady and as nonchalant as he could manage.

'As I told the gatekeeper, it was the quickest and most expedient way to solve the problem. Besides which, it is the Earl of Shrewsbury's money, not mine.'

Chapter Four

Isolda felt her jaw drop and, all at once, something she'd taken for a kindness, even if an unexpected one, took on another, more sinister form. Robert's face rose up before her, his hand outstretched too, silver pennies glinting in his palm. During the whole half year of their courtship, he was always quick—too quick—to pay for everything she and her mother needed in those hard months after her father's death, be it food, clothes, fuel, even a new pony for the cart when the old one died.

At the time she'd thought him over-generous, if a little foolish, and more than a little overbearing when he waved aside her protestations, as if she had no pride or means to provide for herself, her mother and Jac. He wouldn't even let her pledge to pay him back, saying they were gifts, that he was rich and that he loved her.

With hindsight, she realised he was simply trying to buy her and that his gifts were a means to a despicable end. And now the awful thought leapt into her head— was Henry Wevere doing the same thing? Not trying to buy *her*, of course, but to bribe the yeoman farmers in some way?

'The Earl's money?' She rounded on him. 'Then that act of bounty was a trick—or something even worse?'

His brows rose. 'Such as what?'

'Perhaps the Earl means to *buy* information from his tenants!' Suspicion after suspicion raced onto her tongue. 'Does he think his farmers would stoop so low to accept his bribery? That honourable men would betray one of their own for ten pieces of silver, like Judas did?'

'I didn't hand over quite that much,' Wevere replied, a note of flippancy inciting her anger even more. 'And, just to be clear, John Talbot may direct me to do his work, but the way I do it is up to me.'

'And how exactly do you intend to do your work?' she demanded. 'By enlisting the burgesses and merchants, whose rights you are, after all, here to uphold!'

Wevere brushed back the forelock that blew over his brow as a breeze picked up. 'I have heard some very interesting things from them already.'

Isolda nodded to another of the farmers, a latecomer, who was writing his mark on the list of loans to be repaid, glad of the chance to break the hold of those piercing green-gold eyes. 'I don't doubt it,' she retorted. 'And I can guess well enough what sort of things, Sir Henry!'

'Hal.'

Annoyingly, the diminutive suited him. It made him seem younger, less serious, less threatening, almost friendly, instead of a greyhound on the scent of its quarry! But the nagging doubts persisted. He *must* have some hidden motive for paying the farmers' tolls with his—or rather the Earl's—money. After all, most of the people in this town and surrounding lands, herself included, were loyal to the Duke of York. Wevere and his overlord were Lancastrians, and Ludlow was now in their hands. That alone made it impossible to trust him.

And as for that friendly little shortening of his name—

no, she wasn't going to be fooled into that either, even if she'd been so foolish as to call Robert 'Robby' as he'd asked her to! It hadn't taken her long to revert back to using his proper name—among others!—when she'd discovered his true character. But it had been a valuable lesson and one she would never forget nor repeat.

Friendship with a handsome and charming man, which had been the nature of her association with Robert to begin with, could become something that appeared real but was false, leading to betrayal and hurt and shame. And the worst thing of all had been her own sense of powerlessness as it had all unfolded before her, too fast to keep up with, let alone stop.

'*Sir Henry* is good enough for me, thank you,' she said with a nod of farewell. 'And now, as the day is marching on, I must be about my business.'

But it was as if he hadn't even heard her. 'Then I must continue to call you Mistress Breydon, not Isolda? A pity.'

It was somewhere between irony and complaint, and the hint of amusement beneath it irritated her even more.

'As is fitting! Goodbye, Sir Henry!'

Isolda began to walk away, not as quickly as she would have wished since it was muddy and slippery underfoot. It was a warm November and the weather had been wet rather than cold, but suddenly, and oddly, as a watery sun crept higher in the sky, it seemed like summer.

Henry Wevere, instead of leaving her, followed at her side, his steps in tune with hers. The edge of his cloak brushed hers occasionally, and once the touch of his arm, as he stepped to one side to let someone leading a donkey pass by.

However, he made no attempt at conversation and the silence grew as discomfiting as his presence. Isolda bore it as far as the last of the beast pens and then stopped and turned to him. 'Do you not have other things to do, such as arresting the town's *malcontents*?'

'Which ones?' He smiled. 'To know them, I shall need more information first.'

'Well, there are many here who will give it you, though it'll be lies!'

'Then why don't *you* tell me what is true?'

The expression on his face seemed genuine, no cunning gleam behind his frank stare, only an unmistakable challenge. She'd invited that challenge, of course, and now had only herself to blame that he'd issued it. That didn't mean she had to take it up, though. She could let him find out for himself, that was what he was here for after all.

Isolda told herself she should walk away, and as quickly as possible. His presence in the town, uncomfortable as that was for most of Ludlow's inhabitants, had intruded too closely, and too personally, upon her. From the night he'd come to her rescue in Narrow Lane when, thank God, her night's work had already been completed, to his scrutinising stare in the church on All Saints' Day and his visit to her house afterwards.

His too-keen, too-accurate insinuations, the probing questions that she'd found so difficult to evade…and then that unexpected touch of his hand on hers—a tender rather than ensnaring touch that she hadn't made any attempt to escape and which suddenly made her hand tingle all over again.

All of that should make it imperative to avoid Henry Wevere at all costs, and yet…something held her, some inexplicable urge to discover who and what this man really was beyond his Lancastrian colours and official role of investigator. Some hidden force that compelled her and drew her to him that had been sparked the very moment she'd seen him from her window.

That and the urge to lead him a merry dance. It was both amusing and satisfying that the quarry he sought was right in front of him and he was completely unaware of the fact!

The irony of it could work to her advantage though, could it not? She still wouldn't trust him, nor the strange and confusing feelings he evoked in her, but she might *convince* him that the accusations in her poems were well founded. And even if she failed at conviction, she might be able to gauge better the sort of man he was and so arm herself against him. She wasn't the innocent and gullible soul she'd been three years ago when Robert had entered her life, but the cruel lesson of misplaced trust that she'd learned from him was a blessing now.

'You have already seen at the toll gate what life is like for the common people here,' she said. 'One of poverty, hard work and suffering at the hands of the rich.'

'I would like to see more—much more.'

'Very well, let me show you!' Going to one of the pens which held some young rams, Isolda greeted the shepherd. 'Not so many this year as last, Wat. Only three?'

The man, who was one of those that had accepted Wevere's coin at the gate, shook his head. 'Two of my ewes aborted in the spring, Mistress Breydon, and one died from the blood loss. Since certain folk began fencing off the common land, there's been less grazing for my stock.'

Isolda let out a heavy sigh, loud enough for Henry Wevere to hear. 'You're not the only one to have suffered, Wat. I've spoken to many others who have lost their grazing rights also.'

'Aye, too many,' Wat agreed. 'And if it snows bad this year...'

The shepherd's prediction was clear enough without the words. There were noticeably fewer beasts for sale this winter fayre than the last, and those that were looked thin. The lucrative days of the export of wool to Flemish markets were over and she herself had had to adapt. These days, she bought less wool from the farmers, though still as much as she could afford, which she then sold to small spinners and weavers nearer home to produce the cloth that was sold in English and foreign markets.

'Times will improve, Wat, if the authorities in this town do right by the farmers.' Isolda spoke to Wat but her words were aimed at Henry Wevere. 'And once your grazing is restored to you all.'

Isolda bid the shepherd good day and good luck, and moved on to the next pen, which held a cow that she knew belonged to a yeoman farmer by the name of Ned of Burford. Greeting him, she gave another heavy and deliberate sigh, well aware that Wevere's face was thoughtful as he listened intently.

'Isn't that old Daisy? Surely you're not selling her, Ned?'

The man touched the brim of his hat. 'I am, Mistress Breydon. She's seen near twenty winters now and she'll not last another on the little amount of hay in my barn. Best she go while she can still walk to market.'

'You have no hay?' Isolda prodded delicately, not wanting to rub salt into his wounds but eager that the truth came out. After all, Wevere had asked for it. 'Did you not gather the Lammas harvest before the rains came?'

'It wasn't that, mistress, though there was little enough to gather, to be sure.' Ned, who suddenly looked older than his ancient, speckled cow, rubbed his nose. 'We've less use of the common land lately, with all these enclosures on Whitcliffe and certain folk penning ground that used to be open and free to all.'

Isolda felt anger and sadness well up into her throat but before she could think of some words of comfort and hope, even though there was little of both to be had, Henry Wevere spoke, not to her but to the farmer.

'Who is it that has enclosed the common land?'

Ned hesitated and glanced at her. She gave a nod, her heart starting to beat fast.

'Well, Sir Knight, there be a number of them. In my case, it is Adam Knyghtone's and Philip Gryme's beasts that graze where mine used to do.'

'These men are burgesses of the town?'

The farmer nodded. 'And officers of the Palmers' Guild, too rich and too powerful for the likes of me to challenge.'

'Have you reported this to the bailiff?'

'If Tom Hoke was still in office, yes, I would have done, as he's a fine and upstanding man.' Ned, with a sudden flare of fiery spirit, spat on the ground. 'But he's a good Yorkist too and so was ousted for no cause other than that. And the new bailiff won't listen to the likes of us!'

'Why not?'

'Because Ralph Shearman be tanned from the same hide as the rest of them, sir, and worse than many. His sheep graze on common land too, instead of ours, as was given us by right in the old days.'

'I see.'

Isolda held her breath and watched as Henry Wevere's eyes travelled slowly over the adjoining pens, all of them pitifully underfilled with beasts. She saw his mouth tighten, a muscle flex in his jaw as he placed a hand on Ned's shoulder.

'I wish you good luck in selling your cow.' To her astonishment, he pulled Daisy's ears gently. 'If you cannot, come and see me before you leave Ludlow. I am lodging at the castle. Ask for Henry Wevere.'

They moved on, Isolda biting back the longing to ask what he meant to do about the injustice he must now surely see all around them. But she held her tongue, the awareness of him walking so closely at her side making her feel far too aware of *herself*.

They passed on, through Drapers Row and the High Street and into the square, where certain of the womenfolk of the town eyed her with a mix of judgement and dislike. When her father had been alive it had been different. Even though he was a Flemish incomer they'd respected his skill at business, and her mother was a Shropshire woman so, as a family, they'd been well liked.

But after Jacob Breydon's death and his wife's departure to Tewkesbury, things had changed. The ridicule Isolda had suffered over Robert had turned to gossip and scorn as she'd chosen to remain unwed. She often wondered if there wasn't a certain amount of envy, as she'd weathered the economic storm as efficiently as her father would have done. And shame too, as she spoke out against those who profited, despite the slump, by imposing higher taxes on the excuse that more money was needed for the upkeep of the streets and town walls.

The day she'd spoken out publicly against one of the most notable merchants for fixing the weight of wool in his favour, she'd thought the townspeople would put her in the scold's bridle! They hadn't, of course, but it had set the seal on her strained relations with her fellow merchants irrevocably and for ever.

Whatever the reason for the town's dislike of her, she hardly pondered over it now, nor let it bother her, as it once had. When her mother had gone and left her alone, apart from Jac, she'd felt so alone, so vulnerable, afraid even at times. But she'd grown stronger, more independent because of that aloneness, since there was no alternative but to survive a situation that she had, after all, created for herself.

And today, like all market days, Isolda neither acknowledged the good and the great, nor spoke to them, stopping only at the stalls that belonged to the poorer people of Ludlow. At each and every one, the same story was told. How times were so hard now with abuse of grazing rights, higher taxes on goods and dwindling corn supplies to feed their animals. The stories of woe and injustice went on and on, not in mean and complaining tones, but in voices hoarse with distress and fear for the future.

When they had traversed the market square, at the end of which stood her house, Isolda stopped and turned to look up at him. 'Well?' she demanded. 'Whom do you believe *now*? The Twelve and Twenty-Five who govern this town, but do so in a way that benefits only them? Or the tales you have heard this morning from folk who deserve to prosper and be happy but are not?'

The sun had reached its noonday height and as she waited for his answer Isolda felt perspiration trickle down between her breasts. The wool that lined her cloak started to prickle her skin and her bodice, not tightly laced, suddenly hampered her breath.

She was acutely aware of the curious glances of those who passed by, heads that bent close and mouths that whispered behind hands. Aware too of the flash of jealousy on the face of Alice Shearman, the daughter of the bailiff, who gawked at them like a plucked duck. Or rather, Alice gawked not at *her* but openly and unabashed at Henry Wevere!

'Every silver penny has two sides, Mistress Breydon, and I will need to listen to both.' His gaze dropped to her mouth, lingered. 'I admit that I am convinced that the common land is being illegally usurped and that many farmers have lost grazing rights.'

'And what do you mean to do about it?'

His lips twitched and his eyes lifted and twinkled into hers. 'At this very moment, you mean?'

Isolda stared. Had that been half a smile? 'If possible, yes!'

'I am here solely to uncover the writer of the poems, not local inequalities.' If it *had* been a smile, even half a one, it had gone. 'But it is clear the two are connected—though I hardly see Ned or Wat penning such verses... do you?'

Her heart lurched. 'I... No, I doubt it very much.' She cursed the quiver in her voice, put there because that glimpse of humour had been attractive, and disarming. 'But when you have made your mind up which is the *right* side of that penny of yours, be sure to let me know!'

'I shall do so. But, in return...' He paused and suddenly it was as if the sun's bright rays pinned her to the spot. 'There is something I would hear of *you*.'

Hal watched Isolda's reaction closely. They were standing so close anyway that it would have been impossible to miss it. Surprise, suspicion, a flash of alarm and finally a belligerent wariness.

'And what is that?'

She was guarded now whereas before, as they'd walked through the market, she'd gradually relaxed in his company, spoke freely and in friendly tones. Not to him, admittedly, but to the farmers and shepherds and simple country women, who'd all responded to her with warmth and affection.

'Just this,' he said. 'Is it the case that *you* shun your fellow merchants and their womenfolk, or that *they* shun *you*?'

'What do you mean?'

He gestured to the young woman in the ridiculously long hennin nearby who stared at him with unabashed lust in her dark eyes. 'You have spoken to almost every commoner here today,' he went on, looking back into the far more interesting eyes of Isolda Breydon, 'and yet you have not spoken to anyone of your own standing. Why?'

The bustle around them seemed to grow quiet, the lowing of the beasts becoming muted as a strange sort of thudding filled his ears. It took Hal a moment to realise it was his own pulse.

'Is that relevant to your investigations?' she said at last, her tone evasive.

'It might be,' he responded.

A tinge of pink crept into her cheekbones. 'Or it might be none of your concern!'

'Perhaps not,' Hal agreed, 'or then again, perhaps it might. I won't know until I hear your answer.'

They seemed to be talking on two completely different levels, and she seemed as aware of that as he was. Could she see the desire in his eyes? Sense the instinctive reaction of his male body to her allure? If so, she needn't worry. He'd schooled himself long since not to act as he would have done once.

'Well?' he prompted.

'The higher-ranking people of this town and I have little in common.' Her shoulders lifted but there was nothing nonchalant in the shrug. 'They think me bold for stepping into my dead father's shoes and running his business, and are jealous because I do it as well as they do, better than many.'

There was both pride and pain in the way she said it, and something besides desire struck at Hal's heart. A recognition of the inner woman not just the outer one, of the courage and the honesty that she possessed in abundance, which made her beauty rare indeed.

'So it is envy rather than dislike?'

'Oh, they dislike me too, make no mistake about that!' She gave a bitter little laugh. 'They consider me proud, outspoken and brazen and I think them haughty above their station and as spiteful as cats.'

Proud and plain-speaking, yes, Hal had seen that for himself, but brazen? The painted girl in the hennin headdress was the epitome of the word, as she sailed back past them, with a hiss worthy of any viper. In comparison, Isolda's simple gown and surcoat, the woollen cloak discreetly lined with coney, the worn gloves and equally worn shoes did not make one think of the word brazen at all.

Nor did her response to the girl's taunt, as she granted the precariously balanced hennin a pointed stare and a lift of her brows, and Hal found himself even more intrigued.

'Is that one of the cats you mentioned?'

'Oh, yes, she's the most spiteful of the lot, in fact. It doesn't take much to make Alice Shearman show her claws!'

Hal watched the girl—a relative of the bailiff from her name, a daughter perhaps—glide around the stalls as if she were crossing an icy lake rather than a muddy square. She looked back over her shoulder suddenly and threw him a pert yet sly smile. Then the doe-like eyes slid from him to Isolda and sharpened into knives.

He knew women well enough to recognise jealousy when he saw it. He knew too the games of coquetry and conquest, and once had been an adept player. He'd found he was attractive to women and had taken full advantage of that in the past. He'd lain with serving girls and widows, whores and ladies, and had thought himself a fine fellow as he'd boasted to his fellows about his conquests.

Even before he'd reached manhood he'd known he didn't want to settle for the stolid, respectable life of a weaver. Something within had driven him to ease the dull work with the pleasures of the flesh, the oblivion of ale, the thrill of gaming, as he'd sought in vain for a purpose to his life other than the one he'd been born to.

Before St Albans, the girl in the hennin would have drawn him. He'd have allowed her shallow beauty to lure him, aware that, with a little wooing and flattery, he could bed her. Now Alice's empty shell left him cold, but the quiet dignity of Isolda Breydon touched him deeply.

He couldn't obliterate his past, nor the dissolute and idle man he'd once been, but he wasn't that man any more. Now he had a purpose, albeit one he'd never expected back then—to put the needs of others before his own. More, to deny his own needs, pretend they didn't exist, and instead channel all that restlessness in him to the cause of moral good—he who'd once scoffed at morality.

Hal looked again at Isolda and found her staring at him curiously, as well she might! His face heated. What would she say if she could read his thoughts? Would she be surprised to find him, like her, dedicating himself to championing and protecting others, as he should have protected his family? Would she understand? Would she even try to? It appeared not, as she misread his mind completely!

'Don't look so abashed, Sir Henry! The eyes of *all* the men follow Alice Shearman! Why should *you* be any different?'

Hal smiled, letting his gaze flicker to the girl in the hennin, who'd paused at a glove-maker's stall. 'As well they might,' he said. 'She is most...beguiling.'

Her head tossed. 'That is *one* word, at least!'

The retort had more than a hint of scathing in it, though whether the barb was directed at him or at the Shearman girl, he had no way of knowing. Doubtless, Isolda thought *him* beguiled like all the others, but what would it matter to her if he was? It was clear she didn't like him and she didn't trust him. Why should she? His being a Lancastrian, and here in her town, was the least of her reasons.

But perhaps it was best she disliked and doubted him because once he *wouldn't* have been any different. But it wouldn't have been the bailiff's daughter he would have taken in his arms with a careless laugh and stolen a kiss. It would have been the beautiful and proud Isolda Breydon.

Now, though he found himself tempted in a way he hadn't been since then, he resisted. Isolda wasn't like the loose, eager women he'd known in his youth, nor was she like the coquettish Alice. She was a sort he didn't know, but suddenly he found himself wanting very much to know her. To discover if those feelings of dislike and distrust she held for him might even change, the better *she* got to know *him*.

He wouldn't let that happen, of course. If he was other

than who he was, if circumstances were not as they were, he could fall in love with Isolda so very easily. And that knowledge, terrifying and exciting at the same time, brought with it his greatest fear.

To love was to lose, sooner or later, and he had no wish, nor intention, to invite that anguish ever again, even in the unlikely prospect that she would ever be his to lose. So, stepping back, he bowed stiffly.

'I'll bid you good day, Mistress Breydon.'

Her brows rose. 'No more questions?'

Hal shook his head. 'No more questions.' Even as he said it another question leapt onto his tongue, the one he'd wanted to ask all along, although until now he'd not examined his reasons for wanting to know the answer. 'Except perhaps one. Why are you still unwed?'

Her eyes flared wide and her cheeks turned pink. 'Because I choose it.'

'Yet you must have had many suitors?'

A breeze suddenly lifted and the hood of her cloak slipped back to reveal spun gold hair that caught the sun.

'If I have or have not, it is nothing to do with you, Sir Henry!'

'Hal,' he corrected for the second time as those golden coils dazzled him. 'My name is Hal.'

She glared at him in astonishment for a moment and then, with a toss of her head that only made her hair gleam even more brightly, dazzling him again, she turned on her heel and marched away.

Hal watched her go and when the door of her house had closed behind her, he gave a heavy sigh. The girl in the hennin drifted past once more but, ignoring her, he made his way towards the castle gates. He might be a changed man now but he and Isolda might as well have been standing at the furthest reaches of the world, too far apart to ever meet in the middle.

That night, when the curfew bell had sounded and her mother had retired to bed and Jac to his cot in the shop, Isolda drew a small table closer to the hearth and sat down. Rubbing her hands before the fire, she tried not to visualise Henry Wevere's compelling stare or the fall of his tawny hair. She tried not to see the concern on his handsome face when he'd witnessed the poverty of the farmers—nor the way his eyes had followed that cat, Alice Shearman!

But she couldn't dismiss the way his voice had softened when he'd told her to call him Hal. And she couldn't deny either that he'd surprised her that day in ways she'd never expected. She'd sensed, despite her reluctance to acknowledge it, a rare sort of honesty as he'd paid the tolls at the gate, stooped to hear old Ned better amid the noise of the beast market, pulled old Daisy's drooping ears with a tender and careful hand.

Was he to be trusted though, despite all that? Why had he walked through the market with her at all, listening so intently to the tales of woe, if not to gather information to use to his own ends? He was the Earl's man, after all, and a Lancastrian, and surely he knew that the farmers he'd spoken to so cordially today were all for York?

He must know she was for York too, having been born and grown up in the Duke's own town. But, political sympathies aside, she'd trusted too soon and too easily once, where she shouldn't have trusted at all.

Isolda attempted to conjure up the face of her former betrothed, but the knave's despicable features wouldn't form. Only Henry Wevere's face stared back at her out of the glowing embers of the fire. She'd been so neatly trapped three years ago, not because she'd loved Robert but because she'd *needed* him to bring her security and respect. She'd convinced herself that that was enough reason for a loveless marriage, persuaded herself that she could tolerate his rough attentions, even bear the wedding night, and all the other nights...

He'd trapped her but she herself had jumped into the pit. She'd stifled her own inner conviction that she was doing the wrong thing, and had almost sacrificed her freedom to please other people. And now, once more, Isolda found herself questioning her innermost feelings as doubts born of experience encircled her.

No, she mustn't be blinded this time, nor so innocent, not ever again. Instead, she'd gather evidence on which to decide between trust and mistrust—and there was only one place to get that evidence. Lighting another candle, she took out parchment, ink and quill from a small cupboard hidden behind a high-backed bench and began to write.

Mouses and voles, though meek may be bold.
A-scurry at night, they squeak and they fight.
If...

Pausing a moment, Isolda chewed the end of the quill thoughtfully, and as the cat crept out of a corner and settled at her feet she smiled to herself and penned on.

Chapter Five

The following afternoon, Hal stretched his legs under the table in the great hall of Ludlow Castle and read again the poem that had been brought to him that morning. Discovered fastened to the castle gates, it was composed in the same hand as the one that had been pinned on the church door a week ago. This one, however, spoke of mice and voles, not wasps and bees, and though directed with the aim of an arrow, it ended on a more personal note.

If Harry the Cat would catch him a rat,
Then he must be tole he spies the wrong hole.

The last two lines brought a wry smile to his lips. The author was bold indeed to deliver his advice right under the noses of the night watch. Bold enough to risk capture to accomplish his task.

The paper was quite thin, roughly cut and of poor quality, and the dark red ink was common enough. The strokes of the letters had a flourishing sureness of hand, sloping gracefully to the right, the long tails of certain of the letters slanting to the left.

Except in the words *Harry the Cat*. Hal passed his forefinger over the words, obviously a clever play on his own name. Here the writer had paused a second or two, leaving a blot of ink on the *H* and the *C*, and the writing itself seemed less—or perhaps more—convinced of its course.

Hal's mind went back to the incident at the Galdeford Gate the day before. Isolda Breydon appearing from nowhere, like an avenging angel come to uphold the case of the farmers. Was it a coincidence that this new verse should appear the next day—or was he reading too much into these clever, cutting lines?

The thought he didn't want to think—that Isolda Breydon herself was the author of those lines—had barely crossed his mind when Edmund de la Mare, constable of the castle and his host for the foreseeable future, entered the hall. He liked the man, perhaps because, unlike his overlord John Talbot, the constable came from the lower realms of nobility.

'Another one?' Edmund sat down beside him. 'And nailed to the castle gates, I hear. The fellow gets more audacious with every day that passes!'

'How do you know it is a man?' Hal asked quietly.

His companion blinked. 'Well, it must be a man, surely. One of the more educated townsfolk—a craftsman, perhaps, or a disgruntled clerk. A wench wouldn't have the learning to pen poems, even if she could think them up.'

Hal knew his companion was right, of course, but there'd been something in Isolda's face that day in the church, in the furtive way she'd tried to sneak out of the other doorway. And yesterday, at the tollgate, the look of conspiracy that had passed between her and the farmers, the way they'd deferred to her...

He shook himself. She might or might not have written these verses, but he'd wager every piece of John Talbot's silver that she knew who *had*, might even be in league with the fellow. Perhaps that insolent demeanour of her apprentice, with his thick speech and lazy movement, hid a cunning man.

'So...' de la Mare poured himself a goblet of ale, refilling Hal's cup too '...what's your next move?'

Hal took a long drink and considered. 'A visit to the Guildhall, I think. I understand there is a meeting of the Twelve and Twenty-Five this evening?'

He'd interviewed them already, of course, a week ago in this very hall. To a man, they were unanimous in their condemnation of the unknown poet of Ludlow. He'd learned the rhymes had started appearing several weeks ago but the Duke of York, currently in hiding in Ireland, had made no attempt at finding the culprit, doubtless more concerned with coveting the crown of England! And so the verses went on, appearing on the door of the parish church, on the market cross, the Guildhall and the houses of several of the merchants, and now the castle gates themselves.

'Some discussion on rents and tolls, I believe,' de la Mare confirmed. 'I only get involved if I have to. The King has his hands full as it is with the Yorkist threat, and is content to leave the running of his towns to the citizens themselves, as far as possible.'

'A wise decision...or perhaps an expedient one,' Hal mused.

Edmund nodded. 'Expedient, for certain.' He frowned. 'I'm uneasy with York, and his son Rutland, being so near in Ireland. There is talk he will bide his time and strike again through Wales and the March. At least his eldest son, and Warwick, are further away in Calais.'

'Further away, yes, but, of the two, I think that Edward of March, with Warwick's help, will return sooner.'

Edward of March showed military promise but Warwick was clever and without a conscience. The Earl had cared nothing that his victory at St Albans—so decisive for the cause of York, even if fortune had now turned against them—had had tragic and bitter consequences for others who had no part or interest in the quarrels of kings and lords.

Hal's mind went back four years to the time he'd been apprentice to his father, when it had been *his* family that had suffered those consequences, while he'd escaped them. He'd also, though in a way he'd never wished for, escaped the life of a weaver that he'd so despised. After St Albans he'd joined the first Lancastrian force he'd encountered and, as an uneasy peace had settled in England under the King, with Richard of York as Protector, he'd entered the service of Lord Audley of Cheshire as a common soldier.

There'd been no fighting until two months ago, but during the respite he'd learned both the skills of fighting and a little of law, teaching himself the latter. Then, after the battle of Blore Heath last September, he'd been knighted by the King and attached to John Talbot's service, just in time to meet the Yorkists at Ludford Bridge.

Now here he was, a knight of only two months' standing, owner of a gifted manor in the vicinity, which he'd visited only once, and saddled with the lowly role of investigating seditious poetry. Not quite the future he'd envisaged in those days when he'd done everything he could to avoid his loom, but one that atoned, in some little way at least, for his former irresponsible life.

'I'll be away to the Guildhall,' he said to de la Mare, folding the poem into the pouch at his belt. 'Having met certain of the merchants already, I can't help but agree with some of the things this poet claims of them.'

Leaving the constable to mull that over, Hal went out through the castle gates into a bright November day, pausing to look at the houses that stood on this side of the square. The nearest was Isolda Breydon's. It would take no time at all for someone coming out of that house to creep to the castle gates under cover of darkness, catching the guards napping or distracted, or absent from their duty.

Could Jac, Isolda's lad, really be so stealthy, so bold, so clever? Somehow, Hal doubted it, with a feeling based on instinct rather than anything else. His mistress, however, he sensed with the same instinct, might well be all those things. With a sigh, he turned for the Guildhall.

Isolda hadn't seen Henry Wevere since that morning at the market but she'd heard what had gone on in the meeting at the Guildhall the day after. How he'd challenged the Twelve and Twenty-Five on the matter of the increased tolls, how they'd denied any malicious reason for that, how they'd insisted that the murage and the cost of paving the town streets had risen, and so tolls needed to rise accordingly.

She hadn't been at that meeting, of course, being disbarred from joining the Guild, not because of her sex but because they viewed her as an outspoken aberration, and one who questioned every unfair decision they made. But one of the burgesses, less hostile than his fellows, had told her what Henry Wevere's stance had been.

'Fair, not taking one side or the other, but he stated that the matter of the increased tolls would be laid before the Earl of Shrewsbury at the earliest opportunity.'

Now Isolda pondered that stance as she broke her fast before opening the shop. Like everything Henry Wevere did, it puzzled her, unsettled her, and challenged her to dare to believe that he was actually a fair and honest man. To her surprise, there'd been no public announcement of the poem she'd nailed to the castle door a few nights previously. Was that because she'd addressed it to him personally, if not in direct words, or was he biding his time and working out how to catch its author?

It proved a slow morning and she was alone in the shop. Jac had taken her mother back to Tewkesbury, to deliver a consignment of wool to a buyer there at the same time. The parting had been regretful rather than sad. She and Agnes had never been close and she knew she was a disappointment to her mother, who thought her daughter should be wed with children of her own by now. Even after Robert, Agnes had prodded and nagged, and it had been almost a relief when she'd gone to live with her sister.

By noon there had only been two customers and since the sun was shining Isolda decided to go out for a walk. Jac wouldn't return until evening and she wanted to trade some of the eggs she'd gathered that morning with the butcher for a small piece of meat for supper. She might be more fortunate than many in these days of war and taxes and declining markets but thrift was never a bad thing. Her father had taught her that, back in the days when English wool was in high demand by Flemish cloth towns—days long gone now.

She was walking through Harp Lane, her mind pondering the future of her business, when a noise up ahead caught her attention. Shouts and laughter, thudding and scuffling, it funnelled down the narrow street and Isolda soon saw the cause of it.

In the small square between the church and the line of houses that formed Drapers Row, a man was in the pillory. And standing, with legs braced wide and arms folded, head and shoulders above the people that had gathered in front of the spectacle, was Henry Wevere.

Shock and outrage flooded through her and she pushed her way through the jeering crowd to come up, gasping with fury, at the side of the Lancastrian knight.

'Holy Virgin,' she cried, 'this is inhuman! Why is this man being punished so?'

He turned at her voice, his brow set in its usual frown, his tone clipped as he supplied the answer. 'He was caught stealing a loaf of bread.'

Isolda stared aghast at the cringing figure in the pillory. He was terrified, his hands clenched tightly as they stuck out through their holes, and his legs trembling so much they hardly held him up. Pity pierced her heart, for she recognised him as one of the youths who worked in the fulling mills down by the river. A friend of Jac's, he was an honest young man, though poor, like all the labouring classes of Ludlow.

'I *know* this boy, for God's sake!' She rounded on Henry Wevere in fury. 'Dickon is not a thief—he must have had good reason for stealing. He must have been hungry...desperate...'

'Hunger and desperation are no excuse to commit a crime.'

'A crime!' The dispassionate reply infuriated her even more. 'It's not as simple as that! Things are so bad of late that even honest folk are driven to desperate measures to put food in their mouths and keep a roof over their heads.'

His head turned away, a flush colouring his cheek,

his mouth set into a resolute line. 'He is lucky not to lose his hand.'

Isolda's blood ran cold and her protestations froze on her lips. She stared up at him, seeing a completely different man to the one who had paid the tolls on market day and listened so sympathetically to the farmers. Different to the man who'd allegedly been so fair and without bias at the meeting of the Twelve and Twenty-Five. But which was the real one? That man...or this?

Beneath her feet, the earth seemed to rock, loosening the fragile little root of belief that had begun to sprout because of those things. Now...was she seeing him for what he really was? Had that sympathy and fairness and impartiality been a front all along? What else could explain his indifference, his lack of action to stop this horror?

'Then you have condemned him with all the rest?' Her voice began to quiver, not just with anger but with the knowledge that she'd almost been fooled by a man once again. 'Why don't you throw insults too, like they do? Jeer at a boy who is guilty only of trying to survive?'

'His youth is no excuse either.' A muscle clenched in his cheek. 'The baker he stole from must survive too. The law is the law, Mistress Breydon.'

'Law is not the same as justice,' she countered. 'Even *you* know that.'

'No, but it is an effective giver of lessons, albeit harsh ones. I doubt he'll steal again.'

Isolda shook her head, trying to understand him and failing utterly. 'Is that all that matters to you? Do you not feel *anything*?' Gripping his arm, she jerked hard, making him turn to face her. 'How can you stand here and watch a living creature suffer and feel no pity?'

'What in God's name do you expect of me, Isolda?'

Suddenly his eyes blazed and his face wasn't indifferent at all now, but filled with emotion. 'How would you know what I feel or do not feel? Do you think I *enjoy* witnessing this vile spectacle, law or no?'

The words came at her so swiftly, so unexpectedly, that she recoiled in shock. 'I... I...'

But the response Isolda groped for never came as the boy in the stocks gave a hoarse plea for mercy as a cabbage, thrown by somebody in the crowd, hit him square in the face. Everyone laughed and the people seemed to turn into a pack of bloodthirsty wolves as more missiles were hurled—filth, clods of earth, rotten vegetables. Someone pushed into her and the basket she carried fell to the floor and the eggs inside came tumbling out.

'Oh, no!'

Quickly she stooped to retrieve her basket, and the one egg that was miraculously still unbroken, only to have someone pick the egg up and hurl it at Dickon. A curse rushed into Isolda's mouth and she lunged at the woman, who staggered then lunged back, her fingers raised like claws.

'You scurvy wench! You Flemish strumpet!'

Isolda ducked, avoiding the flailing nails, though the vicious words cut to the quick. She recognised the woman as Margery Cottrell, a seamstress who had sometimes bought wool from them. How could she, or *any* woman of the town, act with such malevolent violence?

'How dare you call me names! How dare you torment that poor boy!'

Margery laughed. ''Tis all in the day's sport, my fine lady! There's little enough to be had in this town of late, that's for sure, so can you blame folk for having a bit of fun?'

Fun! Was the woman drunk? Or crazed? Isolda opened her mouth to protest, and then felt strong fingers close around her elbow. An instant later, Henry Wevere's voice came clear and urgent at her ear.

'Come on, let's get away from here!'

Suddenly, she had no will left to argue. Stooping, head bent as more missiles sailed through the air, she followed him blindly through the crowd. It surged and ebbed like an engulfing sea, and for a dangerous moment she thought they were both going to be overwhelmed and trampled underfoot.

But then they were in the churchyard and Isolda leaned against the wall of the church, her knees trembling. 'That...that was awful,' she gasped, fighting for breath. 'What has happened to the people in this town?'

'Something very ugly. I've seen it many times, when a crowd gets out of hand.'

She squeezed her eyes tightly shut, wishing she could shut her ears too to the sounds coming from the square. 'Hounding a boy like that is beyond cruelty. And they are enjoying it!'

Henry Wevere's shadow hovered before her, his lean body a barrier between her and the cold rays of the sun. 'I'm sorry you had to see that, and suffer—'

'Whatever I suffered is *nothing* compared with what Dickon is suffering.' Isolda opened her eyes and glared at him. 'How *could* you let that happen? You could have stopped it—you have the authority to do so, but you didn't even *try*!'

Hal froze, the anger and accusation striking him like a blow, all the more painful because beneath them echoed his sister's voice. A hot wave of guilt washed over him and in its wake the futile anguish of regret for things he could not change.

Whenever Beatrice had accused him thus, as Isolda was doing now, he would have laughed, joked, teased, sympathised or acted, according to whatever wrong she had brought before him. He would have brushed away the tears and if the addressing of the wrong was outside his power would have explained gently that that was the way of things.

He'd known what to do then, how to respond, how to comfort but now...he could hardly gather Isolda into his arms and comfort her because she would surely not welcome it—nor him. But there was *something* he could do, something he'd almost resolved to do just as she'd appeared on the scene. Disperse that rampant mob and allow the felon in the pillory some peace at least, if not his dignity.

'Stay here.'

Leaving Isolda leaning against the wall, praying she'd do as he asked, Hal strode back out of the churchyard and to the front of the crowd, putting himself between it and the pillory. Planting his feet wide, he ducked a flying apple and held up his hand for silence.

Perhaps because the apple had only just missed him, or perhaps because he was a knight and a stranger, or perhaps because they'd had their fun and the novelty had worn off now, silence fell instantly. Clearing his throat, he addressed them with an authority that invited no argument.

'You have had sport enough this day. Return to your homes and let this boy serve his punishment unmolested.'

There were mutterings and mutinous glares, as he'd expected, and another apple was launched, though far wide. Then, gradually, feet began to shuffle and heads to bow. A woman at the back scuttled away, then another, and slowly the crowd did the same, moving off piecemeal like an eddy in the middle of a pond.

He recognised one of the men who'd been in the crowd for a soldier of the castle, either off duty or shirking, and beckoned the man to him. 'You! Come here! Bring this boy some water then stand guard here until I return.'

The soldier did as he was bid, though clearly unwillingly, and Hal, after a quick glance at Dickon to ensure he wasn't badly hurt, and a final warning stare at the stragglers who still hovered, he rescued Isolda's battered basket from where it still lay and returned to the churchyard.

Isolda was where he'd left her, though from where she stood she would have been able to hear what he'd said, and seen the people disperse. But her tone was contemptuous as she snatched the basket he held out to her.

'Why did you not do that earlier? And why did you not release Dickon as well?'

'The mob was a disturbance that needed to be calmed, but the boy's punishment is out of my hands.' The law was the law, no matter how Isolda would have it, but he would speak to the bailiff about Dickon's release. 'I am here on the matter of the poems, nothing more.'

'How *convenient* for you!'

Something struck Hal hard in the chest, for she spoke the truth. He could tell her that he had no power in corporate matters and had been specifically ordered by the Earl not to intervene in the daily government of the town. But to what purpose? At the very best it would sound like an excuse; at worst she would detest him all the more for trying to excuse himself.

'You appear to have made your mind up about me whatever I do, Isolda.'

She shrugged. 'I thought I had begun to know you, but now... I don't understand you at all.'

'Then perhaps you shouldn't try.'

His reply seemed to evoke even more contempt and she spun away and walked quickly towards the lychgate. There Hal caught her up, curling his hand around her wrist and bringing her to a halt.

'Isolda...'

'Let me go!' Her head half turned, the determination in her command matched by the angry spark of her eyes. 'I'm going to free Dickon if it's the last thing I do, and don't you even attempt to stop me.'

Beneath his fingers, Hal felt her pulse beating furiously, making his own pulse quicken too as she tried to pull away, the momentum bringing them both under the shadow of the wooden arch of the gate.

'I will speak to the town authorities on the boy's behalf,' he said, glancing beyond the gate to where a few people still lingered, though none jeered or threw anything at the boy now, since the soldier was doing his duty. But if Isolda attempted to unlock the pillory, the onlookers might not be quite so pliant, and perhaps neither he nor the guard would be able to control them. 'It's too dangerous for you to intervene.'

She turned fully to face him, her chin tilted up, her breath quick and warm at his throat. Her eyes were wide, brilliantly blue, and her mouth was just inches away. Her lips were parted and her breasts rose and fell rapidly as she breathed hard.

'I am not afraid to act even if *you* are!'

Hal *was* afraid. Not of the crowd nor the authorities but of the overpowering urge he had to kiss her. All he had to do was dip his head and let his mouth touch hers. Go further and take her in his arms. Feel her heartbeat match his own, perhaps, as she welcomed him and their two beings became one, for a little while at least.

'Let me go.'

Isolda's command was prophetic, because he *would* have to let her go, one day. He was in Ludlow a few weeks, perhaps a month or two, no more. Even if he failed to catch the writer of the poems, his overlord would recall him to some other duty sooner or later. All at once, the inevitable knowledge of that made his gut twist, and he didn't have to look too deeply to know why.

From the first moment he'd seen her, Isolda had attracted him. Every time he saw her, spoke to her, touched her, that attraction grew harder to resist. He found himself looking for her when he was about the town, eager to see her face, to speak with her. And his nights were full of her, when his need became an aching longing and desire possessed him. She consumed him, her presence constant in his mind, vivid, necessary…

His feelings towards Isolda were the strongest he'd ever felt for a woman. Perhaps, with her, if he acted on those feelings, he could find the happiness that, until now, he hadn't realised he lacked. But if he lost her, as he'd lost his family, by accident or by treachery, or even by Isolda's own spurning of him, he'd finally lose that little bit of himself that still survived. That small piece of his heart that was still whole would shatter into tiny fragments, as the rest of him had done at St Albans, never to be reassembled.

'I said let me go! You are hurting me.'

Her voice broke through his thoughts and Hal realised he still held her wrist. He relaxed his fingers a little but didn't release her yet, lest she march into the midst of that albeit smaller crowd and thus into danger, as she undoubtedly would, oblivious of her own safety.

'If I do, and if I swear I'll speak to the bailiff about the boy, will you promise not to interfere?'

'Interfere?' The word was flung at him like a gauntlet. 'Is *that* what you call it? I would call it going to the aid of someone who needs help. Showing pity instead of cruelty, acting instead of standing apart and letting injustice run rife, *as others do.*'

There was no need for her to elaborate. Among those others she'd included him, perhaps even made him first among them. 'Isolda—'

'No!' Instead of pulling away, as she'd done before, she stepped closer, glaring up into his eyes, her own blazing with anger. 'I don't want to hear your excuses and I will tell you now that talking to the bailiff will achieve nothing!'

'Even so—'

But this time she didn't even wait to hear him out. Nor did she try to break free. Instead, raising her arm, she curled the fingers of her trapped hand into a fist, as if she would strike him to achieve liberty. But as she did so, Hal saw something that made his heart lurch and sink right down to the soles of his feet.

For upon the cuff of the long, close-fitting sleeve of her cream-coloured kirtle sat a small red spot of ink.

He stared, wishing he hadn't seen it at all, or was imagining it, or that he could just pass it off as something else. Here was the evidence he sought—evidence he didn't want to find, not on her. But find it he had. And now, since he couldn't pretend it didn't exist, he had to ask. It was his duty to ask, even if the question tasted like poison on his tongue.

'What do you know, I wonder, of mouses and voles, Isolda?'

Chapter Six

Isolda felt the blood leave her face. 'Mice?' she misquoted. 'Voles?' Shaking her head, she attempted a laugh, dismayed to hear that shake too. 'What is this? A puzzle?'

His eyes never left hers as he turned her wrist so that the incriminating spot danced between them. 'And a pretty one, in red ink and elegant letters.'

Isolda cursed silently, rueing the ink she'd spilled on her sleeve the previous evening and hadn't removed. 'I don't know what you are talking about.'

'Do you not?' A frown darkened his brow. 'Then perhaps a cat called Harry will complete the puzzle for you.'

She tried to smile but her lips seemed to have frozen and wouldn't obey. 'I'm afraid I am no good at riddles.'

'Perhaps not at solving them…but I suspect you are more than adept at posing them, and in verse too.'

Isolda swallowed, found her mouth dry, her breath hard to draw. He could not fail to see her discomfort, she knew, but he still had no proof—nothing beyond a stain on her sleeve to trap her with. 'Let go of my wrist, you are hurting me.'

Immediately, his fingers slackened but he didn't release her. 'Is that better?'

'No! It isn't better at all,' she muttered, though he

hadn't hurt her at all, though fear raced along her nerves and churned in her stomach. He might have no real proof but that didn't mean he wouldn't try and get some, and if he did, she—and the whole cause—would be lost.

'Why don't you put me in the pillory and have done with it?' Panic flooded through her, panic she mustn't give way to, nor reveal either and so condemn herself. 'Throw filth like the rest of them did at Dickon? Gloat while they torment me as they tormented him?'

He made no reply for a long moment but they were standing so close that his gaze penetrated all the way down inside her and his warm breath fanned her face.

'For pity's sake, desist!' she implored him, twisting her arm but to no avail. 'Because if you think I will talk nonsense with you about mice or voles or cats, you are mistaken.'

'*Am* I mistaken, Isolda?'

The question was murmured, low and quiet, but it resounded like a bell in Isolda's ears and went clanging all the way through her. Her heart leapt and got lodged in her throat, its frantic beat stopping her breath for an instant. He knew! He might not have the proof to actually arrest her here and now, but he knew.

Lifting her head, she straightened her spine and forced herself to be calm, or at least appear so. Bluffing would be as useless as struggling. Even brazenly lying would make no difference. She had to outwit him instead.

'What does Harry the Cat think? He is so clever after all—can he not solve puzzles all by himself?'

Henry Wevere's mouth tightened and she let her own form a satisfied smile. They both knew she'd admitted everything and yet admitted nothing. If he met her challenge, then she would have to endure whatever came. If he did not...

'Or is he a mere kitten, running after balls of wool until he gets completely tangled up, paws and all?'

His face flushed and as he drew a sharp breath Isolda feared she'd gone too far. That he *would* actually drag her off to the pillory or, worse, to the strong room in the castle and get his proof, by whatever means he could. She braced herself and refused to allow her limbs to tremble as a long, taut moment of tension played out.

The space they stood in became so silent, so stretched to breaking point, that it took her several seconds to realise it was he who trembled, though with what emotion it was impossible to tell. The muscle that jerked in his cheek was the only movement of his face, the rise and fall of his chest the only signal that he still breathed.

'So...' His voice came at last, still low, still quiet, and full of something that was more promise than menace. 'It is a game of cat and mouse you would play, is it, Isolda?'

'I would prefer to play no games at all,' she countered as his thumb brushed gently, just once, over the inside of her wrist where the pulse beat maddingly. It was a movement so intimate, and so at odds with the sense of stalemate, that Isolda couldn't prevent the flare of surprise in her eyes, nor the jolt of shock that made her almost drop the wrecked basket she still somehow clutched in her other hand.

And then, abruptly, he released her and, stepping back, he sent her a bow. As he straightened up again, unbelievably, a smile touched his mouth—though not one of humour.

'I think we both realise the game has started long since, as long ago as that night in Narrow Lane. However, this is neither the time nor the place to play it out. But we will speak again of this...very soon. For now, good day, Isolda.'

Isolda didn't wait twice to be dismissed. Spinning on her heel, she hooked the handle of the basket over her elbow and rubbed her wrist furiously, as if she might erase his touch altogether. Blindly, her thoughts reeling and her cheeks burning, she marched along Harp Lane, pushing past people in her way, and cursed vehemently at that little red spot of ink that had damned her.

Damned her but nothing more! Why had he not arrested her, there and then? Or at least detained her for further questioning? And if it was a game he was playing, when would be the time or place to play it out? She had no answer to those questions but one possibility surfaced to chill her blood.

He must be planning to trap her, surely, knowing, as she did, that a spot of ink on a sleeve was insufficient to prove she was the poet. And so, now her suspicions were justified, she must tread more carefully than ever before, though in ways she hadn't imagined.

For that touch upon her flesh had sparked strange feelings she'd never experienced before, startling responses that had overridden even alarm and fear. Potent emotions, unwelcome and yet unstoppable, had rushed in upon her as they'd stood face to face, heart to heart, and they'd had nothing to do with cats and mice at all.

Hal watched Isolda leave, her head high, though her steps were unsteady and a little too quick. She didn't look back but she must have felt his eyes follow her. She must also know that he knew it was she who'd penned those poems, and that his course was now clear—or should have been.

All he had to do was search her house, find parchment and quill, then interrogate her as to what use they were put. And he should do that at the soonest opportunity before she had time to destroy all evidence. But Hal didn't move. His feet felt as if they'd sunk into the cobbled street, his duty with them. His hands clenched tightly at his sides and sweat bathed his palms. Duty yes, but what of conscience?

If he arrested Isolda, questioned her, and she admitted it, what would he do then? Put her in the pillory, as she'd taunted earlier? In prison even? And all for standing up for right against wrong, justice over injustice, for having the moral courage that he'd lacked, as he'd stood and watched with all the others, albeit wishing he could spare Dickon his fate. And suddenly the shame of that dug like talons into his conscience.

Hal turned and, throwing his cloak over his shoulder, marched back to the pillory where a few people still lingered. They stopped and stared open-mouthed as he unlocked the bolts and slid the top bar up and away, freeing its occupant as he should have done an hour ago.

Supporting the boy lest he fell, he inspected Dickon's forehead, where blood indicated that something harder and more cruel than eggs and vegetables had struck. Then, satisfied that he'd suffered no further harm beyond fright and indignity, he pulled a handful of coins from his purse and pressed them into Dickon's hand.

'Pay the baker for the bread you took and then go home, lad.'

The boy stared at him in disbelief, then with a swift nod and a choked thanks, closed his stiff fingers over the money. Hal gestured to the soldier he'd stationed there earlier. 'Escort the boy and should anyone ask, you may inform them that the Earl of Shrewsbury's officer has authorised his release.'

The man nodded and the two made tracks towards the street where the baker's shop was located, while Hal strode in the opposite direction, across the square, looking neither left nor right, acknowledging nobody. Ludlow by day always seemed to be teeming with people, and ever since St Albans, when he'd pushed through streets swarming with soldiers, he'd hated this hemming in of bodies. Today he felt himself being crushed from all sides, even though no one actually touched him.

For it wasn't just a crowd that engulfed him but a realisation that threatened to render him immobile and tear him in two at the same time. His duty over the last four years had gone unquestioned, even unexamined, by himself because he'd instinctively, deliberately, acted on the side of the law, whomsoever laid down that law, be it the King, his earls or the corporation.

Now it wasn't as simple as the law. For Isolda Breydon surely acted as she did for the right reasons, even if what she did was wrong in itself. His footsteps faltered. Was it wrong, though, to speak out, albeit in secret and on parchment, against injustice that otherwise would go overlooked and unchecked?

'Wevere!'

A bellow like that of an enraged bull sounded and Hal saw Ralph Shearman thundering towards him. Surely news of his freeing of the boy in the pillory couldn't have reached the bailiff already? Or could it? Since his arrival in the town less than a fortnight ago he'd discovered that the very walls that enclosed Ludlow had ears, that the council was a close-knit and self-serving one, and that people like Ralph Shearman pursued lawbreakers like a hawk did its prey, but his hand never seemed to fall upon anyone of his own kind.

If Hal did his duty and arrested Isolda, he was bound to pass the matter to the town authorities, since the Earl deemed this a local matter not a Crown one. Sherman's hand would not only fall upon her person, but would crush the spirit, the freedom, the beauty and the goodness out of her. He couldn't let that happen!

Ralph Shearman, lumbering to a halt in front of him, didn't bother with a greeting. 'Why haven't you caught the scoundrel who is putting damn lies into verse and decrying the good men of this town? As far as I can see, you've done nothing since the day you arrived here!'

Hal drew a breath, let his lungs fill slowly, and let the air out again. 'On the contrary,' he said. 'I have just this very moment released the boy you put in the pillory.'

Shearman gaped. 'You did what?'

'I released the boy in the pillory,' Hal repeated. 'I don't know how long he'd been in there but he'd clearly paid for his misdemeanour.'

'You took it upon yourself to override the law of this town?'

'Yes. The boy had learned his lesson, so I sent him off with a warning and some coin to pay for the bread he'd taken. I doubt he'll repeat his folly.'

Hal was almost certain of it. The fear in the boy's eyes, the choked thanks, had convinced him that the boy wasn't a criminal but, as Isolda had said, merely hungry and desperate.

'But, to return to your concern that I am doing nothing to apprehend the author of the poems,' he went on, 'I am pursuing my investigations in my own way. If you don't like it, you are welcome to refer yourself to the Earl of Shrewsbury.'

With that, Hal walked past and on, breathing deeply to rid himself of the stench of corruption that emanated from Shearman's every pore. It had been all he could do to stop himself telling the bailiff exactly what he thought of his person and his methods of running the town. Perhaps he *should* have unburdened himself with some choice words because now his throat was thick with dread and his heart thudded against an impending and inevitable weight of disaster.

He wasn't answerable to the men of this town but he was accountable to his overlord, John Talbot. And when the Earl asked the question Shearman had just asked, which then would supply the answer? His duty or his conscience?

That night after curfew Isolda closed the door of her house and cursed the full moon and the clear frosty winter sky that was lit by thousands of bright stars. In a trice, it seemed, the mild autumn had turned to a harsher, if beautiful, season. At least poor Dickon wasn't in the pillory tonight. Her apprentice had told her how Henry Wevere had released him, and that the bailiff, though furious, had not taken steps to undo that act of mercy.

Mercy, pity, feeling…all the things she'd accused the Lancastrian knight of lacking, but now…

Jac, at her side, interrupted her thoughts as he cursed too and pulled his cloak around him. 'We'll needs be careful tonight, mistress, 'tis as bright as day!'

Isolda nodded and pushed the dilemma out of her mind, for now at least. There were more pressing things to do than ponder the imponderable. 'Then best we go separately, Jac. Me to the Guildhall and you to the church, and we must be quick about our work.'

'As fast as beetles, mistress.'

With a grin and a tug of his hood up over his head, Jac was gone, creeping—indeed like a black beetle—along the side of the square in the direction of the church. She watched him until he'd passed the corner of Drapers Row and then quickly crossed the square. It was risky in the moonlight but she passed unseen and darted down Mill Street. So far, all was well.

An uneasy feeling crept down her spine all the same and, feeling as if a hundred eyes watched her, she turned her head swiftly to look. There was no sign of anyone following her but the sensation persisted.

The Guildhall was all in darkness and, unrolling the parchment and muffling her tool with her cloak, Isolda nailed it firmly to the door. Her heart echoed each thud of the hammer, which she had to drive hard into the thick tough oak. It was as the last nail went home that a hand grasped her shoulder.

She spun around, raising the hammer high to defend herself, and saw the face of Henry Wevere. His other hand came up to still her arm, though she was too shocked to have wielded her weapon anyway. Neither of them spoke at first. What was there to say, after all? He'd caught her and there was no excuse nor lie that would explain what she was about. All that was left was to face the consequences.

Lowering the hammer to her side, Isolda took a deep breath. His silence was unnerving enough but the expression on his face was awful. He looked...wounded, as if she'd driven those nails not into the door but into him.

'So... I suppose you're going to haul me off to the gaol now?'

'Why did it have to be *you*?'

She smiled, her lips stiff but not with cold. 'Why not me? Would you have rather it was someone else?'

To her astonishment, he nodded. 'Yes, I wish it had been anyone *but* you.'

'But you should be pleased! Now you have the proof you needed. The town and the Earl will cheer you!' She stared boldly up at him, fear drying her throat despite her brave words. 'How did you catch me anyway? I felt I was being watched but saw no one.'

'We waited outside the castle gates.'

'We?' Suddenly, Isolda's fear became terror. Jac! 'Who else is with you? There's no need to search further now you've got me.'

'My squire followed your apprentice in the other direction.'

'Jac...has gone to visit his friend Dickon, to see he is recovered from his time in the pillory.'

As she said it, the puzzle reformed in her head. Why had he released the boy? Because she'd shamed him into doing so, or because he really did feel pity, and was capable of mercy? Did he recognise, after all, the difference between tyranny and fair rule, and if so...?

But the thought was left unuttered as Wevere stepped closer, his eyes searching her face for truth or lies. 'So stealthily? And after curfew?' He shook his head. 'I think it's rather more sinister than that, Isolda.'

'You can do whatever you like with me.' Isolda's defiance turned to a plea. Jac must not be caught as well. 'I'm ready to face whatever comes. But not the boy, please! He's...'

'Innocent?'

'Innocent and ignorant!' She flung her head up. 'He knows nothing.'

They stood in shadow, for the moon was behind the rooftops, its beam peeping through the chimneys like an emerging halo. Wevere's face was in shadow too, his eyes glinting harsher than the frost upon the cobbles. But when he shook his head, a strangely defeated gesture, a seed of hope sprouted.

'I wish to God, Isolda, that I also knew nothing.'

Isolda fought to control that hope, lest it be shattered at once, before she'd had a chance to build on it, to turn it to persuasion, to appeal. 'You *could* know nothing... if you chose to.'

'Would that it were that simple.' His breath touched her face in a cold mist. 'But it isn't simple at all, is it?'

His hands closed around her waist and the hammer, that she'd been clutching all this time, clattered to the floor. The echoing ring was loud in the quiet street and from somewhere a dog barked and then fell silent.

'Isolda...'

Whatever it was he was about to say—or do—Isolda never discovered because a shout sounded then from the top of the street, as loud and as clear as a trumpet.

'Ho! Hal!'

They jerked apart, Hal turning his head at the same time as she did. At the top of the street, illuminated in the moonlight, two figures stood. One was upright and supporting the other figure, who sagged limply with buckling knees and drooping head.

'Come quick, Hal.' It was the voice of the squire, Simon. 'The boy's hurt.'

Chapter Seven

'No!' Furiously, Isolda pushed Hal away and began to run headlong up the hill. 'If you've harmed him, you'll pay for it!' she yelled as he caught her up and ran at her side. By the time they reached the top of the steep street, the boy had fallen to the floor, the other kneeling over him.

'Get away from him!' Isolda shoved the squire aside and dropped to her knees. Jac lay on his side and at once she saw the flow of blood that seeped from his stomach into the grooves of the cobbles beneath him. Hal came to squat beside her and put his fingers to Jac's throat, feeling for a pulse.

'He's alive,' he said. 'We'd best get him to St John's Hospital. Help me get him up, Simon.'

The two men lifted Jac gently into a sitting position, the boy giving a groan that was pitiful to hear. Isolda put her hand to her mouth to stifle a groan too as Hal pulled off his cloak and wrapped it around the boy, packing some of the material into the wound.

'It'll prevent us leaving a trail of blood at any rate.' He glanced up at her and his voice softened. 'And hopefully he'll be warmer too.'

Simon taking him under the arms and Hal under his knees, they lifted Jac between them. The boy was heavy and, pausing a moment to adjust to the burden, they turned back down the street and headed for the Mill Gate, Isolda walking alongside.

Mercifully, the guard obeyed Hal's order to let them through, and also his explanation of having found an injured youth who they were taking to be treated—which was the truth, after all. Violence, even murder, was a common event in Ludlow.

They hurried on, threading between the dark houses of the weavers' and fullers' quarter, where all was quiet. The river flowed slow and thick to their right, and their footsteps crunched on the frozen ground. Isolda went ahead now they were off the main streets, keeping her eyes peeled for any obstacles in their path, though the moon shone so brightly it might well have been daylight.

'How far away are we now?'

From behind her, Hal's whisper sounded urgently and she stopped. Jac's body hung limply and looked utterly lifeless.

'The road is just beyond this alley,' she said, her voice low. 'Is he...?'

But Hal jerked his head. 'Keep going.'

They went quicker now and soon came out onto the road. Opposite and a little way down stood the St John's Hospital. Isolda's heart lifted when she saw the candlelight above the door lintel and in no time at all, it seemed, Jac was being laid down on a trestle bed in the infirmary with two of the brethren bending over him.

The Prior, Thomas Oteley, had been roused and came to the bedside, his face grave as he spoke quietly with Hal, asking the circumstances of the boy's attack. Isolda, one ear listening to Hal's answers, watched and felt useless as the brethren peeled away Jac's clothes and inspected his wound.

The boy seemed smaller somehow and, naked to the loins, looked thinner, vulnerable. The narrow gash in his right side, just below the ribcage, indicated that the weapon had been a knife, not a sword. A coward's weapon, she thought, the tool of a murderer.

She shuddered and, drawing a deep breath, addressed the brother nearest to her. 'Will he recover?'

'It is too early to tell. He has lost much blood.' Perhaps seeing her stricken face, he added a consolation. 'But he is strong and young, so there is hope.'

The brother on the other side of the bed sighed as, sitting Jac up gently, they began to wrap a binding around his wound. 'We see this all too often. Ludlow has become a town of cutpurses and quarrelsome young men who draw their knives as eagerly as they do a cup of ale.'

Isolda doubted it was either a quarrel or an attempt at robbery that had brought Jac to this but something more sinister. The brethren finished their work and one of them, seeing the blood on Hal, and Simon's hands, offered the bowl and a cloth. After he'd washed his hands clean, Hal spoke again to the Prior.

'I will pay for his care here, of course, should he live through the night.'

The words sounded ominous, and all of them knew that Jac's pale face, the hollows of his cheeks, the blue shadows beneath his closed eyes, boded ill.

'One or other of us will sit with him the night through.' The Prior looked kindly down at her. 'I'll send you word of his condition on the morrow, Mistress Breydon. With God's mercy, he will mend.'

They made their farewells and, outside on the street,

Hal murmured a few words to his squire. The man nodded and disappeared into the night. Then Hal took her elbow. 'We need to talk.'

But instead of heading in through the Broad Gate, and from thence to the gaol, as she'd expected, they turned for the river. The tension in him was palpable as, reaching the centre of the Ludford Bridge, he released her and planted his hands on the stone wall.

Isolda shivered with cold now that delayed reaction set in, and she drew her hood up and her cloak more snugly about her. Hal went on staring down at the running water below, then across at the opposite bank. He was silent so long that she'd begun to believe he had no intention of talking at all, when his voice came low and heavy on a misty breath.

'So...what do we do now, Isolda?'

Hal stared at the cluster of houses on the sloping ground above the river, dark and yet glistening with frost, where the weavers, fullers and dyers lived. While they'd been carrying the wounded boy he hadn't even noticed them, nor the smells that accompanied their work. Now, in the still, sharp air of the night, the odour streamed into his nostrils like a cold and choking fog.

His house in St Albans hadn't stood by the river. His father had been a master weaver and therefore they'd lived in a more respectable part of the town. But the smells had been the same, especially when the wind blew from the south, carrying the stench like a pestilence. The pestilence had struck, once, when he'd been fifteen, but his family had survived it, until the worse pestilence of war had killed them all.

'What do you propose we do?'

Isolda's voice, cautious and wary, cut through his thoughts. She was hovering a foot or so away, staring at him as if she expected him to suddenly pull out an assassin's knife too!

'I have little say in the matter, after all,' she continued. 'I am your prisoner, am I not? And so is Jac...should he live.'

'He is in good hands,' Hal said, for that at least was true. 'If the blood loss is not too much, he has a fair chance of recovering.'

'So you can imprison him or, worse, hang him?'

He turned to look at her. She was pale in the moonlight and frost seemed to shimmer in her eyes, on her lashes, on the wisps of hair that framed her face below her hood. A shiver passed through him that had little to do with the cold that had penetrated right down to the marrow of his bones, for his cloak was still in the infirmary, soaked with Jac's blood.

'I doubt it will come to either.'

'It mustn't! You've got the real culprit now.' The assertion was bold, proud, but the defence of her accomplice spoke loudest of all. 'Take me if you must, but Jac must not be punished. He just did what I told him to do.'

'In all truth, I don't want to arrest either of you.'

The remark seemed to surprise her. 'The town will demand it.'

'The town will have to hear about it first.'

'And...will they hear about it?'

Hal shook his head. 'Not if we are careful.'

'We?' She stepped closer and peered up at him. 'Have you changed sides then, Henry Wevere? Do you fight on the side of right now...or are you still the Earl's good solider?'

'I am not a soldier at all, not really. I am a knight, newly made and of little standing, who has taught himself something of the law. But I was born the son of a weaver.'

'I don't understand. How could a weaver's son become a knight and a lawyer too?'

The night was so still, the river so slow, the moon so bright it seemed as if they'd left the real world and entered another world entirely. Perhaps it was the unreality of where they were, who they were, which loosened his tongue and led him to talk of things he'd never spoken of to anyone.

'Four years ago, during the battle at St Albans, I saw what soldiers do in times of war, how they become like wild beasts, bent on killing, unmoved by death. I realised they don't even see the people in their path, the innocent who have nothing to do with battles or quarrels but who just want to live their lives as best and as happily as they can.'

Her eyes were huge now, dark against the paleness of her face, but she said nothing, just waited for him to go on.

'I was safe enough, up in the clock tower with my friends, all of us bursting with excitement. We watched the Yorkists butcher the Lords Clifford, Somerset and Northumberland in the market square, wound the King with an arrow. I remember how my heart pounded and my blood raced, how thrilling I found the battle, since I had no allegiance to one side or the other.'

Hal stopped. The weir showed like the edge of a sickle under the moonlight, the water running over it slow and thick as the frost pressed down upon it, trying to turn it to ice.

'Then I smelled the smoke and saw the flames, heard the crackle of burning wood.'

There was horror now, not just curiosity, on Isolda's face, as if she dreaded to hear what he would say next but wanted to hear it all the same. What would she think of him, he wondered, if he told her how he had lived while his family had died?

'Warwick's forces came in through the gardens and houses in one of the streets,' he finished instead, 'and took the Lancastrians by surprise. They won a swift victory but left destruction and death in their wake in the town.'

Her face went even paler. 'But what—?'

'What does that have to do with you and Jac?' He deflected the question. To answer it here and now would make it even more brutal, more painful than it already was. 'Nothing—and everything. Innocent people died that day in that fire and I swore then, as I watched those houses burn…that I would do everything in my power to prevent the powerless suffering a similar fate.'

'But you didn't come here to *protect* the innocent and the helpless! You came to seek them out and arrest them!'

Hal stared towards the far bank and its huddle of dark houses. The weavers and dyers and fullers and their families were doubtless all asleep, warm in their beds, safe… Yet that could change in a heartbeat, a breath, a blink of an eye.

'I didn't know the whole story then,' he said. 'I had only the facts…not the truth.'

'The truth being…?'

He looked back into her face. 'That the men who accuse you are themselves criminals, and of the worst kind, because they care only for wealth, power and their own skins. And chief among them is the bailiff, who is as rotten as the law he lays down in this town.'

'Is…that why you freed Dickon today?'

There was a hesitation before he replied. 'You heard?'

'Yes...but I didn't...'

'Didn't believe it?'

Her head shook. 'Didn't trust it.'

Hal almost smiled at her frankness. 'What you mean is, you didn't think I would do the right thing. That I could feel pity, show mercy.'

'No... I don't know.' She glanced away, her brow knitting. 'What you did for Jac tonight, yes, that was merciful, but what you and I consider right and wrong may be very different.'

'Perhaps...and perhaps not.'

Her gaze flashed back to his. 'What do you mean?'

'Before he swooned, your apprentice managed to tell Simon how he was attacked, and by whom.'

In the moonlight her face went paler still but her voice came quick and urgent. 'Tell me who it was!'

'He was knifed at the church door. There were two assailants, and one of them he named as a servant in the employ of Ralph Shearman. A man by the name of Perkin.'

Hal watched her expression carefully but if he'd expected to see surprise there, he was disappointed. Shock yes, outrage too, but she wasn't surprised, a fact that she confirmed.

'I know him. He's a brute, always ready with his fists... but a knife...' Her hand went to her throat. 'My God, to think him willing do Shearman's vile work like that...it is horrible.'

Hal stared at her. 'But you already accused the bailiff in your verses.'

'Yes, but I had no real proof of his wrongdoings, no sure way to expose him—he is too powerful.'

'We'll find proof, Isolda, no matter what we have to

do to get it. I want to help you, but if we are to expose Shearman we need to work together.'

'We?' Her head shook, not in denial but in confusion, her gaze suddenly wary, as if even now she thought he would trap her. 'Why would you aid me?'

'Do you not know?' Hal stepped closer to her, lifted his hand, touched his fingertips to her cheek. Her skin was smooth and as cold as ice, her eyes as brilliant as the stars in the sky. 'After all, it was *you* who told Harry the Cat that he was looking in the wrong place!'

Isolda felt a flush flood into her cheek where his fingers rested, strangely comforting, and yet not comforting at all. Even more unsettling was the notion that, far from arresting and imprisoning her, Henry Wevere was implying that he was willing to join forces with her. Help her bring down the very men he himself had been sent here to support.

For once her instincts, always so dependable, deserted her and left her floundering in uncertainty. Did he mean it? Could she—should she—trust him? If she did and he proved as false as Robert had been, and worse, her fate would be sealed. And yet, was it not sealed already, whatever she did, as he'd caught her in the act this very night?

'I suppose it would be foolish,' she said carefully, 'as well as pointless, to deny now that I wrote those verses.'

The river oozed sluggishly below them and somewhere up on Whitcliffe Common an owl shrieked. From the leper hospital at the other end of the bridge a bell tinkled and a spot of light shone through the narrow window of St Catherine's chapel where, as a child, she used to go and try and peep through that window at the old hermit who lived there, long dead now.

'No.' Hal's voice was as soft as his touch. 'There is no point in denial now.'

She wasn't a child any more but, until this moment, Isolda realised she'd never experienced any of the womanly responses that his simple gesture evoked. Never once with Robert had she known the quickening of her heart that she felt now, the breath that became hard to draw, the pulling of something heavy low down in her belly, the limbs that had gone as weak as water. Until now, she'd felt none of that at all.

'Then I will not try,' she said.

She knew she should step away from those unsettling sensations, guard herself against soft touches and even softer words. But she wasn't able to move. His eyes bored down into hers and she shivered, the hand on her cheek icy but steady. His head dipped and his breath, not cold but warm, was like a mist that both separated and connected them.

That he, like her, felt both cold and hot, suddenly seemed to bring them together in a way she'd never known with Robert. For a long moment they stood without speaking, as if they both waited for something irresistible and inevitable, something that she'd not waited for with her betrothed, ever.

And then a footfall sounded, followed by the chink of iron, loud as a bell, from the wall over the Broad Gate. The guards above changing duty, the sound cutting through the silence of waiting and shattering it.

'Tonight, after what happened to Jac, it is not safe for you to be out of doors after curfew.' Hal's fingers trailed down her cheek, and his hand dropped away. 'I'll see you safely home.'

No, it wasn't safe at all, but it wasn't the point of a

knife, the bars of the gaol or even the hangman's noose that suddenly frightened Isolda, but something invisible, intimate…something that threatened to change her whole life if she allowed it to.

Fear struck at her heart, sharper than the icicles under the arches of the bridge beneath them. Her stomach churned and sweat bathed her palms as she felt herself stripped bare, exposed down to her very bones. That intimate touch of his hand had resonated far deeper than the skin. Deep enough to hover over her heart, reach inside, and touch all the feelings that she'd locked away there three years ago.

The frost must have numbed her wits! Or the moon dazzled her eyes, making her forget everything—the pain and shame of Robert, her fight against injustice, her poems, even who she was. Perhaps the stars had twinkled too brightly, like a witch's magic rod, and turned her into a woman who wanted things she shouldn't.

A man's kiss on her lips, a man's arms around her. But not *any* man—only *this* man who stood in front of her, his mouth suddenly not stern at all, but beautiful and wholly compelling.

'Yes, thank you.' Isolda turned on her heel, her voice unsteady, aware of the trembling of her limbs, that she hoped would be taken for cold. 'I would be grateful if you accompanied me home.'

She didn't want to *become* that woman, willing to let herself be like clay in the hands of a man she'd only known for a fortnight! A woman fooled into betraying everything she was for the sake of needs she'd thought absent but that now she realised she possessed.

And a man, furthermore, who had power over her now after discovering she was the writer of the poems. For that alone, he was not to be trusted, not even after what he'd done and said that night. Robert had been kind too, and clever, and she'd fallen for his courtesy and charm like the most naïve of females. Who was to say that Henry Wevere wasn't even cleverer?

They walked back over the bridge, his hand briefly touching her spine as he guided her back the way they'd come, making her quiver. The smells of dyes and washed wool seemed stronger, the crunching of frost beneath their feet louder, the river deeper in its icy flow. In fact, everything seemed too clear in the moonlight, the night air too sharp, the sting of cold like shards of glass upon her face.

And clearest of all was the shocking self-discovery Isolda had made that night. Somewhere deep inside her, buried but alive, was a living, needing, *demanding* woman of flesh and blood that, now the outer defences had been probed, though not breached, threatened to claw a way out.

To her relief, Hal said nothing as they walked on, side by side, and she made no attempt at conversation either. So the voice of the guard at the gate in the wall came gruff and startling.

'How does the boy, Sir Knight?'

Hal's reply was short, and she sensed he didn't want to tarry. 'Well enough.'

They passed through the arch and climbed Mill Street. Halfway up, and in full moonlight now, her poem shone white upon the door of the Guildhall. They stopped as if each read the other's mind.

'What about…that?' Isolda asked carefully. Down on the bridge he'd said he'd help her, but had that been true? Or had he been dazzled by the moon too, numbed into impulse by the glittering sky, and was now regretting that promise? Was he even—and God forbid the thought—planning to trap her by gaining her trust first?

She waited for his reply but instead he crossed to the door and retrieved the hammer which she'd dropped on the ground, hours ago, it seemed. Coming back to her side, he handed her the tool, his voice a whisper.

'Conceal it under your cloak, lest we meet anyone.'

Taking the hammer, she slid its handle into the girdle at her waist. 'And the poem…?'

The church bell tolled thrice and Isolda felt her heart beating ever louder as Hal's eyes flickered once more to the door and then came back to hers.

'I think we'll leave it where it is.'

'Why?' she asked, unable to keep a note of suspicion out of her voice.

'So that the Twelve and Twenty-Five see it tomorrow, of course.' A ghost of a smile touched his mouth. 'Wasn't that your—and Jac's—intention tonight?'

Isolda nodded, her mind whirling as they walked on in silence, although now the night seemed full of sounds. Their breathing, their footsteps, her heart, even the quiet had a voice. One that grew more and more insistent to be heard as they neared the top of Mill Street, yet to cross the square. There he drew her aside and into the darkness of a narrow alley between two houses.

At first, Isolda thought he'd seen someone abroad and meant to hide until they'd passed by. But there was no one, only they two. And then his arms went around her and the warmth of his body struck hers, and softly he kissed her.

His mouth was gentle but she could feel his heart beating as fast as hers did, faster even, and his body trembled as if he no longer shivered with cold but with feeling.

The same way as she shivered. Isolda curled her hands

into the folds of his cloak, the rough wall behind her digging into her shoulder blades as his mouth pressed harder, his lips seeking, his breath mingling with hers.

In the cradle of her hips she felt his loins harden, the way Robert's had done when his ardour had got the better of him. She'd resisted him each and every time because she hadn't wanted it, nor wanted him. He hadn't lit a spark to her senses, not made her blood warm, her heart pound, her belly swoop and hollow. Robert had caused nothing but empty resignation in her and often resentment, nothing like the violent responses she experienced now.

She wanted Hal, *all of him*, with a craving that shocked her. She quivered with longing for him, so much so that had he not been pressed so close, her legs would have failed to keep her upright. She needed him in a way she'd never needed, nor ever dreamed she'd need, a man.

But Hal wasn't just a man, he was…different. She knew that with a certainty that she couldn't explain. And as she wrapped her arms around his neck, pulling him closer so that his kiss deepened even more, Isolda didn't even want to try to explain anything. The taste of him, the weight of his body as it covered hers, his ardour, and hers too, needed no explanation. It was the most natural thing in the world.

Finally, he broke the kiss and stepped back, his eyes glittering brighter even than the frost underfoot. 'I don't know whether to curse you or myself for that!'

The remark wasn't angry, or accusing, or wondering. Nor was it a jest, but was said so solemnly, with so much intensity, that it sent a tingle down her spine. He took her elbow and they resumed their walking, just as the stars began to disappear into the eerie, slowly emerging hue that preceded the dawn.

And Isolda knew the woman inside her, the one she'd locked away after Robert, with heart dented and pride in tatters, had broken the first bar of her self-sealed prison.

'It's best if you return home alone.' They stopped at the opening of the street. 'I will watch you to your door from here.'

Isolda nodded and then lifted her mouth again and he took it, swiftly, briefly, passionately.

'Go.'

She did as he bid, quickly crossing the square to her house and turning the key as quietly as she could in the lock. Just before she pushed the door shut again, she found him where he still stood in the shadows and, even across that distance, their eyes locked with the same irrevocable intensity as their lips had. Then, with a nod, he turned and vanished.

Chapter Eight

'My man denies it vehemently!'

Hal looked up at Ralph Shearman from behind the long oak table in the great hall of Ludlow Castle. Beads of sweat glistened on the bailiff's heavy forehead and dripped down the bridge of his nose.

'I would hardly have expected him to do otherwise,' he said. 'Nevertheless, the boy recognised him very clearly.'

'Then it is the word of a miserable Flemish wool washer against that of a respected man of the town.'

The arrogance jarred along Hal's nerves and the fact that the bailiff was right irritated most of all. 'I trust a jury would be unbiased.'

'If it comes to a trial at all,' Shearman sneered. 'I hear the boy is unlikely to live.'

Hal had three pieces of parchment on the table before him. One was Isolda's poem left on the Guildhall door, which had been brought to him that morning. The second was the one Jac had been nailing to the church door before he was attacked. And the third was a bait for the man glowering down at him.

'Which would suit you very well, I suspect,' he said, casting that bait smoothly.

The bailiff pounced like a raging boar, thumping his

hands down upon the table, making it rock on its legs. 'Are you accusing me of compliance in this incident, Wevere?'

'Not yet, no.'

'Not yet?' The man blinked, his breath coming rank and laboured between his fleshy lips. 'That sounds like a threat to me!'

'Take it as you please.' Leisurely, Hal indicated the third parchment. 'We have here the words Isolda Breydon's apprentice uttered before he swooned, as related by my squire, who found him at the church door.'

'And what was he doing there after curfew, if not up to no good?'

'Granted, we discovered this on him...' Hal indicated the parchment, which was crumpled and stained with blood. 'That he meant to pin this on the church door is undeniable. What concerns me now are his reasons for doing so.'

'Reasons be damned! The boy got what he deserved.'

'Not in my opinion. Murder, or attempted murder, suggests that the contents of this poem are justified.' Hal looked Shearman straight in the eye. 'All that remains is to prove it and punish the perpetrators...and their master.'

The bailiff's face went from crimson to ashen and then back again. 'By God, I'll go over your head to the Earl himself with this, Wevere! Never mind a jury, it's clear to me that *you* are biased, and towards the wrong cause!'

'If by that you mean I favour right over wrong, then you are correct.'

But even as he said it, Hal knew he *was* biased and had been ever since he'd seen Jac bleeding into the cold cobbled ground, the victim of a cowardly attack in the dark. Even so, the vicious assault on the boy might not have swayed him so completely, nor so soon, had he not stood on the bridge afterwards with Isolda.

The slow flow of the river, the icy rime on its banks and on the roofs of the workers' houses beyond, had sharpened his senses to the point that every glint of frost, every icicle of frozen water, had pierced through his skin and set his heart a-pounding and his blood afire.

As he'd told her what had happened at St Albans—part of it, anyway—he'd known then which side he belonged on. And when he'd reached out and touched her cheek...and later, when he'd drawn her into the shadows...kissed her...

'You jumped-up peasant's whelp!'

Shearman's insult jerked Hal out of his thoughts, but the bailiff was stating fact, up to a point, anyway.

'My father was a master weaver, a burgess like yourself, and therefore hardly a peasant.' In a flash, his voice changed. 'And, as much as I abhor violence, should you repeat that insult towards my family ever again, you'll face the point of my sword, Shearman, in full view of the entire town.'

The bailiff's fists clenched on the table top, so hard that the flesh of his fingers bulged around the bands of his jewelled rings. Hal had kept Shearman on his feet instead of inviting him to sit during the interview, but even though the man towered over him, seated as he was, he knew he had the upper hand.

'And now...' he said, infusing a curt dismissal into his tone. 'My squire will see you out.'

Shearman's whole body quaked like a pot ready to burst and then he gave a dismissive and offensive gesture. 'I'll see myself out!'

As he turned and strode down the hall, Hal let out his

breath and grinned at Simon, who came and perched on the table top.

'Well...' His squire grinned back. 'I think we've made an enemy there, Hal.'

Hal nodded. 'And a formidable one.' He looked down at the bloodstained parchment. 'But at the end of the day, a spineless one.'

'Yes, the man's a coward, sending his henchmen to do his dirty work.' Simon scratched his chin. 'You think him guilty?'

'Undoubtedly, but it won't be easy proving it,' Hal replied. 'He's right when he says it's the word of a respected townsman against the Breydons' apprentice. By the way, has the Prior sent word of Jac this morning?'

His squire shook his head. 'Not yet. Shall I send someone to enquire?'

Hal thought for a moment. 'No, I'll go myself...and from there to see Mistress Breydon. She will be anxious to know of his condition.'

The prospect of seeing Isolda again sent a thrill along his nerves, followed swiftly by excitement, anticipation... and fear. Isolda reminded him too much of Beatrice, not in her looks but in her passion and compassion, her determination to stand up and speak out against wrongdoing. Until St Albans, his family had never suffered oppression and tyranny, only the day-to-day unfairness of life, hardship too at times. In this affair at Ludlow, however, danger as well as injustice lurked. There was so much at stake, so much to win or to lose, and Isolda was at the centre where that storm would rage, should it break.

'But I'll speak to Edmund de la Mare first.' Hal got to his feet. 'And alert him of our suspicions about the attack of last night, which I suspect he has heard of already.'

But, going in search of the constable, he learned that de la Mare had ridden out to discuss some business with the lord of the manor of Ledwyche, and wasn't expected to return until later that afternoon. He would have to wait, but first, to the infirmary and then to Isolda's house. But, as he went out into the daylight, he found there was no need to go anywhere, for she was walking across the inner bailey towards him.

Isolda saw Hal's lean and simply clad figure descend the stone steps from the great hall. Her feet faltered, but only for an instant, long enough to see the look of shock then pleasure that rippled over his face. She forced her feet to resume their course, her eyes fixed on his face. Halting almost exactly in the middle of the bailey, they spoke at the same time.

'I've been to see Jac—'

'I was just going to enquire—'

He was the first to smile, banishing the atmosphere of nervousness and uncertainty. 'It seems we are both of the same mind this morning, Mistress Breydon.'

Isolda smiled too. 'It does indeed, Sir Henry.' A little silence followed, into which fell the memory of his touch upon her cheek the previous night, the gentle strength of the arms that had drawn her into the shadows, the light yet ardent press of his mouth upon hers.

She cleared her throat. 'Jac is well, the bleeding has stopped and the Prior thinks he will make a full recovery.'

His eyes searched her face. 'And you? How do you do this morning?'

'Well enough, thank you.' Isolda took a breath and gathered her courage. 'I am here, as no doubt you have guessed, to speak to you of…last night.'

She'd lain awake for hours after going to bed, thinking of Jac, possibly at death's door, and of the evil intent of the cowards who'd attacked him, and of their master, who was the most evil of all. But when she'd finally drifted off to sleep, her dreams had been full of Hal.

'I am ready to pay whatever price I must for what I did,' she added, her cheeks colouring as those dreams became vivid once more, the nearness of him in the flesh now stirring her senses. 'But, in return, I demand that the *real* criminals of this town are brought to justice, as you promised you would do...last night...on the bridge.'

His gaze scrutinised hers and then he nodded. 'Come inside, Isolda.'

He gestured, not towards the great hall but towards the chamber block adjacent, and they went in through the smaller entrance to one side. Isolda followed him up a stone staircase to an upper floor, where he pushed open a door, standing aside to let her enter first.

As she did so, she saw at once that it was his own private bedchamber. On one side was a large arched window and in the far wall a fire glowed in the hearth, banked low. To the right of her, the bed was visible, the heavy curtain that divided the sleeping area from the rest of the room drawn back to reveal it neatly made. Rich green curtains surrounded the bed itself, also drawn back and tied to each of the four posts.

All this Isolda took in as Hal went up to the table in the middle of the room, upon which sat a piece of parchment. She knew exactly what it was, of course, without having to approach and inspect it. It was one of her poems and although it lay flat it was creased and its corners were curled, as if it had been read over and over.

He turned suddenly. 'I brought you here, Isolda, so

that we might have more privacy to talk than we would have in the hall.'

'I didn't think you'd brought me here for anything else,' she retorted, lest he suppose she'd agreed to come to his chamber for any other reason! 'Is it to be a private interrogation then? No witnesses?'

'It's not going to be an interrogation at all.' His brow furrowed. 'Do you not remember my saying last night that I intend to help you?'

Isolda remembered with acute clarity everything he'd said last night, but in the cold light of day none of it seemed real or believable. 'Yes, but I thought...'

'That I didn't mean it?'

She nodded. 'How can I trust you? How do I know that you are not simply trying to trap me?'

His face darkened. 'I have no need to try and trap you, Isolda. I already have you.'

Leaving that remark hanging in the air, he poured ale into two cups from a pitcher on the table, and held one out to her. Isolda took it, her fingers trembling a little as they brushed his.

'You are cold?'

She shook her head. In fact, she was warm, too warm, despite the subdued fire in the hearth and the draught that came in through one of the glazed windows and touched the back of her neck. 'No, I'm not cold.'

They drank in silence for a moment, holding each other's gaze over the rim of their cups. Between them, a host of unspoken words seemed to pass—unspoken yet understood. Yes, he had her, but strangely, Isolda felt neither trapped nor afraid, though perhaps she should have done.

But the truth was, last night, when Hal had spoken to her on the bridge, she'd seen a vulnerability in him that she'd never seen in any other man. Honesty too, and the courage to reveal himself where another man would not have been so weak. Or so strong.

And before that, when he and his squire had carried Jac, not to the gaol but to the hospital, Hal's cloak stemming the flow of blood, he'd put compassion over his duty. Surely that proved he was trustworthy?

As if he'd read her mind, he put his cup down. 'You can trust me, Isolda. All I said and did last night, I meant to say and do.'

She stepped forward and placed her cup down on the table too. Did that 'all' also include the kiss? And the way he'd taken her into his arms, the warmth of their two bodies coming together in the shadows? It seemed not, as he went on.

'But today we have to think carefully, and cunningly. We must plan how we go about this, and for that we need to keep our heads clear.'

The words, and his meaning, were more than clear. Last night, they had both lost their heads. Their feelings had run high and in the wrong direction, tossed awry by the events of the night. Whatever had happened wasn't what she'd intended or wanted, and neither it appeared had he. Holy virgin! He'd even said he didn't know whether to curse her or himself for it! How stupid she'd been to dismiss that remark, to focus instead on what had caused it, to let herself believe, to hope...

'Yes,' Isolda said firmly. 'If you mean to help me, then we will need all our wits about us to snare Shearman.'

'I cannot promise we will succeed; you must know that from the start, Isolda.'

She nodded. 'I know. But at least we can try.'

'The bailiff is a powerful man and he has the support of many of the burgesses of the town.'

'And we are only two.' She turned and went to stand at the window, looking out over the bailey. 'But two bees can drive a bull to distraction.'

Hal smiled to himself, despite the enormity of the task ahead of them and the risks involved, more so for Isolda than for himself. He, after all, had the protection of the Earl of Shrewsbury, whereas she had only *his* protection. A thin blade of fear drove itself into his heart as the waiting storm suddenly blew nearer. He would need all his advantage of position, all his legal knowledge, meagre as that was, and as much military skill as he possessed if he was to aid her and keep her from harm.

He'd always protected his sister and brother, both younger than he, but on the one day they'd needed him most of all he wasn't there. That loss, that guilt, that regret, had changed him from the idle, reckless youth he'd been into what he'd thought he'd become—a measured and dispassionate man. But was he being just as reckless now by embroiling them both in a conflict they might well lose?

'Isolda...' he began. 'It is not just one bull we are facing but a whole town full of bulls.'

The sunlight behind her framed her figure, like an angel in an alcove. She *was* an angel, championing the oppressed as she did, with no thought to her own safety. Every time she'd stolen out at night to nail those poems onto doors she'd risked arrest or injury, like that which had happened to her apprentice last night.

His heart shuddered violently. If Shearman's henchmen had attacked Isolda and not Jac, it would have been *she* who was discovered lying in a pool of blood, her life hanging like a thread of wool in the wind.

'I know that even better than you.' She turned to face him and the fragile beauty of her face made his breath catch. 'But I've never been afraid of bulls.'

Hal crossed over to the window and looked down into her eyes. Their colour was enhanced by the dark blue gown she wore, their long lashes making them seem larger, more vivid, even more beautiful.

'Nor have I,' he said. 'Especially those that bellow the loudest. And we may be small bees, Isolda, but together we will fly as high as it takes and sting as hard as we have to.'

A smile pulled at her lips. 'Have you set all my poems to memory then?'

'As it happens, I have,' he said, smiling too. 'One about cats and rats in particular.'

Her head titled, her hair catching the sunlight, a blush colouring her cheek. 'Did you suspect it was me, right from the start? That first day you came to my house?'

Hal shook his head. 'Then I half suspected Jac, but later, when we walked through the market, hearing your defence of the farmers, the way you spoke with them, I think then I began to wonder. Though I should have guessed that day in the church, when you and your mother tried to creep out of the other door.'

Her gaze searched his face. 'If you hadn't caught me in the act last night, you might never have had proof, for all your suspicions.'

'No, perhaps not. But when I read about Harry the Cat, I *knew* for certain then that it was you.'

'I wrote that the night of the market. I hoped, after you

paid the toll money for the farmers, and listened to old Ned, and later, when you freed Dickon from the pillory...'

Her voice faded, as if uncertainty still lingered, so Hal completed the sentence for her.

'You thought I might be sympathetic to your cause?'

She nodded. 'I felt you were not a man to stand aside and let wrong prevail over right. I wouldn't have given myself away, of course, but I considered asking you for your aid.'

'And what if I hadn't believed you?'

'Then I would have continued writing the poems until someone *did* believe them.' She gave a little shrug. 'That's why I addressed that last to you. There was no one else who could, or would, listen. You at least are a stranger, impartial...and I hoped you were honest too...perhaps even trustworthy.'

Hal's breath caught. Stranger he might be, but her safety had suddenly become far more important to him than any cause. 'All the same, it might be safer if you stopped writing these poems, Isolda.'

'Never! How can I, while such despicable men rule this town? After what happened to Jac, who will be the *next* to feel the murderer's knife, Hal? No, I cannot cease, not until this evil is exposed and stamped out!'

He knew then it was useless to even try and argue or persuade, but at least Isolda wasn't alone any more. He would help her. After all, fighting wrong and upholding right was what he'd dedicated himself to over the last four years, so how could he do anything else?

'Then promise me you'll be careful,' he said lightly, yet with a warning beneath the words that she couldn't fail to grasp. 'The next time it might be someone other than me who finds you.'

There was a pause before she replied. 'You sound afraid.'

Afraid? Yes, but not of Shearman and his sort, not of what the Earl would say should they fail, not even of the King if he chose to intervene. But he was terrified of failing Isolda, and worse, of caring more about her than about their cause, of coming to love her...

Even as the word formed itself in his head, for the very first time, Hal knew his feelings for Isolda were already ones of love. Not the fierce bond of love he had for his family, but the irresistible and eternal love of a man for a woman. The most violent of emotions, the easiest to embrace, the hardest to forget.

'Fear can be a good thing,' he said. Turning away from that knowledge—too momentous to think on yet—he went back over to the table, touched a finger to the parchment lying there. 'It can—and has—saved many a life.' And many a heart too, no doubt. But it wouldn't save his if he gave it now, to her, whether she wanted it or not. 'But if you cannot be afraid, Isolda, then be careful and wise, not just bold.'

'Let them do their worst. I do not fear any of them!'

'No, I have discovered that.' Facing her again, he adopted the voice of plain reason. 'But it won't just be us. It will be Jac, and Ned, and Wat, and all the others who have complaints against the leaders of this town.'

She was silent a moment, chewing her bottom lip. 'You are right. They will have to come forward in person and put their complaints before a tribunal.'

Hal stared, mesmerised, at her mouth. 'It won't be poems on doors any longer, Isolda, but words spoken under oath at the bench before a jury.'

Her voice, which had sobered a little with worry, suddenly brightened. 'But you are a lawyer, are you not? I remember you said so on the bridge.'

He'd said a lot on the bridge. 'I have some knowledge of law, that I have made pains to learn, but I am not a lawyer.'

'Even so—'

Hal interrupted her. 'And I have learned enough to know that one honest judge and any number of ardent claimants may not be enough to vanquish the corrupt.'

Abruptly, she pushed herself away from the window and marched across the room towards him. 'Stop talking as if we have already lost, Hal! Yes, I understand we may lose—our freedom, our lives perhaps, as well as our cause. And yes, I know we need to step with care, keep our heads, be cleverer than they are.' She planted her hands on her hips. 'But we must be bold too, confident, fearless, not fearful. We must use surprise and take them off-guard…like you took me off-guard last night—'

She stopped suddenly, as if out of breath, or out of words. And, just as suddenly, Hal needed to hear what she'd been about to say next.

'When I caught you, you mean? Or when I kissed you?'

Chapter Nine

Isolda felt herself blush furiously, but one of them had to say it sooner or later, and she was glad it was *he* who'd had the courage that she lacked. 'Both!' she said.

Below, in the castle bailey, the bustle of the day was going on. Voices floated upwards, boots rang on cobbles, a horse neighed in the stables, a clink of metal sounded piercingly. She waited for him to speak, desperately trying to read his mind, his expression. However, when he finally responded, his words were clear as a bell.

'The first I expected and intended. The other I did not.'

A strange pang struck Isolda's heart. 'Well, as to the first, I will go on writing my poems, as I must do until we bring these men to justice. As to the latter…well, that is best forgotten, is it not?'

'It would be for the best, yes.'

She walked back over to the window and looked out. The sky was blue and into it smoke from the myriad chimneys of the castle rose in wisps. A dog barked and jumped around two men who were drawing water from the well, for the kitchen no doubt, laughing at some jest or other.

A jest. Yes, perhaps that was how she should view that kiss last night. Men were notorious for grabbing maidens around the waist and planting meaningless kisses on their mouths, whether they wanted them or not. And yet, when Hal had kissed her, whether he'd intended to or not, it hadn't *felt* meaningless. It had seemed full of meaning, of passion and feeling and, even though it *had* caught her off-guard, somehow it had felt inevitable.

After Robert, she'd never imagined she'd ever kiss a man again, nor want to, but now... Now...she didn't know *what* she wanted. What she *did* know was that her life since then had been lacking, and that her fear of being betrayed, lied to, shamed and humiliated—all the things Robert had done to her—had created that lack.

She turned back to face Hal and, giving herself a mental shake, pushed all thoughts of that kiss and its meaning, or lack of meaning, away.

'So...now we've agreed to forget...that.' Why couldn't she even say the word *kiss*? Had she become a coward now too? 'How do we proceed from here? Do we confront Shearman?'

He didn't respond for a moment and then his shoulders squared, as if he too had pushed that kiss of last night resolutely away. 'First, we talk to all of those who are being unjustly treated. Those farmers who have lost their grazing rights or their homes, or cannot pay taxes and tolls set too high.'

'To encourage them to speak out in the court?'

'That...and to convince them that they are not alone, that we are on their side, openly and legally, not secretly, under cover of dark.'

Isolda knew he meant like a criminal. A sudden shudder went through her as once more the undeniable realisation struck her. If it had been anyone else other than Hal who'd caught her last night, her fate—and Jac's too—would have been very different.

The fact suddenly made her ashamed—and grateful. Crossing back to where he stood, she halted before him.

'Thank you,' she said simply, because there was so much more she could have said.

'It's a bit too early to thank me, since we may yet lose.'

'I don't mean that. I mean thank you for...what you did for Jac last night, for not arresting me...for helping me instead.'

A strange expression coloured the depths of his eyes. 'I could not do otherwise, Isolda.'

'Most men in your position *would* have done otherwise, without a second thought.' She paused. 'Why are you so different, Hal? Is it because you were born the son of a weaver that you understand and sympathise?'

His body stiffened and, although they were standing so close she could have touched him, he seemed to move a great distance away. Then he said the strangest, most startling thing.

'I have a debt to pay, Isolda, one that I will have to go on paying my whole life long, but I will do it gladly.'

'A debt of money?'

He shook his head. 'A debt of honour.'

'Is someone holding you to this debt? Will they not relieve you of it, whatever it is?'

His gaze suddenly grew dark with unmistakable sorrow. 'They cannot. They are dead.'

Isolda touched his arm in a gesture of comfort. 'Dead? Oh, I'm so sorry, Hal. Who were they? When did they die?'

The answer came so bluntly that it took her breath away. 'My family, and they died four years ago.'

Isolda's mind raced. The battle at St Albans had been four years ago. On the bridge he'd spoken of the burning houses, the deaths of the people inside them. And as he'd spoken she'd heard anguish in his voice, the same anguish she heard again now, as he strode to the door and opened it.

'Someone will escort you to the gates,' he said, then called to someone without. 'When you arrive home, can you compile a list of all the people we need to talk to? I'll come to your house shortly after Vespers.'

She couldn't move for a moment, even though it was clear she was being dismissed, and in the most abrupt of ways. Instead, she stood reeling, at what she'd learned about Hal's family, at the terrible look on his face, the quiver of his arm as it braced the door open.

'Hal...?' Isolda began, but the man he'd called for appeared just then and the moment was lost. So, instead, she crossed over to the door, pausing on the threshold to look up into his face. It was white, the lips pressed tightly together, bloodless.

'Thank you, Sir Henry. Until later then.'

She followed her guide down the stairs and across the bailey. At the nape of her neck the hair tingled, and she knew Hal watched her from the window of his chamber. As she passed under the main gates its shadow covered her like a cloak of ice and a chill slid down her spine as the inevitable and horrifying question filled her thoughts.

Had his family been among those who'd died in the fire at St Albans?

After Vespers had ended that night, Isolda waited for Hal. She counted the hours with each toll of the bell, long after curfew had sounded, and finally, as the night stretched out and everything in the house and the town settled into silence, she assumed he wasn't coming.

Unbraiding her hair, she sat at the table next to the fire where she composed her poems and began to comb out the thick tresses, trying to ignore the sense of disappointment that had gradually replaced the anticipation she'd felt earlier.

Before her, the list of names she'd set down on parchment seemed to dance in the flames. Eight and thirty of them. It wasn't a large number, not compared to Ludlow's population, but these were the only ones she was confident would speak out. Others were too afraid for their livelihoods and their homes should they dare to challenge the powers of the town. Isolda had put her own name at the top of the list but omitted Jac's name, although if they lost this fight they would *all* suffer, not just she.

The knock when it came startled her. Jumping up from her chair, she pulled a shawl around her shoulders and went through into the shop to open the door. Hal stood there, rain driving like silver spears behind him and the night outside bitter, as if snow might follow close on the heels of the deluge.

She held the door ajar and felt the wet and the cold enter with him. He shivered and the skin of his face appeared stretched and pale. Had he got so cold just walking the short distance from the castle?

'Are we alone?'

Isolda nodded, her mouth suddenly dry, heat rising into her cheeks. 'My mother has returned to Tewkesbury.'

'Good.'

Hal removed his cloak and he looked down at the garment, as if wondering what to do with it. Isolda took it from him and, shaking it out, hung it on a peg in the wall. Then she gestured to him to come through to the hall, where she poured him a cup of ale.

'Sit down and get warm.'

She spoke as if she was greeting a traveller lost in a storm or a casual visitor, or one of her customers come to buy wool. But Hal was none of those. He did as he was bid, taking one of the two chairs next to the fire, his attention going immediately to the list on the table top.

Isolda retook her seat and waited in silence as his eyes travelled down the list of names she'd written out, sipping his ale as he read. The fire was a good one and she sensed the cold leave him, his limbs relaxing as if his very blood was thawing. Warmth stretched out towards her too, making her kirtle and the shawl she'd pulled around her shoulders seem suffocating.

'Those are the only ones who I'm sure will come forward,' she said, removing the shawl and setting it aside, wishing she'd left her hair plaited as perspiration bathed the nape of her neck. 'But once they speak out, others may follow, if things go our way.'

'We may be able to add another name to this list.' He put his cup down and, leaning nearer the fire, rubbed his hands together. 'I went to St John's Hospital before coming here.'

Isolda's heart staggered to a halt and a sick feeling dropped into the pit of her stomach. 'Is Jac...?'

'He is well. I didn't see him, though I was told he slept comfortably, so did not wish to disturb him. I went instead to speak to Prior Oteley, in whom it seems we have an ally.'

'You told him of our plans?'

'I had no choice. It seems Jac, in his delirium last night, spoke aloud and lucid as to what happened, and who the perpetrator was. When Oteley asked me if it was true, I decided to test him and it appears he is in sympathy with your cause.'

'Our cause,' she corrected.

He gave a slow nod. 'Our cause.' His gaze was bright in the firelight and his hair gleamed like bronze as it fell thickly over his brow, his expression eager and alive.

'Then the sooner we begin, the better.'

Drawing their chairs closer together, they bent over the list on the table once more. Hal asked her meticulously about each name, where the man lived, what his trade was, his family. One or two who would have too much to lose should they fail, they set aside for the moment, preferring to involve them only if necessary. By the time they'd finished, with the list reduced to thirty, Isolda felt he must know each and every one of them as well as she did.

From without, the church bell sounded the hour of midnight. The rain still fell on the cobbled street outside but inside all was quiet. The cat slept in front of the fire, its paws twitching now and then as it dreamt.

It was as the last note of the bell faded that Isolda realised how close they were sitting. His bent head almost touched hers, and his forearm rested alongside hers on the table top. She became aware, slowly but so potently, of the warmth of his flesh seeping into hers, the strength of muscle and sinew hard against the softness of her sleeve.

She knew she should shift slightly so that they didn't touch, but somehow she didn't want to. Whether it was the silence, the comforting crackle of the fire, the sense of peace that pervaded the house, she didn't know but she felt...*comfortable* sitting there with Hal in a way she'd never been when she'd sat with Robert.

Being with Hal was pleasant—more than pleasant... right. As if he belonged here in her house, not like a welcome and occasional guest, but as a permanent inhabitant. As much a part of her home and her world as the oaken beams of the roof, the smell of wool from the shop, the rustle of the autumn rushes on the floor.

Was that because he was a weaver's son, not a nobleman or a merchant? Or because he was Hal?

In any event, it was he who shifted, rolling his shoulders and putting down the quill with which he'd been marking the names. The fingers of his right hand were stained with ink and he rubbed them absently on his hosed knee. With a start, she realised his thigh too had been pressed tightly against hers—but that too had been pleasant...right.

'We will start with those who live in the town itself, I think.'

Isolda gave a nod of agreement. 'Tomorrow?'

'Yes, at first light.' He stifled a yawn. 'As for tonight, I'm tired and I expect you are too. I should go.' Folding the list, he put it in the pouch at his belt. 'I'll take this with me, however, as it will be less suspicious if found on me than it would be found on you.'

'Because it will look as if you are investigating the innocent?'

He smiled. 'But I will be investigating the *guilty*, as we both know.' Then, reaching out, he took both her hands in his. 'And I swear to you, Isolda, I'll do all that I can to bring them to account.'

It was all Isolda needed to hear. Now she began to believe that they not only couldn't fail, but they wouldn't.

'I know you will, Hal.'

Their gazes held for so long it seemed as if she might drown in those green-gold depths. His eyes truly were beautiful and mesmerising, and yet, for all the bright passion that gleamed in them now, there seemed a darkness deep within them. He couldn't have been more than a few years older than her twenty-two summers, yet at times he seemed far older than his face or his body portrayed.

It was on the tip of her tongue to ask him why he was always so serious when a log settled and broke in the hearth and a glowing shard of wood fell out onto the floor. Before Isolda could move, Hal had leapt to his feet and, reaching for the iron tongs, swiftly picked up the fallen debris and threw it back onto the fire.

It was such an ordinary occurrence, one that happened frequently, and yet his chest heaved as if he struggled to draw his breath. His eyes were not mesmerising now but wide with alarm and Isolda saw beads of sweat had broken out on his brow.

'There is no need for concern, Hal,' she said, rising to her feet too. 'Cinders are always falling out of the hearth. Once, the cat's tail got scorched—'

But he cut her off. 'Fires are dangerous, Isolda, and should not be treated so lightly.'

'I know that!' She didn't mean to snap a response, but did he think her a child? 'But there really was no danger of the house burning down!'

As soon as she said it, Isolda knew she shouldn't have. His expression froze and his eyes flashed with such pain that she felt it too.

'I'm sorry,' she said quickly.

'Why should you be sorry?' The question was as sharp as the point of a dagger.

'Because of what happened at St Albans, your fear of fire—'

Again, he cut her off. 'Fear?' He shook his head. 'No, it's not fear, Isolda.'

'Then what is it?' she pressed, anxious to know, to understand. 'Was...someone you knew, or were close to, burned in the fire at St Albans?'

He gave a nod. 'I thought you might have guessed who it was by now.'

'Your family?'

'My parents, my sister and younger brother.' A choke entered his voice. 'They all died...while I lived.'

Isolda's gasp of horror cut Hal to the quick and when she reached out and touched his arm he couldn't help it, he recoiled, and her hand dropped away again. In the stunned silence that followed he could hear the rain outside, so heavy it gushed off the roof of the house like a waterfall. Why couldn't it have rained that May day in St Albans? But if it had, would it have made any difference?

'Hal... I don't know what to say.'

'There is little *to* say.'

He saw her struggle to respond and hated himself for rejecting her sympathy. But sympathy was only a step away from pity and that was the last thing he wanted, especially from her. If it had rained that day, he might not have slipped out into the sunshine to watch the battle. If it had rained, he might have remained indoors, died with them.

'Well, to say I'm sorry for your loss sounds...inadequate, but I am sorry, nevertheless. It must have been a terrible accident—'

'Accident?' He shook his head. Rain or sun, it would have made no difference, But if there had been no battle at all, his family would still be alive. 'It was no accident, Isolda.'

'But you said...'

'I know what I said. And yes, if you take it one way, it *was* an accident. But if Warwick hadn't directed his forces there, if the soldiers hadn't been so heedless, if their commanders had had better control, it need never have happened.'

'No one can foretell what might or might not happen, Hal, especially in the midst of a battle, surely?'

'One can make choices, though, and that's what Warwick did. His choice brought death to my family, and I…'

Hal heard his voice break as a fire, as awful as the one that had consumed his home, consumed him too. He struggled for words but none would come, and the only sounds were the crackle of wood, the rain on the roof and his awful rasping breath.

'You weren't there?' Isolda finished his words for him, ones she sensed accurately that he couldn't bring himself to say. 'You were watching the battle from the church tower with your friends?'

'Friends? They weren't even that!' Suddenly, all the pain inside him seemed to dissipate, as if his lungs had collapsed and left his body completely empty. 'No, I wasn't there, Isolda. But I should have been. I should have been working alongside my brother that day, as I'd promised my father I would do.'

'If you *had* been there, you might have died too.'

'You say that as if it is a *blessing* I didn't. You are wrong.'

She was silent for a moment, as if desperately seeking words to counter his. 'I think it is more wrong to wish yourself dead when you were given life. That is wicked, Hal, because your family wouldn't wish you'd died too. They would be glad and thankful that you escaped the fire, that you lived.'

Hal felt the blood drain from his face. He'd never thought that, nor had anyone said it to him before. He'd never even said it to himself because he couldn't allow himself that easy escape from guilt, the possibility that he might be forgiven. And now, to hear it from Isolda, he rejected it too, as he'd rejected her sympathy.

'Do you not know, Isolda, that there are worse things than death? If you knew how I was back then, you would not be so quick to pity me now!'

'Pity? Is that what you think...?' Suddenly, concern and pity—if that was what it was—vanished, and anger took their place. 'What would your family feel if they could hear you speak of their deaths so glibly? Worse, with words of self-blame that are meaningless?'

'Meaningless?' He shook his head savagely. 'You have not understood. I broke a promise, shirked my duty, and my family died.'

'I have understood perfectly, Hal. But can't you see, they would have died even if you *had* been there?' She looked away, took a breath, and then her eyes locked on his again. 'I am sorry for your loss, but I also have lost a father and a brother, and my mother has lost a husband and a son, both gone long before their time. You are not the only one to know grief so do not speak as if you are!'

A sense of utter shame fell over Hal and his gut clenched as if a well-aimed kick had connected. Holding out a hand, he took a step forward, but she spun away from him.

'I am sorry, Isolda—'

But again she cut him off. 'Do not be! If you yourself hold your life so cheaply, why should I trouble to care?'

His hand froze in mid-air, hung there, his fingers quivering. The question wasn't one that needed an answer and yet an answer—or rather a question of his own—was imperative.

'Do you care, Isolda?'

She spun back to him, her eyes full of an emotion that filled her voice too. 'You know I do!'

Suddenly, as her words thudded into his heart, an urgent knocking came at the door. Hal looked sharply at Isolda, the tension of a moment ago suspended, though not forgotten. 'Are you expecting anyone?'

She shook her head. 'At this hour? No, of course not.'

The knock came again, more urgent. 'Mistress Breydon! Open up, in the name of God.'

Isolda ran to the door but Hal put himself in front of her before she could open it. Motioning to her to wait, he spoke through the wood. 'Who is without?'

'It is Brother Peter, from St John's.'

Pushing him aside, Isolda wrenched the door open and a sense of dread flooded Hal's heart as he recognised the man who stood there, rain falling like needles over him. It was one of those who had treated her apprentice's wound.

'What...what is amiss?' she asked in breathless tones. 'Is it Jac?'

The man nodded, his face beneath his cowl telling everything even before he spoke.

'I have sad news, Mistress Breydon. The boy is dead.'

Chapter Ten

The rain drove through the door and into Hal's face, the news turning the night chillier still. 'What did you say?'

'The boy is dead,' repeated the man. 'Not half an hour since.'

'But I spoke with the Prior earlier this evening. He was well then. How in God's name can he be dead?'

There was a hesitation and then Isolda ushered the man inside and closed the door. 'Speak, Brother Peter, for pity's sake. How did he die? Was his wound really so bad?'

Peter shook his head. 'The Prior suspects poison, Mistress Breydon.'

'Poison?' She gasped in horror. 'But…that's not possible! Why would anyone wish to poison him?'

Hal knew the question was both foolish and futile. Poison was a cunning weapon and easy to wield, and the *why* was cruelly obvious, to him at least, if not yet to Isolda.

'Was the boy left alone?' he demanded. 'The Prior assured me that someone would sit with him constantly.'

Brother Peter shifted his feet and wiped a hand over his face, which was dripping with rain. 'Someone was with him for the most part…but this afternoon, when he seemed so well…he may have been left alone for some of the time, while we prayed or attended to other duties.'

Hal's heart heaved at Isolda's stifled sob. The impulse to take her in his arms was almost overpowering and, to conquer it, he rounded on the hapless cleric. 'We will come immediately to speak to the Prior. Go ahead and tell him to expect us within the half-hour.'

The man left and, shutting out the night, Hal turned to Isolda. She stood, white with shock, the cat winding around her ankles as if it sensed her distress and was trying to comfort her.

He too went to comfort her but she spun away, her hands gesturing futility. 'Jac...poisoned? I cannot believe anyone could do such an evil thing!'

'I can believe it,' Hal said grimly. 'After the attack on his life failed and the knowledge that he would recover became known, there was bound to be some sort of foul play. I should have expected it and prevented it.'

Her eyes, bright with anger, found his. 'You think Shearman is behind it?'

'Who else? Jac named his man as one of his attackers and, even though the knave denies it, if it came to court, he might lose his nerve and admit the bailiff gave the order. Shearman couldn't take that risk.'

She shook her head, helplessly wringing her hands together. 'If only I had acted alone, not involved Jac in this business, it would never have happened. He would be alive and well, not...dead by murder!'

'Don't think like that, Isolda. Jac was in this by choice, was he not?'

'Yes...but that is little comfort.'

Hal knew the truth of that. Not that he'd sought comfort after the death of his family, turning a deaf ear to the condolences his friends and the townspeople offered. Why they hadn't blamed him, he'd never understood. Now he began to understand, however, as she paced the room, berating herself with bitterness.

'He caught me...writing my verses one night and, even though he couldn't read, he knew what it was. He begged to be allowed to help. I refused, time and again...but he kept on asking, and in the end I...'

'You said yes.'

She nodded. 'It seemed the best thing to do, not least for secrecy, lest he speak of it to any of the townsfolk, but I was so alone and...'

A sob swallowed whatever else she was going to say. But she didn't need to say it. Hal knew the torment she was putting herself through, for he'd put himself through that same torment, not once but many times.

'I know how you are feeling, Isolda,' he said, stepping closer, touching a hand to her shoulder. 'But you mustn't blame yourself for this, not now, not ever. Jac would not do so.'

Those words, or similar, had been said to him many times, but they'd made no difference. And suddenly he needed those words to make a difference to Isolda. This situation was not the same. He'd been young, idle, reckless, not deserving of comfort, whereas she was only trying to do the right thing.

'In time, you will see that, and remember him as he should be remembered—as your friend as well as your helper. For tonight, would you like me to go alone to the infirmary?' he offered. 'Find out from Thomas Oteley exactly what happened?'

She shook her head. 'No, I want to go. I need to see Jac. To say goodbye.'

Hal's heart heaved again as it shared her pain. He'd gone too, four years ago, to another infirmary where his brother lay. To find out about unjust death too and also to say goodbye, for Will's burns were far too severe to hope for any recovery.

Then, he'd been mad with rage and grief, and over the years those feelings had remained, buried deep inside him. But he hadn't realised self-pity had joined them, not until Isolda had accused him of such before Brother Peter arrived.

Now he felt only shame because, as well as accusing him and rightly so, she'd tried to help him and he'd spurned that help. Instead, he'd raged at her, and at himself, until she too had become angry. He'd told her she hadn't understood but it was *he* who'd failed to understand, or even to see, her kindness.

'Then dress warmly,' he said, a hoarseness in his voice. 'The rain is harsh without.'

'I'll get my cloak,' she said, a choke in her voice too.

Hal watched her go into the passageway that separated the shop from the hall, then he took down his own cloak from its peg. It was still damp and as he threw it around him he shivered as foreboding, not just wet wool, enfolded him. The situation had suddenly turned very ugly, the danger that had hovered was now within touching distance, so close that his scalp prickled.

It was all he could do not to run out into the corridor after her, dagger in hand, lest that danger come and he not see it in time. The house seemed filled with menace, the shadows from every corner stretching out long fingers, not towards him, but towards Isolda. What if that danger came when he wasn't with her? What if those fingers crept unseen, unheard, and reached her before he could?

Sweat broke out on his brow and Hal almost did reach for his dagger, but he stilled his hand, forced himself to think. There was nothing in the shadows of the house, at least not tonight. But poison could find its way into any cup, any time, and Isolda was not safe now, anywhere, not even in her own home. Windows could be broken, doors forced, houses burned to make it look like an accident.

Accident! He shuddered, remembering Warwick's verdict on the death of his family, the Earl even blaming them for leaving a brazier burning on a hot day in May. How lightly, and how cunningly, that word *accident* could be used by those with evil intent.

Hal swore to himself then and there, as he awaited Isolda's return with every sinew taut, every nerve alert, that there would be no more *accidents*. It might have been she who'd spoken glibly when she'd said she cared about him, despite even the anger and self-pity he'd shown her, but he knew at that moment that he cared for her too much to allow anything to happen to her.

In the corridor, Isolda took down her cloak, her hands hardly knowing what they were doing. The candlelight from the shop cast her shadow in front of her and it seemed as if Jac's spirit had returned to the house To steady herself, she leaned her forehead against the wall for a moment and breathed deeply.

No, Jac wouldn't blame her. Hal was right. But that wouldn't stop her blaming herself. Her apprentice—who had become her family, too—had entered into this venture willingly and eagerly, and with all the vigour of youth. He'd enjoyed thumbing his nose at Ralph Shearman and his like, mimicking their strutting about the town behind their backs. Time and again, she'd warned him to be careful, less exuberant when they went out at night to do their work, but he'd only listened with half an ear.

Now…how could she ever forgive herself for his death?

Isolda thumped the wall and fought down tears, her throat swallowing as if she were drowning. Pinning poems on doors was not a crime that warranted such cruel punishment, but it wasn't about rhymes any more, was it? The enemy had gone too far now, beyond what even she knew them to be capable of. And for that she'd make them pay, even if it cost her life too.

Hal's voice sounded quietly behind her. 'Isolda?'

She hadn't heard him approach, so quietly must his feet have moved.

'I'm all right,' she said quickly.

'Are you?'

His hand touched her shoulder and Isolda squeezed her eyes tightly shut. She wouldn't cry! She hadn't cried since her father and brother had died. She hadn't even cried over Robert, for God's sake, not once. But she'd been angry more than hurt when her betrothed had revealed himself for a rogue, cruelly calling her a slut for being so easily wooed. Hate had swiftly replaced bewilderment and shock—hate for herself as well as for him, for being so credulous, so trusting, so utterly foolish.

'*Are you*, Isolda?'

The repeated question was quiet, his hand on her shoulder tender, caring. His presence was like a blanket she wished she could fold about her, burrow into its comforting folds, go to sleep and wake up on the morrow to find this was nothing but a nightmare.

Although she tried hard not to, Isolda shook her head, the pain, the grief, the guilt twisting in her heart. 'No, I'm not all right really, Hal.'

In an instant, though there was nothing hurried about it, his arms went around her. His chin came to rest on the top of her head and suddenly she *was* swaddled in a sort of blanket after all. But better than a blanket. Warmer, stronger, safer.

Isolda let herself be held, just for a moment. How long was it since anyone had held her like this? Had she *ever* been held like this? No, not quite. This wasn't the way her father, her mother, her brother had ever held her. This wasn't the way Robert had held her, ever. This was…innocent yet intimate…unexpected yet right.

'You don't need to be all right, Isolda. Not for me, not for anyone.'

She felt Hal's breath on her hair as he murmured the words. Not trying to help or resolve or advise, but just being there in this moment, with her, for her. Isolda counted in her head. How long did a moment last? Could one make a moment last for ever? Should one want to? And, if not, why did she want *this* moment to last for ever?

One moment became two, and then three, then four. Time stretched away into a sort of void and everything else receded. Suddenly afraid, though of what she knew not, Isolda tried to drag reality back.

'We should go…' she said, her tone reluctant, even to her. 'To the infirmary…'

'Not until you are ready.'

Why wasn't she ready now? She wanted, needed, to see Jac, speak to the Prior, get to the truth of what had happened, but just standing here in the dark, with Hal's arms around her, felt so right that she never wanted to go anywhere at all.

'Then…just a moment more,' she whispered.

'Yes, a moment more.'

Her very existence seemed to hang on that moment. The rain fell, the house slumbered, and the dead slept.

As if the world outside was counting the time down, the church clock struck the hour with two solemn notes that echoed and died slowly away into eternity. It would be wonderful just to stay here, as if this was eternity too, with no beginning and no end. Pretend Jac wasn't dead, that there was no injustice or corruption in the world. Pretend that there was only peace and stillness and Hal and love...

Love!

How could she even *think* of such a word when Jac lay murdered? How could she think of such a word in connection with Hal, for surely she didn't love *him*? Or did she? Had he, like the rain outside, dripped into her heart without her knowing it?

Isolda shivered, though not with cold, then shifted herself from within the fold of his arms. 'The Prior will be waiting for us,' she said.

He looked at her keenly for a moment, his eyes gleaming in the dim light that seeped into their little haven, and then nodded. 'I will bank down the fire and put the candles out.'

She watched him do so, swiftly and with care, as he removed the burning logs from the centre of the hearth, swept aside the ashes, waited until the ashes had cooled a little and then swept them back over the logs, dousing the smouldering wood to embers before placing the fire cover securely on top.

Isolda waited patiently while he extinguished the candles, leaving one alight, which he brought back into the shop with him. If he hadn't told her about the death of his family at St Albans—and how they'd died—she wouldn't have waited patiently at all. But now she understood.

'Ready?'

She nodded and, pulling her cloak about her, preceded

him to the door. There he blew out the candle, left it on the window sill, and they went out into the rain. He took her hand gently in his and the realisation she'd dismissed, and denied, as he'd held her so quietly and so tenderly, hit her like a bolt of lightning.

She *did* love Hal. She loved him with all her heart, all her soul.

Hal held Isolda's hand firmly in his as they hurried across the square. He could have excused it, said it was in case she slipped on the wet cobbles, or that she might not see her way clearly in the dark. But he didn't excuse it. Perhaps tomorrow he might. Perhaps tomorrow he might regret that he'd ever held her as he had, deny that he'd have held her as long as she wanted him to, for ever if need be.

He would certainly rue the inappropriate desire that had rushed through him and heated his blood. For what purpose did desire have? He could never marry Isolda. He could never marry anyone. And she was not a woman to be tumbled for sport and then discarded, even if he was that sort of man, which he wasn't, not any more.

He'd sworn to himself never to love a woman, have a family or a home, the day he'd stood in the burned-out ruins of his home. Seeing that smouldering shell where all the people he loved had died had broken him. On his knees, heedless that the wood still scorched, he'd wept as that fire—though doused—withered him too.

The pain was the worst he'd ever known, the desolation unbearable, and he knew he could never survive such loss a second time. His own life wouldn't matter, but the lives of anyone he loved—no, he couldn't risk that. Better surely not to love, and so he'd sworn a vow that he'd kept ever since.

He'd not been tempted to break it, not even in his loneliest moments, at the darkest hour of night, when love made its absence agonisingly present and wrung his heart, not just his body. Not until now. Not until Isolda.

He glanced at her as they turned down Narrow Lane, the place where he'd encountered her being accosted by that oaf of an archer, so long ago now it seemed. Remembered how, when he'd tried to assist, she'd swung her fist at him! His fingers tightened and hers answered. How far they'd come since then. And how far apart they still were and must remain. Even if he hadn't vowed as he had, he'd already discovered that Isolda was her own woman, one who neither wanted or needed a man, be he lover or husband.

'We'll go through the Broad Gate,' he said. 'It'll look less suspicious if we use the main route and with luck the guard will ask no awkward questions, but accept our explanation that we're going to visit the boy.'

Even in the dark, he saw the shadows in her eyes. 'It will be the truth, after all.'

Hal swallowed down a surge of anger at Ralph Shearman and led them onward down the hill. However, he was wrong about the man at the gate, or rather the four guards who, on their approach, stepped out and barred their way, pikes planted like a wall in front of them.

'I've had orders to let no one pass, Sir Knight.'

Hal glanced at each of their faces in turn. Two were men of the castle, but the other two were townsmen and that set his senses on alert. 'By whose orders?' he asked of the guard who'd addressed him. 'Not Edmund de la Mare's, I'll warrant.'

The man shifted his feet uneasily. 'The order came from the bailiff, Sir Henry.'

'Why?'

'There's been some mischief at the infirmary. One of the brethren has been accused of murdering a patient there, and he's taken to his heels. The hue and cry has been raised.'

No sooner had the words been uttered than the town bells began to ring. In no time at all the town would become more like a hunting ground, and Hal's blood ran cold at the fate of the hunted.

He heard Isolda utter an oath and then she snatched her hand from within his and stepped forward. 'The dead boy is my apprentice and I demand to be allowed to see him.'

'His body is no longer there, Mistress Breydon.' This time it was the guard's eyes, not his feet, which shifted. 'It has been taken away for investigation.'

'Taken away by whom?'

'Orders of the bailiff.'

'Never mind the bailiff! We know—'

Before she could finish, Hal stepped forward. 'You recognise me?'

'Of course, Sir Henry.'

'Then you'll know I act with full authority of the Earl of Shrewsbury. Lord Talbot will demand to hear the full details of this, and so I will tell you again to let us pass and speak with the Prior.'

The man shook his head. 'I cannot.'

Hal felt a thick web of deceit and danger close around them. All the town bells were ringing now, their clamour echoing far up into the night sky. By the light of the torches that hung on the gate, the points of the four spikes glinted wickedly. Rain fell like rods of steel and spattered ominously on the cobbled street. He had a knife at his belt but no sword and, anyway, solving this with violence was not a solution at all.

'Very well,' he said, infusing a bite of irritation into the words. 'It seems we will get no further tonight.' He looked closely at each guard in turn. 'In case I forget your faces...'

Leaving that unveiled threat hanging, Hal took Isolda's hand again and they turned back the way they'd come. Once out of earshot, he bent his head and whispered, 'Keep walking and don't look back.'

'Shearman is quick indeed to cover his tracks!' she muttered, her pace quickening to keep step with his. 'Jac's corpse must barely be cold!'

Hal agreed. 'A little too quick perhaps.'

At the top of Broad Street he could see torchlights as men answered the call of the bells. The sound of doors being slammed and feet running echoed around the streets and town walls. No good going the way they were headed, that was clear, so he turned them left into a little lane, and then right into another that twisted between low-storeyed houses.

'We must get to the castle, inform Edmund de la Mare about this.'

'Can the constable be trusted?'

Hal nodded. 'I think so, from what I've seen of him so far. He's not enamoured of Shearman at any rate.'

A noise sounded from behind them and swiftly he drew Isolda aside into the cover of a doorway, placing his forefinger on her mouth to warn her to keep quiet. She pressed herself close as, above the pealing of the bells, the sound of trudging boots and the scrape of metal came nearer.

For the first time that night Hal thanked the rain, for the men strode past without looking left or right, their heads bent and their hoods up. One of them cursed the weather and then the sound of their footsteps faded and melded into other noises further away.

'Are they gone?' Isolda's whisper was muffled against his tunic.

'Yes,' he whispered back, letting the word brush the top of her head. Even through her hood, the thrill of just touching her with his lips rippled along his senses. Why, whenever he was near Isolda, did he want so very much to hold her in his arms? To touch her with his lips when, for the last few years, he'd never wanted to do any of those things with any other woman?

'Though we'll not move just yet,' he added. 'We'll wait until it's safe.'

Shouts went up from myriad parts of the town, men howling like hounds sniffing out their prey. A light flickered on the wall opposite and Hal's nerves jolted as a doorway further down opened and shut again, then a voice called and boots raced on cobbles.

It wasn't safe here at all, but if they were discovered he'd have to just bluff it out—or fight it out, depending on who discovered them. The hue and cry weren't looking for them at least, but if Shearman's henchmen discovered them it would be a different matter.

But if he was truthful with himself, it wasn't safe anywhere if Isolda was with him, and that danger came from within not without. Even when she wasn't with him, his thoughts constantly sought her, wondered where she was, what she was doing. Even when—especially when—he reread her poems and she was there, in the room with him, speaking the words in a voice low and sweet.

Everything about her was so familiar to him, as if he'd known her always, not just two weeks. She'd burrowed into his heart without him even realising it. And that was what frightened him. Now she was part of him, what would happen when he lost her, as he would one day? Either she herself would make an end when their cause was won, or he would be called away from Ludlow to other duties, or…

No! Hal shook his head, pushing the pain away before it possessed him. Soon he would be gone, whatever the outcome, and when he was away from her, perhaps then she would fade, leave him bereft, yes, but able to go on as he'd always done. And one day he might even forget…

The commotion was moving swiftly through the town now, urged on by the clamouring bells. God forbid they apprehend that poor brother of St John's, whether he be innocent or guilty. There was nothing worse than a mob of men out for the kill. Hal knew that better than anyone.

Boots sounded again, running towards them down the lane, but the lone figure passed by without looking right or left. Another one out for blood! Why did men, even the most idle, leap up eagerly from their beds when the opportunity for violence presented itself?

'We dare not stay here any longer,' he whispered, shaking that unanswerable question away. 'Your house isn't far and the rain is heavier now. We'll go slowly, ducking into cover if needs be.'

She tilted her head to listen. 'There is no one nearby now at any rate.'

Hal stepped out and looked up and down the lane. Likely the mob was gathering in the square, before spreading out to search the town. He wrapped his gloved fingers around hers once more. 'Keep close,' he murmured, 'and step as soundlessly as you can.'

Together they crept onwards in the shadow of the wall,

with Isolda on the inside. Every now and then he brought them to a halt and listened, but thankfully, the noise was always ahead of them now, not behind.

It seemed an age before they reached the square, and there they discovered a large body of men gathered, with torches and various weapons in their hands. And in their midst, standing on an upturned barrel, was Ralph Shearman, his voice and his bulk, if not his face, unmistakable.

Hal swore softly. 'We'll never make it across the square until they move off.'

But Isolda pushed past him and just in time he drew her back into the cover of the lane. 'What in God's name are you doing?'

'I'm going to confront Shearman, of course! Accuse him in front of everyone of Jac's murder! Why else would he take the body away if not to hide his crime? That poor wretch they are hunting may have held the cup, but it was Shearman who filled it!'

'It would be folly to confront him tonight,' Hal argued. 'That crowd is bent on violence and Shearman has them in his hand. They'd never believe you, even if they give you the chance to speak.'

'We are dressed like everyone else, in cloak and hood, against the rain. We could at least merge with the crowd and so hear better what he's saying.'

'I can hear well enough from here, and I can guess the rest,' he said. 'The brother, whose name is Matthew, has not been discovered in St Laurence's so they are going to the other churches and chapels, in case he has sought sanctuary in one of those.'

'If he has, that doesn't mean he'll be safe. I've seen felons and the like dragged out of Ludlow's sanctuaries before now and killed by the hue and cry before they've even had a chance to plead innocent or guilty.'

Hal nodded. 'And Shearman's too careful by far to let him escape and live to plead at all.'

At last, the crowd began to disperse in various directions, Shearman at the head of the group heading towards Galdeford, where the Augustinian Priory lay. Others went towards the Carmelite and Dinham chapels, while others spread out into the streets, several men heading straight towards them.

Hal looked swiftly around, got his bearings. They were in Narrow Lane, which ran parallel to Mill Street, and Isolda's house was at the other side of the square, too far away. They'd never make it there safely, not now, and it was too risky to try and reach the castle.

'Is there a good neighbour who would let us shelter under their roof for an hour or two?'

Isolda shook her head. 'No. I would trust none of them.' Her brow creased and then cleared. 'The Guildhall! Of course, no one would think to look there for us, I'm certain. It'll be locked, of course, and the door is sturdy, but there are windows.'

Hal remembered the building and the door well enough, as he'd caught her pinning her poem there the night he'd kissed her. It was almost too ironic. 'Very well,' he said. 'We'll risk it.'

Going back the way they'd come, they crossed through into Mill Street and reached the Guildhall in a matter of minutes. Taking an alley that led into the gardens beyond, where the building had windows aplenty, Hal chose the furthest one. He was reaching for his dagger, intending to use its hilt to break the thick glass, when the sound of it shattering made him jump.

He looked up to see Isolda holding aloft a large stone, which—having made the first crack—she now used again and again, with surprising strength and with unbridled relish, until there was a gap big enough for them to climb in through.

She turned to him, her eyes ablaze. 'Oh, I've wanted to do that for such a long time!'

Hal smiled. 'That I had gathered.' He wrapped his cloak around his fist. 'I'll clear any jagged edges so we can pass through safely.'

The sound of breaking glass had been loud, too loud, but hopefully, with all the other noise going on in the town, it would go unnoticed, or else those folk in the neighbouring houses would think it looters and stay safely in their beds. However, as he knocked away the remaining shards around the frame, the sound of running feet came to his ears.

'Quickly, inside!'

Hal helped Isolda through the window, heaved himself up and tumbled down onto the floor next to her just in time. The mob thundered by, their torches casting flickering flashes of light into the dark room, and then was gone. One by one, the bells in the town stopped ringing and the night crept close and enfolded them completely.

'So…what now, Hal?'

Chapter Eleven

Isolda's heart was pounding against her ribs and she shook with exhilaration. Her legs felt so weak that water, not blood, might have flowed through her veins. Above her head, the cold air whistled in, echoing the breath that rasped in her throat. Hal was breathless too, and it was a moment before he answered her question.

'We wait.'

In the near-dark, sitting as close as mice in a trap, Isolda suddenly had the urge to giggle. The lines of her poem on mouses and voles seemed to have become reality, but a reality she'd never envisaged when she penned that verse about Harry the Cat, telling him he was seeking the wrong hole. And now here they were, both of them in a sort of hole together!

'The commotion all seems to be in the main streets of the town.' She could hear clearly through the stillness of the cold night, the noise of doors being pounded on and the shouting of men's voices. 'Perhaps we are too close to the castle for them to think of searching here.'

'Perhaps. But I suspect they'll search everywhere, beyond the river too, and on the common, unless they find the man in sanctuary in one of the churches.'

The remark brought a sobering sensation in its wake.

'Do you really think one of the brethren would have poisoned Jac?' she asked.

'I think it is possible, though whether in full knowledge of what he was administering or in ignorance will remain to be seen. I doubt Thomas Oteley would be involved, though those who enter a religious house do so for many reasons, not all of them holy.'

Hal shifted and then his arm and his cloak were around her. Isolda leaned into his warmth, twisting slightly so that she fitted into the crook of his shoulder. 'How long will we have to stay here?' she asked, aware that she could easily have stayed there for ever, sitting on the floor like this in Hal's embrace. 'We must be gone by daylight, else we'll be discovered.'

He nodded, his chin brushing her head where her hood had fallen back. Damp tendrils of her hair lay against her cheek, from when she'd unbound it earlier, thinking Hal wasn't coming, in preparation for bed.

'We'll stay until it quietens down, then try and make for the castle. The constable will have heard everything by now, of course, though from the wrong mouths.'

Quick sorrow, followed by anger, filled Isolda's heart as she remembered Jac, lying dead, God only knew where. Perhaps Shearman would dispose of the body in secret, even throw it into the river so it would be carried far from Ludlow, to ensure his guilt would never be proved.

A dog barked in the street outside and both of them lifted their heads to listen for any accompanying human sound. There was none and their heads both lowered at the same time, their faces turned towards each other, their mouths close. It was the simplest and most natural thing in the world to let their lips brush, meet, cling softly, then part again.

'What we said earlier, Hal...about forgetting that we kissed last night.' Isolda searched his gaze in the dark. 'I think I *like* it when you kiss me.'

There was a little pause before he answered. 'I like it too.'

'But it's not only kissing, is it?' she said, placing her palm on his chest, over his heart, feeling it beat strong and fast. 'It's touching...holding...being like this...together, every time we meet.'

'Yes.'

'But...do you think we should?'

Another pause. 'Do you?'

Isolda didn't know whether she did or not, because at that moment the things that she should want—freedom to be her own woman, to live her own life—seemed very far away. Extracting herself from Hal's embrace, she sat up and, drawing her knees up to her chest, wrapped her arms about them.

'I was betrothed once, three years ago,' she said abruptly, as there seemed no other way to even begin to explain feelings that she was no longer sure of. Wants that she wasn't sure she wanted any more. 'He was a merchant of Bristol, a man called Robert.'

'I had heard of your broken betrothal.'

Isolda gave a quiet laugh. 'I don't doubt it! I'll wager you've heard the whole story from many a gossiping tongue.'

'Is the story true?'

'That depends on which version you've heard. The likes of Alice Shearman will have told you I'm an...unnatural woman, the sort who doesn't like men. Others will tell you I considered Robert beneath me, not good enough.'

'And neither is true.'

'No.' Isolda stared out over the room, her eyes having adjusted to the darkness now, picking out the long table down its centre. One by one, to help her focus, she began to count the chairs lined up on either side.

'I thought at first I could come to love Robert,' she said after she'd counted five chairs. 'He was handsome, attentive, amusing, rich...not that the latter point mattered. And he seemed to love me, though now I know he didn't. How could he when he loved half a dozen other women?'

'You mean he had other sweethearts?'

'Not just sweethearts, but wives too, at least three.' Isolda went on counting along the row of chairs. Twelve on the side nearest. 'A visiting merchant, also from Bristol, told me—perhaps out of spite or to make mischief. And when I asked Robert outright it if was true, he admitted it.'

Her eyes went to the chairs on the opposite side and she began to count them, too. 'He didn't even see anything wrong with it, and said I only had myself to blame for being such an innocent! As if it was a cruel game he was playing, even though bigamy is a crime in the eyes of the law and the church.'

'Was he arrested?'

Isolda shrugged. 'I never heard anything of him after he left Ludlow. He's not been back since as far as I know.'

'No doubt the law caught up with him somewhere, some time.'

'I hope so.' Ten, eleven, twelve. Twelve on the far side, too. The chairs that seated twenty-four of the Twenty-Five that governed the town. 'He didn't break my heart,' she went on, 'although it felt like that at the time. It was the shame of it, the fact I'd been so easily deceived that really hurt.'

The remaining chair, the most ornately carved, the

most important, the most impressive, was at the head of the table. Ralph Shearman's chair. Strangely, seeing it and knowing the character of the man who sat in it made it easier to speak of Robert who, for all his faults, still fell short of the bailiff's sins.

'He charmed me from the start,' she went on, 'with his knowledge and business skill, the chance to discuss wool with someone who seemed so different from my fellow merchants, who didn't hold the prejudices they did. My mother took to him at once, saying how good it would be to have a man in the house again. I liked him too at first, but I should have realised what he was when...'

Isolda drew a breath, let it out again. 'As our wedding day approached he pressed himself upon me more and more, and every time he did I liked him less and less. He claimed his love for me drove him to distraction, that he couldn't wait. He always sought my forgiveness for his passion—until the next time. That alone should have showed me his true nature.'

'It sounds like you were not the only woman he fooled, Isolda, so there is nothing to be ashamed of. You were a victim.'

'And a willing one, even if not for the same reasons as those other women.'

'How so?'

Isolda turned to face him, what she had to admit tasting sour on her tongue. 'I thought marrying Robert would make me respectable in the eyes of the town, that the people here would accept me, even like me, instead of ridiculing me for trying to run the business on my own.'

In the dark she saw him frown. 'Did you want that respect and liking so badly?'

'At the time, yes. Or rather, I thought I *should* want

it, for the sake of my mother, and my father's memory. I'd always wanted to go into the wool trade, even when a child, but my father didn't agree.'

'Was he a hard man?'

She nodded. 'He loved me, I think, but had little patience and he couldn't see my dreams. He thought business was for men, not women, even though my mother sometimes helped him in the shop. So I hoped that Robert and I could work together, be partners as well as husband and wife, to compensate for...the rest of married life.'

'Yet you have succeeded without Robert, or any man.'

'I think it is more a case of succeeding *because* of Robert, and to prove my father wrong, as much as to fulfil a dream. But in the process I've discovered that it's hard to walk alone through life, to struggle constantly to be heard, less still be taken seriously, and harder still to be an outcast among your own kind.'

'Even when you walk head and shoulders above your fellow merchants, as you do?'

'Is that what you think?'

'It is one of the first things I learned about you, Isolda.' His gaze never wavered from hers. 'You are honest, compassionate, courageous, strong and yet—'

'Yet foolish, impetuous, proud and selfish! Is that what you were going to say next?'

His teeth gleamed as he smiled. 'Proud, yes. Impetuous, perhaps. But you are not foolish, nor selfish either. You stand up for those who suffer and speak out against wrongdoers and injustice, putting the needs of others before your own. I would call that *selfless*, not selfish.'

'Stop! You'll be calling me a saint next!' Isolda felt her cheeks burn and was glad of the darkness so that he couldn't see her embarrassment. Not only at praise she was not used to, but at the knowledge that she *did* have needs that were craving to be met. Needs that she'd not had at all, not let herself have, until Hal had come to Ludlow and into her life.

'I suspect the yeoman farmers already do talk of you in saintly terms!'

'Well, they are perhaps a little biased!' She ignored the jest and took a deep breath. 'Hal…the reason I told you about Robert is…well, there was a consequence of that, a decision.'

'What was it?'

She looked away. 'Months later, when Robert had ceased to exist for me, I realised how close I'd come to sacrificing everything I believed in. Perhaps fear was at the root of my need to be like everyone else, but I nearly lost myself completely, and I'll never do that again, not ever.'

There was a long silence before he asked the inevitable question. 'Is that why you are yet unmarried? I'm sure Robert wasn't the only suitor—there must have been many others.'

Isolda nodded. 'I spurned them too, even though my mother urged me to wed. But isn't it better to live a life alone and free than to be invisible and chained to a life you hate? To be of no significance, not even to yourself?'

'A life without love.'

It wasn't a question, nor even a statement…more an agreement. She turned to look at him, the shadows cast by the darkness making it difficult to read his expression accurately. 'There is more in life than love, Hal. Love isn't everything.'

He nodded slowly. 'No, not always, and not for everyone either. One can choose to live without it.'

'Have *you* so chosen?' Isolda's heart suddenly lurched with fear as an unthinkable thought struck her, one that had to be voiced. 'Or...do you have a wife, a family, too, somewhere that you have neglected to mention?'

He gave a soft chuckle. 'Do you think me a man like Robert then? Do you think I would kiss you as I did, had I a wife somewhere?'

'I don't know. Would you?'

His head shook. 'No.' There was a pause but when he spoke again the words were not ones she expected. 'And as it happens I agree wholeheartedly with you about love. Better to live a life free from cares and loss and pain, because those things always go hand in hand with love, no matter what kind of love it is.'

'Yes.' Isolda nodded, not sure any more if her agreement was as certain as it would once have been. 'Far better.'

A short silence fell between them, a silence alive with things it seemed they thought but were reluctant to say. It was almost as if those unsaid thoughts were the same for him as they were for her, and that he was equally unable to articulate and understand them.

But how could she tell him she loved him after all she'd just revealed? How could she admit that what she'd *thought* she wanted—a life without love, filled with independence and work—was not what she wanted now? How, when she didn't understand any of it herself, could she hope that he might understand too?

Outside, the night had grown quiet, the noise in the town suddenly ceasing, leaving an eerie void in its place. Hal got to his feet to peer cautiously out through the window.

'The street is clear now. I think we can risk it.'

Isolda placed her hand in his and he drew her to her

feet. For the briefest of instances, he held her against him, their fingers entwined between them, his breath warm on her face.

'I'll go out first,' he whispered, 'in case it's not safe. Get a chair so you can climb out after me, but wait for my word.'

Isolda crossed to the table, reaching for the nearest chair. Then, on an impulse, she took Ralph Shearman's grand chair instead, with a stab of righteous spite that she didn't even try to stem. Dragging it to below the window, she waited for Hal's voice.

'Come now.'

Climbing up, she heaved herself onto the sill, where Hal's hands were waiting for her. As he helped her through, her gown caught on a nail and there was a tearing sound as the material ripped at the hem. When she landed on her feet she reached for it, thinking perhaps she could repair the gown, but Hal's voice stopped her.

'Leave it! I hear footsteps. Quick, we'll go by way of the river to the Dinham Gate and into the castle.'

Hand in hand, they ran through the Guildhall garden and across Christ Croft Lane into the orchard of St Thomas's Chapel. The sound of the river grew loud as they crept along the town wall to the gate, crouching low lest anyone see them.

Luck was with them—or perhaps it was Hal's boldness that carried them through. The two men on duty there jumped to attention as they approached, and he addressed them in authoritative terms.

'Doubtless you've heard the hue and cry in the town. Has anyone passed this way tonight?'

'No, Sir Henry, though they searched the chapel and

beyond the walls earlier. We heard it was one of the brothers from St John's they were after. Is that so?'

'So I believe. But due to the crowds in the streets, and for reasons of privacy, I'm conveying this lady into the castle via this gate.'

Even in the dark, Isolda saw the smirks on the guards' faces. Hal's implication needed no further explanation. They obviously, and naturally, assumed he was taking her not just into the castle but into his bed! She didn't know whether to blush, giggle or protest, and in the event had no time for either as the guards stood smartly aside to let them pass.

Hal led her up the stone steps onto the top of the wall, through an oak door in a tower further along, and out again onto the next wall. She followed him along the parapet and into yet another tower where they turned down a staircase and into a corridor.

He opened a door and ushered her in and she realised that it was his own chamber, where she'd come to surrender herself for her actions only that morning. Before he closed the door behind them he took up a candle and lit it from a torch that flickered in the corridor wall. Then, as he lit another candle from the first, bringing light into the dark room, Isolda shivered, though not with cold.

Now that they'd reached a place of safety, at least for the moment, the danger without seemed greater than ever. Jac was dead, a violent mob was hunting Shearman's scapegoat through the town, and now, here she and Hal were running and hiding like criminals too.

'Drink some wine.'

Taking the silver goblet he held out to her, Isolda drank deeply, finding that she was parched. Gratefully, she sank into the chair he indicated next to the hearth and, leaning back, closed her eyes, keeping them closed as she listened to Hal bring some life into the fire. Slowly, feeling came back into her frozen feet and the bottom of her gown began to steam.

She heard the chair opposite creak and she opened her eyes to see Hal leaning forward and looking at her anxiously.

'Are you all right?'

She started to say she was fine, then changed her mind as suddenly her weariness, the exertion of the night, Jac's murder all merged into one terrible maelstrom. 'I don't think I've ever felt so tired in all my life,' she admitted.

He nodded. 'It is always like that when one comes through danger and finds oneself alive and unharmed.'

'Not everyone is alive and unharmed though, are they? Jac...' Isolda swallowed a sob and took another sip of her wine, feeling it rush like quicksilver through her veins. 'And now the town is out hunting that poor man from the infirmary, who may be innocent for all they know.'

'I'll go and see the constable in a moment. It's not far from dawn now, and on the morrow we shall act.' He took a gulp from his own goblet, and she saw how tired and cold he was too. 'Tonight, we must rest, however, and make the most of a few hours of respite.'

Isolda knew he was right. Even if Ralph Shearman himself walked in through that door right now, she doubted she'd have the strength even to move. 'I'll never be able to sleep tonight, no matter how tired.'

'You *will* sleep, Isolda, and you'll sleep here, where you'll be safer.'

All her tiredness fled and she sat upright in her chair. 'In the castle?'

'In this chamber. For your own safety, no one must know you are here.'

She turned her head and eyed the one bed in the room. 'Surely you don't mean...'

'I do indeed.' He rose to his feet and she saw his gaze flicker to the bed and away again. 'The bed curtains will give you privacy, and when I return from speaking with the constable I'll sleep in this chair.'

'But...'

He turned, his brows lifting. 'If you prefer, I will sleep in the hall, though that will look suspicious and give rise to speculation.'

Isolda shook her head. 'No, no, I see that,' she agreed, but the thought of spending the night in the same room, albeit not in the same bed, with Hal suddenly had her blood heating and not from the effects of the fire nor the wine. 'But surely, at this hour, will the constable not be abed?'

'Undoubtedly, but what I have to tell him won't wait until daylight.' He moved to a coffer, from which he took a cloth, a long linen garment and a woollen cloak. 'Use these, or if you can find anything more suitable in the coffer, then you are welcome.'

A flush mounted his cheek as he placed them on the arm of her chair. 'I'll take the key with me and lock it from the outside—just in case.'

With that, he left her, the turn of the key in the lock seeming loud in the nocturnal quiet of the castle. Isolda finished her wine then removed her damp outer clothing and shoes and arranged them on chairs around the fire. Her chemise was damp too, and she took it off and put it to dry as well. After rubbing her naked body briskly with the cloth, she reached for the linen garment.

It was a shirt, well-worn but clean and fresh, old-fashioned, like her father used to wear, simple but of fine quality. She pulled it over her head and as it fell to her knees she let herself relish the thought that Hal had worn it.

Isolda dried her hair as best she could and used her fingers to untangle the knots. Then, when all was done, she pulled the woollen cloak he'd given her around her shoulders and sat staring into the flames. The fire was burning merrily now and a delicious sense of warmth and safety shrouded her.

Her eyelids began to droop. Hal could be a long time relating the events of the night to the constable. Should she wait for him...or did he mean her to retire to bed—his bed—at once? She decided she would wait for his return since she wanted to hear what the constable's response was but, even so, before many moments had passed, her head started to nod.

The time passed slowly. From the town, the clock struck four times and Isolda fought to keep her eyes open. In an effort to clear the fog from her head, she got up and moved her clothes a little way away from the fire. As she reached to put the iron fire cover over to keep it in but safely contained, she thought of the fire in her own house. Was that still banked down and safe as Hal had left it?

Now she understood Hal's reaction when the log had fallen from the fire earlier, before Brother Peter had come with the news of Jac's death. From there her thoughts went to St Albans, and she understood too Hal's sense of guilt, as misplaced as it was, and the remorse that had lived with him ever since.

Isolda crossed to the window and looked out to see the rain had turned to a light snow. All was quiet now in the town. The hue and cry had either found the runaway or given up for the night. She yawned, felt herself sway, and put a hand on the sill to steady herself. Perhaps she should go to bed after all, but not sleep, just lie down, close her eyes and wait.

Approaching the simple though sizeable bed, she hesitated a moment and then pulled back the coverlets and slipped beneath them. It was bliss to feel that weight, that warmth, the faint aroma of Hal all around her. From the hearth, the fire settled down to a slumberous glow, the light peeping out of the air vents and the soft crackle of wood comforting. Would Hal ever come to see fire as comforting, warming, necessary instead of a source of horror and death, as it had proved for his family?

Would she, in his place? Before Jac, she'd never known guilt—not that sort of guilt—but now she not only understood Hal but she could empathise too, feel the pain that futile remorse brought with it.

Isolda squeezed her eyes closed, blocked that pain out before it took root. Remorse would not bring Jac back, but at least she, and Hal, could go forward and bring his murderers to justice. They must!

Behind her eyelids, the fire still glowed and the candles on the tables flickered. She realised she hadn't drawn the curtains around the bed, nor the one that separated the room for living and sleeping. No matter, she'd just rest for a little moment, then get up and do so. It was on that thought that she felt into a deep sleep.

Hal slid the key into the lock, paused and then knocked softly. He waited but there was no sound from within so he unlocked the door and pushed it open. The room was dim, just the faintest fire glow through the vents in the guard, the two candles he'd lit earlier still flickering. He looked across to the bed, and his breath caught in his throat.

Isolda had not drawn the curtains and she lay as still as a ghost beneath the thick coverlets. Her breathing came softly to his ears and he stood for a moment, just listening. The lights from the room caught the gleam of the oaken panel behind the bed, the curves of Isolda's body beneath the bedding, the glint of her golden hair on the pillow.

It had been so easy, an hour earlier, to say he'd sleep in the chair…but now. Now the longing to slip beneath those heavy covers and sleep alongside Isolda was almost overwhelming. A longing he had to suppress. Locking the door, he went to the fireside and stripped himself down to his braies and, with the cloth he'd given Isolda, he rubbed his body until his skin tingled.

From down below, he could hear the sounds of soldiers making themselves ready for first light. The law and order of the castle wasn't the authority of the town under usual circumstances, but Hal had convinced the constable that circumstances were *not* usual and it was the town's authorities themselves who were the miscreants. So the constable had assured him that every effort would be made to discover Jac's body and the fate of Brother Matthew.

And now Hal needed to sleep, for an hour or two at least. His body ached and his eyelids were heavy, though his nerves still jangled after the events of the night. But now, in the calm after the storm, the words Isolda had said to him before Brother Peter had come returned to hammer at his skull.

For four years he had wished he'd perished with his family at St Albans. Long years when he'd punished himself for still living. And yet tonight, despite all the danger, he had felt more alive than he'd ever felt and he was glad he lived, because Isolda had changed his beliefs, his heart, his whole world.

He loved her, he knew that. Perhaps he'd loved her from the first. And that made him feel more afraid than he'd ever felt since that time he'd run through the streets towards his burning house.

The loss of his family had been unbearable, yet somehow he'd borne it. He'd thrown himself into action, into work, into duty, and into the quest of doing his best to protect the innocent in times of battle. But those innocents he'd saved from looting and pillaging and raping had meant nothing to him on a personal level.

Isolda had come to mean everything to him, on every level, and the enormity of how much she meant to him, how great her loss would be, was like a crushing weight over his heart. What if he failed her now, tomorrow, in the future? Failed to be there when she needed him most, as he'd not been there for his family?

'Hal? Is that you?'

Chapter Twelve

Hal turned at the sound of his name to see Isolda sitting up in the bed. In the dim light he couldn't see her face properly for its features were shadowed, but her hair flowed down over her shoulders and breasts in a shimmering fall of gold. She looked like one of the angels painted on the walls and ceilings of St Laurence's church.

He'd thought of her as an angel once before when she'd come to the Galdeford Gate and spoke up for the yeoman farmers. Then she'd been an avenging angel, lacking only a shining sword in her hand. Now she was a mysterious, beautiful and beguiling angel, one that called him to rest.

Taking up the candle, Hal crossed over to the bed. 'I thought you asleep. Did I wake you?'

She shook her head. 'No, but I forgot to draw the curtains across.'

Of course! She wasn't calling him to anything at all, but merely needing him to close the curtains and protect her modesty while she slept in his bed, and he in the chair.

'I will do so now,' he said. But as he turned and stretched his hand out towards one heavy woollen hanging her voice came again, less sleepy now than before.

'What did the constable say? I hear noise below. Is anything happening?'

'Edmund is mustering soldiers to go into the town at daybreak, to find Jac's body and to ascertain the fate of Brother Matthew.'

Her head turned towards the window, but no light came through it yet. 'Is it nearly dawn now?'

'Not quite—in another two hours, perhaps.'

'I'm a little cold.'

Hal felt his heart jump. 'I will bring another coverlet.'

Putting the candle down upon the table at the bedside, he went to the blanket box against the wall and took out a thick covering. Laying it over the top of the bed, which already had two, he tried not to look at Isolda. But out of the corner of his eye he saw her slender body, the small breasts below his shirt, the sleeves that were too long and that covered her hands as they lay in her lap.

'Is that better?' he asked as her beauty made his voice tremble with awe.

'Yes, thank you.'

His hand reached for the curtain once more. 'You will be warmer still with the curtains closed.'

'If you shared the bed...' As she spoke there was a tremble in her voice too. 'We would *both* be warm.'

Hal turned back to look at her. 'What?' The question was unnecessary as he'd heard clearly enough, even though he didn't quite believe his ears.

'It is what people do, after all, winter and summer.'

Yes, people *did* share beds. That in this castle of Ludlow he had a chamber and a bed to himself was a rare occasion. Only the rich or the ill slept alone, and he was neither. A tiring woman might sleep with her lady, a squire with his master, and those who were married shared a bed. Children invariably slept together, as he'd done with his brother Will, and now often he slept alongside Simon, when in the field or some wayside inn.

But that was for warmth, for necessity, out of expedience—it was different. Unmarried men and women did *not* share beds for any reason—except one!

'It would not be fitting,' he said, even though every part of him yearned to accept her invitation, lie down beside her, take her in his arms and sleep. Nothing more. Simply sleep.

'Fitting in whose eyes? We are already sharing your chamber. Come, Hal, take your rest properly, for it will be little enough.'

Still Hal hesitated, casting a glance at the wooden high-backed chair next to the hearth that he'd intended to sleep in, or try to. He looked then at his bed, large, warm, inviting, and with Isolda in it to welcome him, if sexlessly—as it should be.

His heart made his mind up for him. 'Very well, if you are sure?'

She nodded so Hal doused the candle in the outer room and checked that the fire cover was secure. Then, his heart beating hard and his breath piling up in his throat, he returned to the bedside.

Isolda had lain down again and drawn the coverlets back a little, inviting him in, and he gave up questioning the wisdom of it and slipped beneath. As one, they both turned onto their sides to face each other, though without any part of their bodies touching.

'I have never shared a bed with a man before.'

She had no need to tell him that, for he'd surmised it from what she'd said about her former betrothed, and the decision she'd made after that to remain unwed. And

Isolda was no strumpet to give her favours to a man out of wedlock.

'Though I suppose you have shared a bed with many a woman, even if it was without love?'

Her question took Hal unawares but his answer came without hesitation, since it was true. 'When I was young, yes. Since then...no.'

'You talk as if you are ancient, yet you cannot be much older than me, Hal.'

'How old are you?' he asked, realising suddenly that he didn't know.

'Two and twenty.' A pause. 'Well over marriageable age.'

He smiled, held her eyes in the flickering candlelight. 'Some might say I am well over the age of wedlock too, at four and twenty.'

'You seem older sometimes, when you are not smiling.'

'Do you think so? Then I suppose I must smile more often.'

Her gaze dropped to his mouth and the coverlet moved as she lifted a hand and touched her fingers there, tracing his lips.

'When all this is over—when Shearman is caught and this town is free of corruption—will you be staying in Ludlow?'

The future had never entered Hal's head. It never did. He lived only in the present, going wherever his duty and his overlord sent him. And the past always accompanied him. Or at least that had been his life up until now. Suddenly, the thought of leaving Ludlow, leaving Isolda, even leaving this bed seemed impossible.

'I don't know yet,' he replied. 'If John Talbot orders me to serve elsewhere, I must go.'

There was a little silence between them, during which she read his thoughts with startling precision.

'And will you mind going? Or will you not care one way or the other?'

Hal took her hand in his, curling her fingers within his own. 'I will mind very much, Isolda.'

And then, suddenly, they were in each other's arms, holding each other close, tightly.

'I will mind too, Hal.'

Against his neck, her words were muffled, but his heart heard them clearly. The leaving, and the pain and the loss that would result, was already unbearable, even though the parting had not come yet.

A sense of utter desolation swamped him and yet he knew it didn't have to be a parting at all. He could request to stay in Ludlow in some capacity. His manor nearby, bestowed on him by the Earl, which he'd visited briefly after the rout of Ludford Bridge, would doubtless bring him back, if only on occasion. Or, given the precarious location of this border town, with the Duke of York biding his time and doubtless plotting his return just across the sea beyond Wales, Talbot might in fact decide to station him here, to support Edmund de la Mare and ensure that when York came, Ludlow would be for Lancaster not York.

But if he stayed his love for Isolda would make it impossible to ever be anywhere else but here, by her side, making her his wife, living his life with her. And when York and Warwick came again to make war, the worst could happen. After all, it had happened at St Albans.

Hal cleared his throat, moved back a little so he could look into her eyes, but the candle had burned low and he couldn't read their expression clearly. He might have no choice in the matter of whether he stayed or went, but he needed to be truthful with this woman he loved, no matter how brutal that truth might be.

'I have never stayed long in once place since I left St Albans, Isolda. I prefer it that way. I am no homemaker or husband.'

Her body stiffened against his but her voice was steady, no hitch in the breath that tickled his throat. 'I *am* a homemaker, I suppose, since I cannot imagine living like you do, but I am not a wife. No, definitely not that.'

And with that strangely distant exchange, as if she'd sensed his fears and shared them, everything was abruptly settled. Isolda would never be his wife, even if he *could* stay. And she could not be his lover, for he would not dishonour her in that way.

Rolling onto his back, Hal drew her close again and then stared up at the ceiling. A hot stinging sensation rose up behind his eyes as the thin sliver of dawn that came through the leaded window thrust like a blade into his heart.

'We should sleep now so that we are rested to face whatever the morrow brings,' he said. 'I will wake you in good time…or if I am still asleep you must wake me, Isolda.'

'Yes.'

She snuggled closer, her hand resting on his chest, her head settling into the crook of his shoulder. In a few moments he heard her breathing grow quieter as she fell into a deep sleep. Hal's eyes remained open and watched the night away. And from the silent corners of the room a sense of loss as great as that he'd felt after St Albans crept in upon him even as the dawn crept in at the windows.

If only he were a different man, if only the world were

different and the past had no power over him. If only he could face his fears and conquer them, tell Isolda of his love and ask her to be his wife, regardless of whether she loved him or not—what then?

'Wake up.'

Isolda woke at the touch of Hal's lips against her ear. Opening her eyes, she saw it was daybreak. 'What hour is it?' she asked, and then needed no answer as the bell for prime sounded.

'Time to get up.'

However, neither of them moved, but remained lying close together as they'd been when she'd fallen asleep. Isolda looked into his eyes and wondered if he'd slept at all. There were dark shadows below and their colour seemed dull in the weak morning light. But his body was warm and strong next to hers, his arms tight about her, and she knew he'd not let her go all night long.

'Did you not sleep?' she asked.

He shook his head. 'No.'

'Why not?'

'I was...thinking.'

'About what?'

There was a little pause before he answered. 'The events of the last few days, the things we have said to each other, the things we have done together. The things we may never do together again.'

Isolda's heart gave a little leap at the edge of sadness in his tone. Did he mean to stay after all? Had he decided that he no longer wished to live as he'd always lived, that he was tired of constantly moving, of having no home... no wife? He'd told her he wasn't a man to settle anywhere, and from what he'd revealed about St Albans she'd understood why.

But a little part of her had begun to hope that he might change. That if he changed she could change too, that together they would find the thing that had always evaded them—the love of a woman for a man and a man for a woman. That she loved Hal was undeniable now. But he didn't want love, he'd told her that too, in plain words. Now...should she question those words?

'We have lived a lifetime, it seems, these last few weeks,' she began cautiously. 'I have told you things I've never said to anyone.'

'And I have spoken to you, too, in a way I've not to anyone else, ever.'

'Do you think...' Isolda smoothed her hand over his bare chest. 'Have we been able to speak so honestly because we are the same, and we want the same things?'

Coward! That wasn't really how she'd intended to put it, but suddenly, after being able to speak so bravely, she felt afraid to say what was in her heart. To speak of love and find him surprised, shocked, even dismayed to hear it.

'The things we spoke about when we were hiding in the Guildhall?'

She nodded. 'When I told you about Robert, and how... why I'd chosen to live my life alone, and you agreed with me.'

'I remember. After all, it wasn't so long ago!' The smile that flashed faded as quickly as it had come. 'Yes, we agreed, we both wanted the same things...but I'm not sure what those things are any more, Isolda.'

Her heart fluttered again. 'Are you not?'

He curled a lock of her hair around his finger and looked deeply into her eyes. 'Yesterday, in your house, when you told me I was wrong to wish I'd died in that fire with my family, I suddenly realised how important life is and how much I want to live it. I realised too how important *you* are, Isolda, to me.'

Isolda said nothing, just held her breath and prayed silently for him to go on. From the window behind him, slanting between the shutters, the daylight grew stronger. The light was grey, the air so still it was unearthly, and she knew snow was falling, even though she couldn't see it.

'And the things we said, just a few hours ago, about my leaving Ludlow...our parting. I don't know if I want that either now.'

'Why not?'

His gaze softened. 'Because I have fallen in love you, Isolda, even though I know you don't want the love of a man, *any* man.'

Isolda looked into his eyes, knowing hers shone with hope. 'That's not true any more, Hal, even if it was just a few days ago.' She heard her voice tremble with excitement as the impossible suddenly seemed possible. 'Since you came...everything changed, and the way I am...was... suddenly felt wrong. This feels right. You feel right... for me.'

His eyes flared. 'Then...do you love me too?'

She nodded. 'I do, with all my heart. I didn't know how to tell you or even if I *should* tell you.'

'Do you love me enough to wed me, Isolda, when all this is over?'

'More than enough! Oh, yes, yes, I would wed you tomorrow, Hal!'

Then words failed her altogether as his mouth took hers, fiercely and with passion. Wrapping her arms around his neck, she drew him near, feeling his body hard and eager against hers. She had no physical experience of men, beyond Robert's clumsy and unwelcome kissing and pawing, and never dreamed she'd ever want…anything like *that*.

But *this*…this was not like that at all. Lying so close to Hal that he and she seemed to become one, she *craved* him, his touch, his kiss, his body, his whole being.

If the knock hadn't come then at the door, Isolda knew that—had he asked—she would have given herself to Hal, wed or not. But the knock did come at the door, and he drew his head back, his eyes shining down at her in a way she'd never seen them shine before. With love…and with joy.

'Perhaps that interruption is fortuitous,' she said.

He smiled and his beauty emanated like the rays of the sun, even though the sun had yet to rise. 'Perhaps… though I will have to bite my tongue so as not to berate whoever it is!'

He kissed the top of her head and got out of bed, drawing the curtains closed again before he went to the door. Isolda listened, recognised the voice of his squire, and while some of his words were indistinct, others she heard clearly.

'Parliament to be held at Coventry…sought sanctuary in the chapel… Shearman…the Breydon apprentice.'

Jac! In the bliss of morning she'd forgotten everything that had happened the night before. How could she have been so heartless, so carefree?

Isolda threw back the covers and leapt out of bed, then stopped, looking down at herself. She wore Hal's shirt and all her clothes were draped before the fire—something Simon couldn't fail to notice. She sat on the bed again and pulled the coverlet up around her, listening to the men's conversation, longing to rush out and join in.

But, biting her lip, she forced herself to wait. And after another moment or two, she heard the door close and she stepped out into the room to see Hal gathering up her clothes. He turned as she approached and she had no need to ask, for he supplied the answer immediately.

'Jac's body was discovered earlier this morning, in Shearman's cellar, would you believe. Edmund de la Mare has ordered Jac to be conveyed to the church.'

Isolda's excitement vanished and a sob rose up into her throat. Whatever happiness she and Hal found together in the years to come, Jac's death would always lie beneath it, and perhaps that was right. Surely joy such as she felt had a price?

'Thank God for that, at least.' Fury rose up inside her like a flame. 'How did Shearman explain stealing Jac from the infirmary?'

'He said because the boy died in suspicious circumstances, he would be safer in the custody of the authorities, lest someone try and dispose of his body to cover their tracks.'

'*He* was the one trying to cover his tracks, the devil!'

He nodded, his face grim. 'But at least Jac will have a proper burial now.'

His tone was also grim, and Isolda sensed there was much more to be told. 'What other news did Simon bring?'

'The Earl cannot come to Ludlow as he has been called to a special Parliament in Coventry, where the rumour is the Yorkist leaders will be declared traitors and be placed under attainder.'

Isolda didn't fully understand the word. 'But surely

York is already declared traitor? What does the rest mean?'

'The flight of the Duke and his kinsmen after Ludford Bridge, their hiding out in exile, did not make them traitors. An act of Parliament is needed, and that is the purpose of the assembly at Coventry. To officially and legally strip them of their lands and chattels, their rights and liberties, and declare them outlaws.'

A pang of sadness, and of apprehension, struck at her heart. She, like most of the people of the town and surrounding lands, had been under the rule of Richard of York for many years. Now, it seemed, their loyalty must be to Lancaster, for the foreseeable future at least, perhaps for ever if the Duke and his sons did not return from exile.

'What will that mean for Ludlow?' she asked Hal.

'Little, I pray, since the town is already being governed by Lancastrians. But it means we cannot rely on the Earl of Shrewsbury to come to our aid, since he will be in Coventry before and during the Parliament.'

Isolda said a silent little prayer for the family of York, and especially for the Duchess and her three young children, still in custody, albeit a comfortable one, with her sister, the Duchess of Buckingham. Then she forced her mind back to things of more immediate urgency. 'What of Brother Matthew?'

He handed her her clothes and pushed her gently towards the curtain. 'Go and dress while I do the same, and I will tell you.'

Isolda did as she was bid, dressing quickly, even though it seemed strange to do so in private after sharing a bed with Hal—though she had not seen him naked, of course, and he had not seen her. She heard him dress with haste as well, his voice muffled now and again as he related what news his squire had brought.

'He has barricaded himself inside St Catherine's Chapel on Ludford Bridge. It is not a legal sanctuary but sacred nevertheless and the constable is reluctant to break the door down. De la Mare has placed a guard there, lest Shearman has no such scruples, so hopefully he will be safe.'

Isolda remembered the night they'd stood on the bridge and she'd looked at the tiny chapel, with its narrow door and two small windows. How the cold had shrouded her and Hal and the frost had twinkled like jewels and the moon had cast an icy reflection on the dark river.

How his touch on her cheek had begun to melt the bars she'd built around her heart. And now...now she was to be his wife! She would never have believed such things could happen in the space of just a few days! But they had. And whatever happened in the months or years ahead between the King and the Duke of York, nothing could change that.

Quickly securing her hair into a braid, though she had no braiding to tie the end, she stepped out through the curtain again, and then stopped dead in her tracks. Hal was still half dressed, having pulled on hose and boots and a fresh shirt, and was in the process of lacing up a doublet on top. His head was bent to his task and his hair was ruffled, falling over his brow and making him seem much younger.

Suddenly, the whole world lurched around her. He was so beautiful and he loved her. And she loved him and so she would pay any price to live the rest of her life with him. When they'd said as much, spoken of their love and the future so calmly and without emotion, as if they were discussing the price of fowl or the texture of wool...she'd almost not believed it, almost thought she'd still been asleep and had dreamed it all. And then, when Simon had come, the dream had all but faded...

Now, as Hal straightened and smiled at her, a wave of love so intense swept her up and carried her across the room into his waiting arms. 'Oh, Hal!'

He crushed her to him, his mouth taking hers with a passion she returned. Because this wasn't a dream; it was real. He loved her, she loved him, and they would be married one day!

'I never believed I could love someone so much,' she gasped against his mouth. 'Never.'

'Nor I...' His lips left hers and, drawing back, he looked down at her, his hand cupping her face. 'And when all this is over, when we are wed, we'll never be parted, Isolda.'

Tears threatened behind her eyelids but she blinked them back. Before then, there was much to be done. Jac to bury, Shearman to bring to justice, wrongs to put right. 'Then let us get our work done quickly.'

He nodded. 'It won't be long now.' Dropping a kiss onto her brow, he bent and reached for her shoes and stockings. 'Today, however, you must go and open up your shop as if nothing is wrong.'

Isolda sat and quickly put on her footwear. 'With Jac dead, it would not be seemly to do business, and neither would I want to.'

'Of course. I'm sorry, forgive me.' He touched her hair, the tenderness of the gesture bringing a lump into her throat. 'Nevertheless, we must behave as if we know nothing, and accept Shearman's excuse for taking the boy's body. If he senses the trap closing, he might yet evade it somehow.'

'I understand,' she said, rising and pulling her cloak

about her. The room was cold and grey in the early morn, with the fire still banked down, but suddenly she didn't want to leave it, nor leave Hal. Going to him, she wound her arms around his neck and gazed up at him. 'I've only been in this room twice but I love it, because it is *your* room.'

He touched his lips to hers. 'If you were already my wife, we would break our fast in the hall proudly, then go out hand in hand before the whole world.' His eyes twinkled. 'But today, since we are unwed, yet both famished and must eat, I think it wiser we take something quickly in the kitchen then leave by the postern gate.'

'Where are we going?'

'First, to the church, to pay our respects to Jac. Then we will meet with Edmund de la Mare, Simon too, and plan our next move. Time is vital now. Shearman has committed murder and he will be desperate and afraid, so now is the moment to trap him.'

'Harry the Cat catches his rat?'

He nodded, his gaze sobering as it bored into hers. 'He wouldn't have done it without the help of the poetess of Ludlow.'

'I will miss writing those verses when this is all over.'

'If you hadn't…' His fingers curled around hers '… I would not have come to Ludlow and we would never have met.'

Isolda went up on tiptoe and kissed his mouth. 'I love you, Hal.'

'And I you.' His smile stole her heart away. 'And if you do miss penning poetry, sweetheart, you can write verses to me, every day if you like, as long as they sing of love.'

Chapter Thirteen

The morning of Jac's funeral, two days later, Isolda went early and alone to the church to say goodbye to her apprentice—though he was much more than that. Gazing at the lifeless figure on the wooden bier in a little side chapel, shrouded in darkest grey and surrounded by candles, it was hard to remember the exuberant boy he'd been in life. And harder still to ever forget how he'd lost his life.

A tear slid down her cheek and she brushed it away. But another slid down, then another, to splash upon the hand she rested on the bier. Tears that were too late. When Brother Peter had brought the news of his death, she'd wished it had been *she* who Shearmen's men had discovered, not Jac, she who'd gone to the church and not to the Guildhall. She rued that they'd ever ventured out at all that night with parchment and nails.

But she couldn't go back in time and wishing would change nothing. Now she had to do as Hal had urged her. Try not to hold herself wholly to blame and focus instead on vengeance upon Jac's murderers.

Much had happened the previous day, while Jac had lain in simple state here. She and Hal had met with the constable and Simon, and they'd talked long about what their next move should be. As the Earl of Shrewsbury could not come to Ludlow, Edmund de la Mare had held an interview with Ralph Shearman at which Hal, as the Earl's officer, had been present. Shearman, of course, had denied everything, declaring the town to be full of Yorkist sympathisers who were trying to undermine the new Lancastrian rule, and the dead boy to be one of York's agents.

Among those sympathisers he named Prior Oteley and all his brethren at St John's Hospital, several of the tradesmen of the town, the writer of the mysterious poems and lastly—and ironically, since *she* was the writer of the poems—Isolda herself. She'd declared hotly to Hal afterwards that the bailiff had been one of the most ardent of Yorkists when Richard of York had ruled the town!

They had decided to tread carefully for a day or two, until the man in sanctuary at St Catherine's Chapel could be encouraged to speak out. Till now, Brother Matthew had admitted no one, but only spoken fearfully to the Prior, who had spent several hours yesterday at the window trying to persuade the terrified man to let him in.

It was as if everything was standing on the edge of a knife. One slip the wrong way and everything could go against them, despite having right on their side. Shearman and many others of the Guild were powerful and had influence, and it would take cunning, not brute force, to defeat them.

Isolda said a little silent prayer for Jac, crossed herself and turned to leave. Just then she heard a noise, a footfall, so quiet it was hardly there at all. A feeling of unease slipped down her spine, for the funeral was at noon and it was barely eleven of the clock and until then she had been the only person in the church.

Her unease was well founded as she saw Ralph Shearman coming down the aisle towards her. In spite of his size and bulk, he seemed to glide not walk, his ermine-lined velvet cloak like the wings of a great bird of prey as it flowed from his wide shoulders.

'What do you want?' Isolda demanded. 'How dare you come here after what you have done!'

The flickering light of the candles that lined the walls made the bailiff looked like the very devil himself as he smiled, not in greeting but with malice. 'I've come to have a little talk with you, Isolda.'

Isolda's eyes darted beyond him, desperately seeking the priest or an acolyte, anyone—but she was alone. How had he known she was here? Had he followed her? Or had he been in the church all along, watching her from a corner?

'What about?' she asked, slowly inching backwards towards the bier. 'I thought you'd done enough talking to the constable, albeit with lies! And why here, a holy place that you should be ashamed to even enter?'

He grinned, his teeth large and square in his jaw, like those of an ogre. She'd never really realised until now how monstrous he was, both his figure and his demeanour.

'About the slander you and your friend Henry Wevere have been spreading about me, among other things.'

'Slander?' Isolda lifted her chin higher and glared at him. 'Don't you mean the truth? About your corruption, your greed, your intimidation of those weaker than you?' She felt her blood begin to boil. 'And far worse too—crimes that you will pay for sooner or later.'

'Have you forgotten how high I stand in this town?' Shearman stepped closer, so close that she caught the hint of wine on his breath. 'Besides which, since we are talking of crimes, I have something to show you.'

Reaching into a pocket inside his cloak, he took out

a piece of mustard-coloured wool. Even before he'd unfolded it and dangled it in front of her, Isolda knew what it was. The torn-off piece of her gown that had been left behind in the window of the Guildhall.

'A cloth?' She laughed, though her throat had dried with dread. 'Why would I be interested in that?'

'Don't play coy with me, Isolda. You know full well what it is, since to my knowledge only you, of all the women in this town, possess a gown of this particular colour and this type of Flemish weave.'

'You are mistaken.'

'Am I?' His head shook slowly with satisfaction. 'You forget, I am a wool merchant too. I know this was material your late father brought back from Bruges with him— for I was on the same ship—and I know where and how it came to be torn off.'

Isolda swallowed. 'You could have obtained that cloth from anywhere. Entered my house in secret and cut it yourself, if indeed it did come from my gown.'

He smiled menacingly. 'Oh, it came from your gown, Isolda, and I didn't have to enter your house, because I got it from the broken window where you were careless enough to leave it.'

'It's a flimsy enough shred of evidence for whatever you are accusing me of.'

'I'm accusing you of entering the Guildhall through that window, which you broke. The reason you did so evades me for the moment, but I will discover it, when I have you in custody.'

'Custody? Are you drunk?' Isolda eyed him squarely, even though her heart was quaking. 'You'd be a laughing stock if you tried to convince anyone I would ever do such a thing. What reason *would* I have?'

'That is what puzzles me, but I will find the reason. I only have to search your house for the gown to prove your guilt. And you forget, as the bailiff, I am the law in this town. I can do anything I want—to anyone.'

The arrogance took Isolda's breath away but he was right. He was the law, be he corrupt or not. Fear began to creep along her nerves and to counter it she launched an accusation of her own. 'Does that *anything* include murder?'

His pig-like eyes flared wide and then narrowed in suspicion. 'Murder? That is a serious word, Isolda.'

'An apt one too for the act you have committed,' she returned hotly. All the necessity to bide their time until they were sure they had Shearman was irrelevant now, for *he* had *them*, albeit for the minor crime of breaking a window and entering into a property. 'An act that you will be brought to justice for, I'll see to that.'

'You?' He moved closer, his lips curling back from his teeth. 'And what can a Flemish wool-monger's spawn like you do to touch me?'

'I can speak out and others will too.' Isolda felt herself begin to shake with utter fury. 'I can't prove it—yet—but this boy here was murdered, if not by your hand, then by your order.'

Shearman's grin slipped. 'And why would I want the life of a miserable guttersnipe?'

'Because of what he knew and who he saw...just before a knife was thrust into his belly.'

'No one will believe you. All the town knew your boy for a cutpurse and a liar.'

'That isn't true!' Isolda clenched her fists at her side, her heart beating so loudly it seemed to fill the little chapel. '*You* are the liar, aye, and thief too, since you steal from the poor and the helpless, bending the laws to suit you, and soon everyone will know it.'

'The word of a whore and a worthless knight against a fine upstanding merchant? No, Isolda, I think not. You might have ensnared Wevere for the moment, but he'll cast you off sooner or later, just like that hapless oaf from Bristol did—what was his name—Robert something?'

Shearman stepped into the coloured lights from the Palmers' window above, his features illuminated with malice. 'And when he does I might take pity on you, if you say you are sorry for the lies you said about me. I might forget about this piece of cloth, and where it was found.' He tucked the cloth back inside his cloak. 'What do you say, Isolda?'

Isolda's heart leapt with hope, for he'd as good as admitted to her, if to no one else, that he was afraid too. 'I'll never take back what I've said, for it was the truth!'

'You little vixen!' Suddenly his hand shot out and closed around her throat. 'But I must admit I admire your spirit, even though I mean to crush it.'

'You can try...' Isolda gasped for air, her hands gripping his wrist and trying to break his hold. 'But you can't stop me! You'll have to kill me and even *you* wouldn't dare to do that.'

'Oh, I wouldn't stoop to those depths, my dear. Your neck is much too pretty to break, easy as it would be. But I'll make a bargain with you.'

His other hand closed tightly around her breast and squeezed so hard that she cried out. But the insult of his next words was even worse.

'I'm not without pity, Isolda. Beg my forgiveness and I'll do right by you. I might even take you to my bed, enjoy you for a night or two, like Wevere doubtless has, and give you a handful of pennies to keep you alive. But if you try and win against me I'll see you'll lose everything.'

Isolda was so weak with lack of breath now that but for Shearman's hand around her neck she might have fallen to the ground. She struggled with all her might against him, her fingernails desperately clawing at his hands and wrists, but making no headway since he wore thick kidskin gloves. Her knees started to give way and her vision blurred and she knew any moment she would faint, and be completely at his mercy.

And then, like a miracle come just in time, the church bell began to peal in the tower above them. A door opened somewhere and footsteps sounded, voices too, and she knew it was the clergy come to prepare for Jac's burial.

With the last ounce of strength left to her Isolda fisted her hands tightly together and jerked them upwards against Shearman's forearm. He was caught off-guard, staggered backwards, and the next instant she was free. Clutching the bier for support, she spat at him like a cat.

'I would rather die than lie with you! I would starve before I took a single penny from your dirty, murderous paws!' To speak, even to breathe, pained her throat but she didn't care. 'You won't silence me, Ralph Shearman. As soon as my apprentice is decently buried, I am going to prove to the whole town that you killed him.'

She saw him go pale, his mouth twisting grotesquely, and if people hadn't started coming into the church Isolda knew he might well have tried to strangle her again then and there, not stopping until his aim was met. As it was, he sent her a look of pure evil and smoothed down his sleeves, like a butcher after a day's work.

'You have made a grave error here today, Isolda, one for which you, and your lover too, will pay dearly.'

Then he turned and marched away. Isolda slumped to the floor, her lungs burning, her flesh smarting from the grip of his fingers. She didn't hear other footsteps approaching, nor know of Hal's presence until he was crouched before her, his hand on her shoulder, his face creased with concern.

'Isolda? What's happened?'

She looked up into his face, saw his squire and Dickon, Jac's friend, standing behind him. Other people were there too, staring with astonished eyes into the little chapel, and as her vision cleared she recognised the priest and some of his acolytes.

Swiftly she shook her head. 'I was overcome with my feelings,' she said, loudly enough for those nearest to hear, anxious to explain why she was on the floor of the chapel. Then, in a low whisper to Hal, she added, 'Shearman was here. I'll tell you later.'

Hal stared into Isolda's ashen face, the red weals around her throat a shocking contrast to the pale cheeks, and the residue of fear in her eyes caused his blood to rage through his veins. As he'd entered the church he'd seen Shearman storming down the nave, his momentum pushing aside those mourners who were already inside. The bailiff's expression had been livid, his fists clenched tightly, his stare seeing no one.

Hal had wondered at the time—now he knew the cause, if not the details.

'Can you stand?' he asked Isolda. 'Or do you need a moment more?'

The fear in her eyes had gone and now courage shone brightly, though she still looked shaken. 'No, I am all right.'

He supported her as she struggled to her feet, her long gown hindering her. The tremble of her body was tangible and it was all he could do not to rush out of the church there and then, and find Shearman and beat the truth out of him. But the church was full now, candles being lit, the mourners standing solemnly in the nave, the bearers waiting...

'Lean on me,' he murmured close to her ear. 'I will secure a chair for you.'

But she shook her head. 'I can stand.'

Hal nodded and held out his arm, relieved to find her grip was strong as she took it, and she let him lead her out of the little chapel and up to the front of the assembly, where a moment later the mass began.

It was a simple enough service, fitting for Jac's standing. There were no nobility or merchants among the assembly, all of the trade, servant and lower classes. Isolda had given money for a grander service than a mere apprentice would usually have, and others who had known and liked Jac had paid for masses for his soul. Hal himself had paid for the ringing of the bell, not once but several times that morning.

Isolda, as was customary, had employed some women of the town to help her prepare the feast, which would be held afterwards in her house, and to which the members of the gathering were invited.

The mass ended, Jac was carried out and buried in a far corner of the churchyard, the land closer to the building being the domain of the richer sections of society. It was cold and snow hovered in the air but did not fall. As the grave-diggers began to refill the earth, covering the boy for ever, Hal stood at Isolda's side while she passed a word or two with the people who had attended.

Her calm dignity amazed him and only he noticed that her face was paler than usual, only he knew that around her neck, beneath the collar of her cloak, red weals marred the soft creamy skin. And it didn't take much of an effort to know that Ralph Shearman had put those marks there. As the last mourner left, making their way to Isolda's house for the feast, and the priest bid them farewell, Hal led Isolda into the shelter of the lychgate and sat down on the resting bench beside her.

Her eyes were dry—in fact, she'd not wept at all during the funeral—but her feelings were clear enough without tears. 'Tell me, Isolda, before we return to your house. What did Shearman do? Those marks on your throat are his marks, aren't they?'

She nodded and drew her cloak up to her chin, as if she was ashamed to let him see them. Of everything, that cut him most of all.

'He was angry. Or rather I made him angry. I told him I knew he murdered Jac and that I meant to prove it. I know we had resolved to use cunning and bide our time, but I was furious that he should come into the church and insult me, insult Jac, insult you, too.'

Hal put his arm around her and drew her close. She was shivering and he suspected it wasn't all due to the cold. 'Never mind that, tell me all.'

'I think, if the priest hadn't come in and the mourners started to arrive, he would have killed me.' Her eyes, which had been fixed on his, widened. 'He has the piece of my gown that was torn off the night we entered the Guildhall.'

'God's bones!' Hal hissed a breath. 'Why didn't I think to retrieve it? But he could not trace the material back to you, surely?'

Alliance with Her Renegade Knight

'It is unique.' She chewed her lip and he saw it tremble. 'My father brought it back from Bruges as a gift for me, the year before he died. It is a certain Flemish wool, finely woven and not usually seen here.'

'Then we can be sure Shearman will know it belongs to you?'

'His daughter will know it already, as I have worn it often, and she always looks at it with envy. Even if I destroyed the garment, he would find a way to prove we were there, Hal.'

Hal cast his eyes about the quiet square beyond, then up at the sky, which had darkened to an ominous heavy grey, despite it being not long past noon.

'Then we must act quicker than we planned. There is no telling what he will do now that he knows we suspect him.'

Her gaze searched his. 'We can do nothing today. The feast...'

Snow started to fall and he pulled Isolda's hood up, his hand caressing her hair as he did so. Everything was quiet—too quiet, as a town always was on the day of a funeral. But below the silence, broken only by the barking of a dog somewhere and the clucking of ducks on the mill pond at the edge of the square, he clearly heard the sound of menace.

Daylight would be gone soon and in the darkness of a winter's night anything could happen.

'After the feast, it might be best if we leave Ludlow.'

'Leave?' She shook her head. 'I am not running away like a coward, Hal. Let them come with their accusations! We have done nothing wrong—it is *they* who are guilty, not us. And if we flee, will we not seem guilty, like poor Brother Matthew?'

'Either way, if Shearman apprehends you for being in the Guildhall when you should not have been, we have little excuse to explain it, and no proof of his guilt with which to defend ourselves. And once you are in his clutches, under the rule of law...'

Hal looked into her face, saw it drawn and pale with dark circles under her eyes, and the vision of those red finger marks on her throat made up his mind. 'No, it's too risky to stay. We'll go to Halton this evening.'

Beneath her hood, her brow creased. 'Halton?'

'I have a manor there.'

'I didn't know.'

'It is only lately become my property. Hopefully, no one will think to look for us there.'

He sensed her hesitate and then, to his relief, she nodded. 'Very well, then let us go to your manor.'

Hal thought quickly. Shearman would know that Halton was in his possession but the manor would still be safer than staying in the town, tonight at least, after what had happened in the church. 'I will leave the feast early, while there are people with you in your house. Then I'll return before it grows dark, with horses. Can you be ready?'

'Yes, but...' Her brow creased. 'My animals... I'll ask Dickon to see to them after the feast, before he returns home. And to come again morning and evening tomorrow, if we have not returned to Ludlow.'

He nodded. 'That would be wise. It will not look strange if your shop is closed for a day or two in respect for Jac. I'll instruct Simon to come on the morrow and alert us to any move the bailiff may have made in the night. And, Isolda...'

On impulse, he bent and took her mouth with his. Her lips parted at once, welcoming him, and a rush of love filled his heart, all the more desperate because of the fear for her that had already lodged there.

A moment later, reluctantly but necessarily given the urgency they faced, he drew back, brushed his fingers gently down her cheek. The neckline of her cloak had fallen open a little and he was gratified to see the red weals were fainter.

'And?' Her gaze searched his, clouded with worry. 'What else were you going to say?'

Hal smiled, though in his breast his heart heaved with worry. 'Only that I love you, more than my life.'

'I love you too, Hal.' The worry vanished and her eyes shone. 'No matter what happens now, I will always love you.'

He drew her to her feet and pulled her cloak more snugly about her as the first flakes of snow began to fall. 'Bring your torn gown with you to Halton. We'll destroy it there, or if you cannot bear to lose it, hide it where Shearman will never find it.'

Chapter Fourteen

Later that afternoon, just as the sun began to sink over the turrets of the castle, Isolda rode behind Hal down the Dinham Road towards the gate, and beyond that the bridge over the Teme that led to Halton. The town walls loomed above them, lit by torches at intervals, the sound of boots and voices reaching down to echo their horses' muffled hoofbeats. The snow now fell thickly and was a blessing, it turned out, as they passed unheard along the track and met no one coming towards them.

At the gate there was only one guard, but there their luck ran out. The man, perhaps suspecting their reason for being out in such weather, challenged them but Hal didn't stop to argue. Reaching quicker than the eye for his sword, he drew it and dealt the guard a blow with the hilt, felling him senseless to the ground.

Isolda expected them to dash at once through the gate, but instead Hal sprang down from his saddle and inspected the prone figure. Then he dragged him under cover of the stone arch and bundled him deeper into his cloak.

Turning to mount again, his eyes met hers. 'No need to let the fellow freeze to death. He'll soon come to, however, so we need to hurry and get to Halton before dark.'

Walking their horses across the bridge, for it was treacherous and slippery, they followed the river north as far as the weir, white and eerie in the gathering dusk, and then once on the Halton road, bordered by stark trees either side, they pushed into a careful canter.

Halton was no more than a league or two distant but was not a place Isolda knew at all, having never had cause to visit. She knew there was a small manor house and some fine woods surrounding it, full of deer and boar, formerly the property of the Earls of Mortimer and then York. She knew also it had passed into Lancastrian hands since York's rebellion against the King, but had not heard the new owner's identity—until now.

They turned off the road and rode through thick oak trees, the ground underfoot so white with snow here that it was almost like daylight. Through the leafless branches, the rising moon behind them dappled their horses with silver. They didn't speak at all as they slowed to a trot when the snow fell thicker, but questions burned on Isolda's tongue.

Why did he reside at the castle in Ludlow and not in his manor house? Where had he lived since leaving St Albans? And now peace reigned momentarily, would he live *here* when not on the Earl's business elsewhere? She had no chance to ask those things as in no time at all, it seemed, they were dismounting and a surprised steward, lantern in hand, was greeting them at the door.

'Who comes here at this hour?'

'I am Henry Wevere, lord of this manor, which I hold from the Earl of Shrewsbury, as you well know, since I was here two months ago, if briefly.'

The poor steward peered closer than began to stammer, 'Sir Henry, I did not expect... We had no word of your coming.'

'I did not *know* I'd be coming again so soon, but now that I am here, please get someone to see to our horses and provide a bed for myself and my guest.'

'At once, Sir Henry.'

They went into the house, bringing snow on their boots, and found the hall lit downstairs and a fire burning in the hearth. A plump woman in a russet kirtle and a faded white coif rose hastily from one of the two chairs placed around it and, her eyes popping, bobbed a belated curtsey.

'This is my wife, Mary, who keeps house, Sir Henry.'

The steward, whose name she discovered was Hugh, took their cloaks and baggage, while his wife hurried aloft to prepare bedchambers. Isolda sank down gratefully into the chair the woman had vacated and stretched her cold fingers out towards the fire. She couldn't feel her toes, so she eased her shoes off and stretched her stockinged feet towards the welcoming warmth as well.

As Hal spoke with his steward she looked around the hall. It wasn't big but was richly panelled in oak on all sides. Candles burned brightly in holders on the walls and on the long table in the centre of the room. The floor was thickly laid with rushes and the shutters over the windows were sturdy and firmly fixed. It was obvious, even though Hal appeared not to live here, that his servants kept his house well for him.

Or rather, for themselves! On the table was the remnants of a meal of roasted goose, bread and cheese, some honey cakes and a large jug of ale. Dismissing his man, Hal filled two cups from the pitcher and brought them over to the fire, placing them on a small table he dragged between the chairs.

'Drink this. It will warm you.'

Isolda drank gratefully, feeling the ale bring heat into her belly. Slowly, her limbs began to thaw and her face started to sting as the fire banished the cold. Leaning back in her chair, she put her cup down then looked across at Hal, who seated himself opposite.

He drained his own cup and, putting it down beside hers, leaned forward and took her hands in his. Immediately, the warmth that was flooding through Isolda's body changed in its nature as a wave of love swamped her.

'It has been a long day for you, Isolda.'

She nodded. 'For both of us.'

His gaze dropped to her throat, and she saw his mouth tighten. 'I'll make Shearman pay for what he did to you today, I swear I will! If we hadn't come when we did...'

Isolda squeezed his hands. 'But you *did* come. He is a coward, Hal. I saw his fear plainly on his face, along with his guilt.'

He nodded. 'At least here, unmolested, we can plan how to prove that guilt.' Releasing her hands, he refilled their cups, passing one to her. Then he sat back and looked around him. 'I never thought I'd ever visit this house again, let alone spend a night under its roof.'

Isolda blinked. 'Then you really have only been here once before?'

'Halton was gifted to me when I was knighted, after the battle of Blore Heath in September, but I had no wish to settle here.'

'So where have you lived these last years?'

He shrugged. 'Wherever my duties took me. In various castles, in Ireland twice, on the road if my master moved his household, in the field when local disputes turned to conflict.'

'That sounds unsettling.'

'It is a normal existence for a man like me, and for all men who serve great lords.'

'Why did you turn from weaving to soldiering?'

'I hated weaving. I was too restless to sit at a loom day in day out, but I had no idea of what else I could do.' He stared pensively into his cup. 'After I left St Albans, I joined the retinue of a minor Lancastrian nobleman, as soldiering seemed the only option for a man unskilled in anything else.'

'Did you take to it well?'

He shrugged. 'It gave me a new life and calmed my wild ways, at any rate.'

'And since then?'

'My first lord died with no sons to follow him and I entered the service of Lord Audley of Cheshire. He was killed at Blore Heath. I fought also that day, the only pitched battle I have faced, and I loathed it from beginning to end. The slaughter, the wasted valour, the reckless charges into death...'

'Yet you yourself claim to have been reckless once.'

He shook his head. 'Not any more, and not just because fighting sickens me. I fled St Albans full of rage and a desire for revenge on Warwick, on the house of York itself. High ambitions indeed for a simple weaver! I fled Blore Heath too, with all the other Lancastrians that still lived, and was rewarded with a knighthood I didn't really deserve.'

'Because you fought well?'

'No, because I saved the life of the young heir to Lord Dudley, purely because I was in the right place at the right time and conveyed him safely to the royal forces at Stafford. The King needs all his loyal nobles alive in these precarious days!' A smile touched his mouth. 'Henry himself bestowed the honour on me, though hurriedly in the field, along with one or two other survivors of the battle. Then I was attached to John Talbot's service, equally hastily, just in time to meet the Yorkists at Ludford Bridge.'

Isolda was silent for a moment. 'You cannot fail to admit you have come a long way for a lowly weaver.'

He met her eyes. 'That is true, but I sometimes wonder if there had been no battle at St Albans, no fire, no conflict between Lancaster and York... Ah, well, perhaps it is too late to wonder now.'

Another silence fell between them and Isolda sensed the time had come to ask the question that had been waiting to be asked ever since he'd told her about that battle.

'How did it happen—the fire?'

She saw shock ripple through him and in the firelight his whole form seemed altered, as if the flames had called up a ghost from somewhere deep within him. Then he nodded, a heavy movement of his head.

'As Warwick led his forces through the houses, mine included, a brazier that had been lighted was knocked over. The house, like all the others in those streets, was built in wood and went up in flames at once. They couldn't get out and so they perished—my parents and sister in the fire, my younger brother, Will, two days later from his burns. Before he died, he told me how it had been.'

Isolda stifled a gasp of horror. 'I am so sorry, Hal,' she said ineffectually, as she had the first time he'd told her, though not in such detail. And she'd berated him for what she'd seen as self-pity! 'Your whole family...'

He cut her off. 'Except me.'

Except him. Because he'd been up on the clock tower with his comrades, watching the battle. He didn't even have to say it—she saw the guilt rise up and swamp even the anger in his eyes—but there was no self-pity in his words now.

'I cannot change what happened then, nor turn back time, Isolda, but I can ensure I never let anyone down like that ever again.'

At that moment Hugh reappeared, to announce that two chambers had been made ready aloft for them, but as the upper level had not been used in many years, the hearths in the rooms were cold, and there were rooks nesting in the chimneys. First thing tomorrow, he would clear the nests away and fires would be made, but for tonight he'd put extra coverlets of heavy down and furs on the beds.

'Though they are motheaten and musty, Sir Henry, I hope they will serve.' The steward spread his hands. 'If we'd known you were coming, naturally, we would have prepared...'

Hal answered without breaking the lock of his eyes on hers. 'Then we will sleep here, before the fire, tonight. Thank you, Hugh. We require nothing more. You and your wife may retire.'

The steward bowed and left, closing the door softly behind him. The wind whistled in as if another door beyond, or a window, was open. And when Hal spoke again it was clear the topic they'd been speaking of a moment before was closed.

'But I'm glad I have this house now. If you had remained in Ludlow tonight, there is no knowing how low Shearman might have stooped. A man who has murdered once will not hesitate to do so again.'

Isolda shuddered as she remembered the bailiff's words, how he'd offered to take her to his bed when Hal deserted her, as Robert had done.

'Is the manor fortified?' she asked, settling back into her chair, the warmth of the fire pervading the room and making the hall look homely. Hal had spoken so openly just now but she sensed there was so much more to be said, though not tonight.

'Not as such.' He took up his cup again and turned it in his palms. 'It was begun as a castle two centuries ago but its outer defences were never completed.'

She looked around the room, at the candles that made the old oaken walls glow, the rich tapestries here and there, the sparse but beautifully carved items of furniture. Would she and Hal live here as man and wife? Would they bring up children in this house?

The notion made her heart skip a beat. Those questions were ones she'd never imagined having, let alone asking, even to herself. Was it all a dream? Had he really asked her to marry him? And had she said yes?

Doubts surfaced, born of worry and fatigue, but insistent nonetheless. When all this was over, when they had no need to work together for justice, would the love Hal had confessed to vanish? Would it prove to be nothing more than an unconscious result of the partnership that had grown up between them?

Isolda felt her face grow hot, the heat travelling down her throat, into her body, leaving her skin bathed not with warmth but with an icy sense of terror. Shearman's sneering warning that Hal would tire of her echoed in her heart, as brutal as his hands around her throat had been. Until that moment, she'd been so swept up in Hal's love, in the fact they would be wed, that she hadn't doubted it, or him, but now...

Now fear gripped her and, from the past, arose the desolation after the loss of her father and brother, the indignation when Robert had left, even the sadness of her mother going to Tewkesbury to live, even though that had been a relief too, as the nagging had gone with her.

She'd thrown herself into work and hadn't let those losses, the underlying loneliness, preoccupy her. She'd even believed herself to be the strong and determined woman she showed the town, as hard as it had been at times to maintain that veneer, but now that image wavered before her eyes.

Now she loved and all the vulnerabilities she knew she possessed, which she'd succeeded in ignoring, or at least hiding, surfaced. She loved Hal and if he too left her, taking her heart with him, would that loss, greater than all the others, destroy her?

'And now you have come here,' she asked, trying to keep that fear from her voice, 'do you see yourself living here, Hal?'

'That will depend on the Earl's duties for me, but yes, I think so—but only if you are living here with me, Isolda.'

Her heart came to life again and, resolutely, Isolda stamped down her fear. She loved Hal and she trusted him. Surely there was no room for doubt, no cause to feel vulnerable, not any more. Rising from her chair, she knelt before the fire and stared into the flames.

'That first day I saw you…something happened to me,' she said. 'I seemed to know you in a way I'd never known Robert. I tried to dismiss it at first, but then in the alleyway when you came to my rescue I felt it again. As if I knew you with my whole soul.'

'Even with a wool sack over my head?'

Isolda glanced up, sought his gaze, saw it twinkle. 'Even then,' she joked in return, anxiously searching his eyes and finding only love. 'Did you feel that too?'

***

Hal put his cup down and went on his knees beside her. Taking her in his arms, he kissed her mouth, her brow, her cheeks, then her mouth again. 'Sweeting, I feel as if I have been waiting all my life...searching without knowing I searched...for you.'

He threaded his fingers into the hair coiled over her ears, loosening the braids until the golden strands began to escape their bonds. All the feelings she'd inspired in him since that first moment spilled out with total abandon, with a need he'd not felt ever in his life before. A need he'd never known he could feel, or even existed in the world.

Or at least in the world he'd created for himself. A realm of guilt and regret and loneliness. A place he'd chosen for himself and that he'd never intended to leave. Until now.

'And now that I've found you, my love,' he vowed, 'I will never let you go.'

The flames from the fire were scorching, making their clothes steam even more, but suddenly he realised those flames held no fear for him. He twisted to the side, however, away from the heat, taking Isolda with him, and laid her down beneath him on the rushes, their mouths still locked hungrily, greedily, together.

'Then you do really love me as I love you?'

Her arms wrapped about his neck, drawing him down closer still, until their bodies touched at breast, belly and thigh. He was a hard as a staff now, his manhood straining against his hose, pressing urgently into the cradle of her hips.

'Can you still doubt it, Isolda?' Hal lifted his head and stared down at her. 'There is no need to, for I will love you until my dying breath and beyond.'

The truth of that shook Hal to his core. Lying here with Isolda in his arms, with all the world outside banished and barred, he knew his love was the sort she really meant. The love that came with knowing, that went beyond the physical, the sort of love that encompassed a man's heart and possessed him—and changed him—entirely.

Beneath him, her eyes shimmered like precious jewels. Her hair glowed like gold and her lips were the colour of dusky pink roses. She was his and he was hers…for ever, no matter what happened tomorrow, or next year, or whatever came to pass between Lancaster and York, they would never be parted.

'No,' she breathed. 'I do not doubt it and never will, though after Robert, I never thought I would trust again.'

He touched his mouth lightly to hers. 'I am not Robert, nor ever could be. He was a fool and, although I may have been foolish many times in my life, I am not such a dolt as to let you go now that I have you.'

Isolda smiled and laid her head against his shoulder, weariness claiming them both. Hal let his fingers play drowsily with her hair, watching the shadows of her eyelashes on her smooth cheeks, seeing how her eyes fluttered closed, then opened again, to seek his.

'We must undress and sleep, sweeting.'

Slowly, without haste, he peeled her gown from her, then her stockings, leaving her only in her soft linen chemise. With the same leisure he removed his own clothes down to his braies and then, to keep out the cold, he rose and fetched a thick murrey-coloured coverlet from the settle at the opposite wall. Dropping down onto his side next to her, he drew the coverlet over them.

But suddenly she seemed wide awake again. 'Do you not…want me, Hal?' Her palm pressed lightly against his chest. 'I know you love me, but do you want me too, the way a man wants a woman?'

Hal felt his heart kick, knew that she felt it too, for she snuggled closer, her body arching against him. Her fingers caressed a path down his chest and belly...lower still.

'Isolda... Can you not see how I want you?' He snatched a breath and his whole body jerked into life. An instant later, he was wide awake too, his blood coursing and every sinew in his body pulling tight. 'But desist for the love of God!'

She gave a soft laugh and her fingertips travelled lightly ever downwards. 'I've never touched a man... like this... I never dreamed it would feel so...delicious!'

Hal chuckled too, though it was heavy with a desire he could barely keep in check. 'When we are man and wife, I will show you how delicious touching...and more...can be, sweeting, but...'

A little frown creased her brow. 'But?'

He captured her wandering hand just in time and brought it up to his mouth, kissing her palm, then curling her fingers within his. 'I have to tell you, Isolda, that in my youth...well, suffice to say, I was seldom without female company.'

Her gaze danced mischievously in the firelight. 'You weren't?'

He shook his head. 'Back then I thought I was a fine fellow, but now I am ashamed.'

'Why?'

'Because I lay with all those women—wives, widows and whores, I wasn't choosy—and none of them meant anything to me.'

'Oh, I see.' The mischief faded into sober curiosity. 'But why are you telling me this now?'

'Because when I lie with you, when we join together fully as man and woman, I want it to be properly done, as lovemaking should be between a husband and wife. I want it to mean everything. Do you understand?'

She nodded. 'I think I do, yes.'

He smiled down at her, her returning smile both warming his heart and humbling his soul. For lying here with Isolda, simply touching her and nothing more, made *him* feel the virgin too. 'I long to make you mine, Isolda. To show you with my body as well as my touch and my lips how much I love you. But until we are wed, I will not.'

'No, I want it to be that way too, Hal.' Her fingers threaded through his hair, traced a path down his cheek, his throat, came to rest at his collarbone. 'But I will count the days impatiently until we are man and wife in every sense.'

'As will I!' Hal took her mouth in a deep kiss, tasting the promise in it, and willed the body she'd inflamed all over again to obedience. 'I love you, Isolda.'

'And I you,' she said.

Then he got up, his manhood proud against his braies despite his will, and built up the fire from the log pile at the side of the hearth. Reaching instinctively for the iron cover, he paused, then left it off. The night was cold and they would need all the warmth they could get.

Tonight, with Isolda in his arms, sleeping safely, he would not think of fear. She trusted him and she loved him. The past, his guilt, had no place here tonight, nor on any other night, nor day either. He had to leave all that behind, go forward with her into the future.

Dropping down beside her again, Hal drew her close once more, the scent of the rose and lavender in her hair, on her skin, greeting his senses. 'Are you warm enough, sweeting?'

She nodded. 'And sleepy.' A sigh of contentment escaped her, tickling his bare throat. 'Lying here with you, before the fire, with the world outside all white with snow, I think I will sleep more soundly than ever in my life. Are you sleepy too?'

'A little. But before we sleep, would you like to hear another story?' Hal shook his head as she gazed questioningly at him. 'No, not another regaling of my shameful youth. You know everything there is to know of that now. I want to tell you how the loss of my family changed me, for I've never told it to anyone.'

She nodded and for the first time in four years he spoke without pain about his sister, his brother, his parents. This was the moment to say it, now, before their future together started properly, so he could live the rest of his life with Isolda with his conscience and his heart clear and clean.

'My family was one of love, of kindness, of generosity, of morality. My father was the most honest man I knew, though he was a hard taskmaster, and my mother was a saint, but quick of temper when riled—and I riled her often enough, God knows!'

'And your brother and sister? Were you very close to them?'

'Yes, though they were younger than me. Will was jolly, good-hearted always, and Beatrice...she was like you, stubborn and unafraid, full of passion for justice and the determination to put wrongs right.'

He paused as the vision of his sister, his brother, his parents seemed to rise from the flames in the hearth and then dissipate, like souls finally going to rest, as he felt his was doing.

'I would do anything for them, but there were bad traits in me too. Ale, dicing, pranks that were harmless enough but wrong…and all those women. That was my youth, Isolda. Because of my reluctance to follow in a trade which bored me, I chose instead, perhaps as a remedy or a release, to be idle, dissolute and wasted.'

'I think many other men have misspent youths too, though they hide it.'

'Perhaps. But that day of the battle, when I was safe and enjoying the spectacle, the fighting, the colours of the knights' banners, their great war horses, the sound of cannon…a day when I should have been beside my brother at the loom, but was not…'

'Your brother would not blame you, Hal. None of your family would.'

'No, I believe that now, though it has taken me a long time to do that, and without you, I might never have done so. But my whole family were lost to me, in a moment, it seemed, and the grief and the guilt, the hatred for the man I was, was like nothing I'd ever imagined. It changed everything—changed me—in an instant.'

Isolda shifted in his arms and raised herself on one elbow, her gaze not sleepy at all now, but understanding, loving, knowing. 'Making you resolve to never experience that sort of loss ever again?'

Hal nodded. 'I decided the only way to avoid it was never to have a family or a home, or love anyone so much that losing them would be unbearable. Even the fear of letting them down, failing anyone again in that way, for whatever reason.' He laid his forehead against hers. 'I will never forget the past, Isolda, but I think I can begin to break free of it at last.'

'You no longer wish you'd died in that fire too?'

'No. I've discovered my life is far too precious to me since you entered it.'

She lifted her palm to his cheek, making him look into her eyes. 'And can you forgive yourself too for something that you were never really to be blamed for?'

'If I can one day, it will be thanks to you. If I'd never met you…'

'But we *did* meet. I believe with all my heart that we were meant to find each other sooner or later, Hal. And you will find forgiveness too, for I will help you look for it.' She snuggled into him, her weariness evident in the limbs that relaxed in his, the little yawn she tried so hard to stifle. 'You and me…our love…and the future…that is what we must cling to now, not the past.'

'I know.' He kissed her lips, her fatigue reaching out and claiming him as well, too strong to resist. 'Go to sleep, my love.'

'Goodnight, Hal…' Her eyes, which had begun to close, fluttered open for a brief instant. 'I'm glad you told me about your family…and everything.'

'I am glad too, sweeting.'

As Hal closed his eyes and began to sink into sleep, he made a vow. He would make Isolda his wife as soon as he could. He would build her a home here in this manor, where together they would raise the family he'd sworn he'd never have. And as the fire burned low and crackled comfortably in the hearth he found a peace that he'd never known.

Chapter Fifteen

The banging at the door woke Isolda with a start. At first, she thought it was thunder but then the sound of men's voices told her it was not. Hal was already on his feet, naked apart from his braies, his hand outstretched in warning not to move or speak.

The room was not fully light, through dawn had broken, and the fire still slumbered in the hearth. All was quiet elsewhere in the house, which made the noise at the door even louder and more alarming.

'What is it?' she asked, sitting up, unable to keep quiet or still any longer. 'Surely no one would come at this hour, and Hugh would not pound the door like that, would he?'

Hal shook his head. 'No, it is not Hugh.' He ran a hand through his hair, tousled from sleep, and cast his eyes around for his clothing and his weapon. 'Quickly, we must get up!'

Isolda leapt to her feet and looked around for her clothing too, which, like Hal's, lay among the rushes on the floor where they'd discarded them the night before. But even as she reached for her gown the door splintered and beyond it appeared dark figures outlined against a dusky pink-grey sky.

'Wevere!'

The roar was exultant, as if he who had roared had won a great victory. Isolda pressed her hands to her heart as men tumbled into the hall and came rushing towards them. Hal bent swiftly for the murrey coverlet on the floor and draped it around her. Then, with a calmness that was admirable, he turned and faced Ralph Shearman, for it was he who stood there.

'I would say good morrow, Shearman, if you'd been invited into my home, and if you'd had the courtesy to knock at the door instead of breaking it down.'

The measured yet contemptuous words caught the bailiff off-guard. His mouth opened and shut and then he gave an ugly sneer, his eyes travelling down Hal's half-naked body to his bare feet, and back up again to his face.

'Well, well, well...it seems I've come at a most inopportune moment—for you and your whore, that is!'

Isolda saw a flush mount Hal's cheek, not one of embarrassment but of anger. He stepped towards Shearman, his magnificent form even more magnificent for its lack of clothing. In fact, next to the other man's opulent blue and gold attire, the ermine-lined velvet cloak and hat and the ridiculous pointed shoes, Hal emanated integrity, honour...and beauty. So beautiful that, even despite the danger that surrounded them, she swallowed in awe, and so much in love that she thought her heart would burst from it.

'If you don't take that word back, I'll ram it down your throat so far that you'll never speak it, nor any other word, ever again.' Hal's threat was made even more menacing by the quiet way it was said.

Shearman moistened his lips and his swaggering stance wavered just a bit. Then he laughed and planted his feet wide. 'I'd like to see you try, Wevere, with four swords drawn against you.'

Isolda's mouth dried. Sherman had three men with him, and Hal's sword was where he'd left it, in its scabbard, propped against a wall. He'd never reach it, she knew, even if he made a dash for it. Besides which, outnumbered as they were, it would be both futile and fatal to do so.

'Don't tempt me, Shearman,' Hal said, 'for it might be worth the risk just to rid the world of your presence, no matter what it cost me.'

'And your whore?' The word was spat out. 'Her sex won't save her. I promise you that much.'

Isolda drew the coverlet closer about her and stepped forward to stand at Hal's side. Lifting her chin, she looked Ralph Shearman straight in the eye. 'I'd gladly die at Sir Henry's side as long as you were hanged for our murders, aye, and the murder of another innocent soul!'

Shearman's gaze slid from Hal to her. 'Murder? Oh, no, not that, Isolda. It'll be a fair act in which you and your lover perish as you try to escape justice. We would have no choice but to cut you down as you fled.'

'And what would we be fleeing from,' she asked again, 'if not from you?'

'The question is—why would you flee at all? And knock the guard on the Dinham Bridge to the ground, though not entirely senseless, as he was able to report who had struck him and where they were making for.'

'I should have hit him harder, obviously!' Hal's tone was dry, contemptuous. 'But it is no crime, as far as I know, to visit my own manor.'

'Bodily assault and flight under cover of darkness? I consider that suspicious enough for pursuit by the authorities.' The bailiff stepped closer, his sneer uglier than ever. 'You accused me, in the church, of poisoning your little apprentice, Isolda, but who is to say you didn't do that yourself, lest he speak of your vile and carnal ways?'

Hal stepped forward, putting her behind him, rage shaking in his voice. 'That is utter slander, Shearman—how dare you speak it!'

The bailiff tutted. 'My word is law in Ludlow and if I say you fled rather than face the humility of being flogged around the town for the fornicators you are, no one will question it.'

'You...!'

Several things happened at once. Hal lunged for Ralph Shearman, his fists clenched. The bailiff lifted his sword but stepped hastily backwards. Hugh the steward appeared through the door behind them with a meat cleaver in his hand. And in the wrecked doorway, the broad shoulders of Hal's squire suddenly blocked out the dawn light beyond. Isolda remembered that Simon had been instructed to come that morning, and now it seemed his arrival was just in time.

'Isolda—into the back room!'

Hal took her arm and, dragging her to the door which Hugh had come in through, pushed her over the threshold, pulling it shut behind her. Isolda stood stupefied for an instant, staring about her, in what she realised was a kitchen-cum-parlour, with a large hearth and a staircase leading upwards on either side of it. From above, there was the sound of feet running, and she knew that Mary had heard the commotion. But she gave that little thought, for on the far wall hung a collection of knives for the preparation of food.

Her stupor vanished. Running forward, she took down the largest and sharpest knife and flung the door open again. It had been the truth when she'd said she'd die with Hal and now, as the scene of violence unfolded before her, Isolda knew that that might well be her fate.

Simon was fighting with two men at once and getting the better of them. Hugh, with his cleaver, was fending off another, being backed slowly across the room but doing his best. Mary appeared from the doorway behind Isolda and screamed. And before the fireplace, Hal, his sword in his hand now, was pitched against Shearman.

Hal was clearly the better swordsman but the bailiff was big and strong and his weight behind his sword was punishing, and frenzied. However, his heavy cloak was cumbersome and slowed him down, whereas Hal's lighter body was lithe and nimble, the firelight behind him flickering over his skin and making him seem of another world, not this one.

Fear clutching at her heart, Isolda called out his name and Hal's head turned sharply. She saw him wince as, taking advantage of the distraction, Shearman's blade found his flank, making blood spurt.

'No!' she screamed, wincing too. Throwing off the coverlet that hindered her, she ran towards him, but Mary's arms came around her waist and she was pulled backwards.

'Ye'll not help matters, Mistress. Stay out of the way and let the men do their work. 'Tis best.'

With a helpless sob, Isolda knew Mary was right. The two men were like demons, lunging back and forth before the flames, the glint of swords deadly, the ring of metal the anvils of hell, the trickle of blood on Hal's side turning his flesh red.

She clasped the handle of her useless knife and willed him to win. He had to win! If he lost, they would all perish. The thought didn't frighten her. If she was at Hal's side, she would take whatever came. But what of Simon, and Hugh and Mary, and Brother Matthew, and Dickon, and all those who suffered at Shearman's hands? They would go on suffering and oppression would know no end.

'Oh, no, no! My poor Hugh, he'll be killed for sure!'

Mary's shriek sent Isolda's eyes darting to where the steward was on his knees, his cleaver knocked from his hand. His opponent, who now she recognised as Perkin, one of the men who'd attacked Jac that fateful night, raised his sword high, and then paused. His mouth pulled into a hideous grin as he took a moment to savour the atrocity he was about to commit.

A moment he would not live to enjoy. Isolda didn't hesitate. She didn't even think. She raced across the room and plunged her knife deep between the man's shoulder blades. He went completely still and his head turned, his gaze astonished, then his body crumpled to the floor. He, at least, would kill no more.

Hugh, his face ashen, gave her a nod of gratitude, then heaved himself to his feet and found his cleaver. Simon had dispatched one of his opponents and the other was disappearing out through the door, as if not even his orders were worth his life.

Only Hal and Shearman fought on before the fire, which flamed higher now, fed by the air from the open doors, as if providing a backdrop for their combat. Or for its conclusion. For, as they watched, Shearman's weapon went spiralling out of his hand to land with a clatter in the hearth.

There was an instant of stillness when neither man moved, as if neither could believe what had just happened. A moment when the onlookers, drawn to see what would happen next, inched forward, Isolda at the front. And then Shearman snarled like a cornered wolf and, with a swiftness that belied his bulk, stooped low to the fire.

Hal's sword was too slow, too late, as it came down on the bailiff's forearm, slicing through the flesh and breaking the bone. Shearman screamed and fell forward, his other hand reaching out, not for his sword but for a burning log. Then, with a terrible and blood-curdling howl, he swung and threw.

The glowing piece of wood arced through the air and then dropped into the rushes nearby. It caught with terrifying swiftness and, even before the cry had leapt into Isolda's mouth, flames snaked across the floor and licked at the red coverlet that lay where she'd discarded it, near her feet.

Hal spun around and was blinded by colours. Red flames, red floor, red walls—everywhere seemed to have been painted in shades of scarlet and crimson. Voices shouted and the forms of people loomed and faded as the crackle of burning wood filled his ears. He saw the frightened faces of Isolda and Mary as they stamped upon the burning coverlet to try and extinguish the flames. Simon and Hugh tore the tapestries off the walls and began to beat out the fire that was eating up the floor rushes.

Hal went to run and help them but fell headlong as something grabbed his ankle. The breath was knocked from his body and, dazed for a moment, he couldn't get up. Fire licked around him and the years between St Albans and now converged into one fiery hellish pyre. The screams and shouts around him echoed back and forth through those years, pulling him with them, towards the same people, the same fear, the same loss.

But he couldn't lose now, not again, not here. This wasn't St Albans, this was Halton, his manor... Isolda! Hal tried to rise but found himself held fast, by what devil, God only knew. The furniture and fabrics were burning quickly now, and smoke filled his throat and made his eyes stream as they sought her.

'Isolda! Isolda! Where are you?'

Answering voices came but Hal couldn't make any sense of what they said. With a curse, he kicked as hard as he could at the ogre that ensnared him. Miraculously, it released him and he leapt to his feet to see people running outside now, though one—a woman—struggled against the man who was dragging her towards the door.

'Hal! Hal!'

Isolda! Hal went to run to her but whatever it was behind him grabbed him again and once more he fell forward. But he wasn't going to let it trap him a second time. With a snarl, he turned and kicked viciously. There was an unearthly shriek, his leg was free, and then someone was pulling him to his feet.

'Can you move, Hal? Are you hurt?'

He knew the voice but couldn't see the man's face. 'Yes, I can move. We must get everyone out, Simon, and quickly! Where's Isolda?'

'Outside, and safe.'

Relief flooded him and, hauling up a man who lay inert on the floor, Hal made for the door, Simon doing the same, with another of Sherman's men over his shoulder. Outside, it was snowing and his feet and ankles groaned in agony as he dropped his burden, surely lifeless, into the snow. Then, from inside the house, a scream rent the air.

Simon touched his shoulder. 'There's someone still inside!'

Hal didn't answer but ran back into the smoke, keeping his bare feet moving swiftly to escape the hungry flames. The noise was overwhelming and sparks danced like stars before his eyes as the entire hall was eaten up by the fire.

'Who is it?' he shouted. 'Where are you?'

'It's Ralph Shearman! I'm over here!'

The shout was cut off abruptly by the awful sound of the staircase collapsing. The ceiling was alight too now and it would only be a matter of minutes before the roof came down.

'Where?' Hal yelled again, leaping to the side as a beam fell from above. 'Call out, man!'

The only answer was the shattering of glass from a window, and he hissed in pain as shards shot into the room and lanced his naked skin. Shielding his face with his arm, he peered through the smoke, coughing and choking, aware that his lungs would not function for much longer. Then, just as he felt his head begin to spin and breath deserted him, a shadow moved towards him, low on the ground like an animal, one hand outstretched.

'Help me, for the love of God!'

Stooping, Hal bent forward to grasp the hand just as a section of ceiling above dropped to the floor. He was thrown backwards, debris slamming into him and his head hitting the stone floor. He lay there on his back for a moment, gasping for air, unable to think, unable to feel anything but pain.

The noise of the fire was all around and everything was red and angry and hellish, but at least Isolda was safe. Beatrice had died, his mother, father and Will too, but Isolda was safe, and Simon and Hugh and Mary were safe as well, outside in the snow. Only he would perish.

But he didn't want to perish! He wanted to live, to

love Isolda, to marry her and have a family again. Turning, he tried to push himself to his feet, but there was no strength left in his arms, so on his hands and knees, his flesh shrivelling in agony, he crawled.

But he couldn't see the door or which direction he should go in, as smoke swallowed him like a dense choking fog. He knew that in a moment his breath would cease and his heart would stop. Like his family, he'd be reduced to dust and ashes. It was ordained perhaps—a retribution that was bound to claim him one day…

'Hal!'

Hal lifted his head and peered into the smoke and fire, tears streaming down his face, distorting everything. His whole body seemed to have been skinned raw and his bones felt as if they had melted to the marrow. And then ghostly hands were upon him, lifting him up, but whose they were, or whether they were taking him to heaven or hell, he didn't know.

'Hal! Hal!'

A form appeared with a blinding light surrounding her. A woman with golden hair and pale skin who knelt and cradled his head, her tears falling upon his face. Lips touched his and, even though an icy cold swamped him, bringing a new agony to his scorched flesh, a sort of peace embraced him.

An angel come to comfort him, to convey him to rest. Whichever world awaited him—the celestial one or the underworld—he was content. Isolda was safe. Hal closed his eyes and the last sound he heard was a sob as the angel kissed him again and then clasped him—body, soul and heart—to her breast.

Chapter Sixteen

Isolda sat on a stone bench in the little room off the infirmary in St John's Hospital, her eyes never leaving the door opposite. Hal lay behind that door, being treated by the brethren for the burns and injuries he'd sustained in the fire at Halton yesterday.

She shuddered. Had all that only been yesterday? And how could so much happen in just one day? And one night. The hours before, when she and Hal had reaffirmed their love, when he'd finally began to forgive himself and find peace and they'd slept safely in each other's arms, had been like heaven. And then heaven had become a terrifying hell when Shearman had come.

One of the brethren brought her a blanket, though there was a merry fire in the room in which she waited, and gratefully she pulled it around her. The hours dragged by. The same brother reappeared some time later with a cup of warm ale, which she drank thirstily.

'Will it be much longer?' she asked, handing back the empty cup with her thanks.

The man shrugged. 'I do not know.'

With that the door opposite opened and Prior Oteley himself appeared on the threshold. Isolda leapt to her feet even before he beckoned her forward.

'Is he...?'

The Prior smiled. 'His injuries are grave but not fatal. He is asleep but you may go in.'

She saw Hal at once, since his bed was the nearest. The brethren who'd been tending him gathered their balms, potions and cloths and left. One of Shearman's men who'd survived the fire occupied a bed on the other side of the room, but she hardly glanced at him as she hurried over to where Hal lay.

Sinking down into a chair at the bedside, she swallowed back a choke, afeared that she'd wake him. Hal's hands and arms were swathed in soft linen up to the elbow and lay outside the coverlet. A bandage was wrapped around the wound in his flank, but his chest and shoulders were bare, revealing the small but numerous cuts that marked his skin.

She couldn't see the lower half of his body, as it lay beneath some sort of cradle that kept the bedcover off his lower limbs. His hair was matted and dirty against the pillow but his face—though pale and drawn—was unmarked by fire and had been cleaned of smoke and grime.

Thomas Oteley's voice startled her. She'd forgotten his presence completely. 'We have cooled the burns and dressed them with a balm of alkanet, hemlock and rose oil. We have also treated and bound the wound in his side, which fortunately wasn't deep. The cuts on his shoulder and chest seem to have been made by shards of glass, but they are superficial and will heal of their own accord.'

Isolda looked up at him. 'Is he...in pain?'

'Yes.'

The blunt confirmation, though said gently, was brutal, and only tempered a little by the Prior's next words.

'Though hopefully there will be no infection of either his wounds or his burns, since he came to us in good time.'

'Yes, we brought him—and the other—as quickly as we could.' Isolda looked over to the other bed, whose occupant fretted and muttered. 'Will he live too?'

'I believe so.' The Prior shook his head. 'Though it will be some time before he is well enough to face a trial.'

'You have heard news of that?'

Thomas Oteley nodded. 'I spoke with Sir Henry's squire and with Edmund de la Mare this morning.'

Hal stirred suddenly, as if their conversation, or its topic, had roused him. Isolda saw him wince as he tried to lift an arm and then slowly his eyes fluttered open. For a moment he stared upwards, his face blank, as if he knew not where he was, and then his head turned on the pillow.

'Isolda?'

The Prior left them, his footsteps silent, only the swish of his robe telling of his departure. She reached out to place her hand on Hal's arm, then hesitated, fearing his body was too sore to be touched. 'I'm here, Hal.'

'Where am I? What day is it?'

'The next day, and you are in St John's infirmary.'

'What hour?'

'It is not yet sunset.' She laid her fingertips gently on his uninjured shoulder. 'Prior Thomas says you are in no danger, and that you will soon heal.'

'I don't remember...' His eyes focused, cleared, became filled with alarm. 'The fire! Were you... Are you hurt?'

She shook her head. 'No, I'm not hurt, nor is Simon, nor Hugh and Mary. Everyone is safe.'

'Shearman?'

'Dead—in the fire.'

Hal's eyes closed for a moment and then opened again. 'It was you, wasn't it, who leaned over me, who kissed me?'

The question caused her heart to jolt. 'Yes, it was me, Hal.'

He nodded, drawing his breath sharply as his head moved on the pillow. 'I thought I heard your voice…but I couldn't see clearly… I was hot and cold at the same time.'

Isolda leaned closer, looked into his eyes, searched anxiously for fever but found none. 'Simon and Hugh brought you out of the house and laid you on the ground, covered you in snow to cool your burns.'

'That was brave of them, but foolhardy. They might not have been able to get out again.' His head turned away and for a moment she thought he'd fallen asleep—until he spoke. 'They should have thought of themselves and left me in there.'

Her heart jolted again. 'Don't say that!'

'It was my fate, Isolda.' He addressed the empty bed that was next to his, not her. 'My time to make amends.'

Isolda followed his gaze, seeing, as she knew he did, his brother lying here, in another hospital, far away and long ago.

'It was *not* your time! And there is nothing to make amends for. Why are you speaking like this?'

His head turned back and he stared at her as if he'd never seen her before. 'My family…died by fire, and now you…*you* could have died the same way.'

'But I *didn't* die. The fire never touched me, I swear it. *You* were the one who could have perished when you went back in for Shearman.'

'It could have been otherwise. He and his men could have killed us all, burned the house to make it look like an accident. I tried to keep you safe by taking you to Halton but I put you in danger instead.'

'Hal...you could not have foreseen any of it, not what Shearman would do, or even that he would find us at your manor...' Isolda paused, sensing what was at the root of his strange and upsetting words '...any more than you could have foreseen the fire at St Albans.'

He looked down at his arms and hands. 'They must have gone through agony and terror worse than hell itself, Isolda. Far worse than I'd ever imagined, even in my darkest nightmares.'

The bleakness in his tone sent a chill down her spine.

'Fire is terrible, God knows, but don't look back, Hal. You cannot change anything. You must look forward now, find the forgiveness you deserve.'

He made no answer and Isolda's mouth dried with fear. Had all those things they'd said as they'd lain in each other's arms before the hearth all been destroyed, along with his house?

'We have won, Hal!' She leaned forward, made her voice light yet urgent, desperate to pull him out of his despair. 'The inquiry will soon be held and even though Shearman has escaped justice on earth, others won't. Ludlow will be free from oppression now and so will its people.'

'Yes, and you will be free too, Isolda.'

She stared at the deep hollows of his cheeks, the dark shadows under his eyes, the sad line of his mouth. And all of a sudden her new world that she'd looked forward to with Hal shattered into a thousand tiny pieces.

This man she was looking at was not the Hal she'd come to know, grown to love, at all. The man who had touched her and kissed her last night then gathered her into his arms in sleep. This man was someone she didn't recognise at all, and the unfamiliarity had nothing to do with his injuries.

'But you must rest before all that.' She swallowed hard, trying to hide the dreadful apprehension in her voice. Even though Hal lay not a foot away, suddenly he had gone from her, left her feeling adrift...and frightened. 'Get your strength back, let your body heal itself.'

'No.' He tried to push himself upwards, wincing through gritted teeth. 'I need to get out of this bed and return to my duties.'

'Hal, you cannot!' Isolda pressed her hands to his shoulders, making him lie back down. 'You must stay here—the Prior said so. Your feet are damaged—you would not be able to walk, even to the door.'

His head fell back onto the pillow and his eyes closed. 'It seems the Prior is right.' He was silent a moment. 'How badly am I burned, Isolda?'

'Not so much,' she replied carefully, shuddering inwardly at how he'd looked when he'd come out of the fire last night. 'Your lower arms and hands, as you know. Your feet and ankles, the right worse than the left. The wound Shearman gave you has been treated. You lost blood, though the others are only small cuts. But you inhaled a lot of smoke, some of which must still be in your lungs.'

His eyes opened and met hers again. 'What of Shearman's men? Did they survive?'

Isolda nodded towards the other bed. 'One lies opposite, wounded by Simon's sword, but brought out by him alive. Another died...by my hand, to save Hugh—you carried him out of the house.' She paused and felt an instant of horror and shame, remembering how she'd driven her knife into Perkin's back. Would she ever forget that?

'And the third fled before the fire started. I don't know if he has been apprehended.'

'Where is Simon?'

Hal's tone now was clear, authoritative, as if none of the bleak and recriminating words of a moment ago had ever been said.

'I don't know. He was here earlier, speaking to the Prior, the constable too, then they left.'

Isolda floundered at the practical conversation but she didn't know how to talk to Hal any more. It seemed as if that fire, even though they'd both survived it, had severed the bond that had formed between them these last weeks. A bond that, in those blissful hours in Hal's arms, she'd begun to believe unshakeable. But now...could it ever be repaired?

'Doubtless, they are searching for the man who escaped,' she said, her voice unsteady, her heart thick in her throat. 'Though perhaps he has not returned to Ludlow.'

'He would be foolhardy to do so, but he will be found, nevertheless.'

As Hal levered himself up onto his elbows, pushing his body into a sitting position against the wall, she made no attempt to stop him this time. But the sweat that broke out on his face was evidence of the painful effort it had cost him as, drawing a breath deeply, his gaze locked on hers.

'Shearman was fortunate to have escaped his fate, though that is a death I would not wish on anyone, no matter what they'd done.'

'Is that why you went back in for him?'

'Yes...though I didn't know it was he at first. I was confused and just heard the screaming, and thought it was... someone else, that I was somewhere else.' He smiled grimly. 'It would have been an ironic sort of justice indeed to die with him, of all people, in that fire.'

Tears began to prickle, hot and fearful, behind Isolda's eyes. She'd seen Hal in many moods during the short time she'd known him, but never like this. Not so bleak or unreachable, nor so dreadfully empty of any feeling at all, least of all feeling for *her*.

'Hal, you are not yourself, can't you see that?' She touched his shoulder again, resisting the urge to shake him, bring him back to her in any way she could. 'You need time to heal, and when you are well again you will not think such morbid thoughts.'

Hal was silent a moment, letting the word sink in. *Were* his thoughts morbid? Perhaps. But they were the only ones he had. He had no thought now of the past fortnight, when he and Isolda had grown so close, of how he had come to love her. No thought either of how they had both overcome their fears and embraced that love and made it the most beautiful, the most natural, the most right thing he'd ever known.

Shearman had come, and the fire had started, and Isolda had nearly died. It didn't matter that she *hadn't* died, that the fire hadn't even touched her. She *could* have died...*would* have died if Simon and Hugh hadn't been there to save her. Because he had failed to do so.

He'd lain helpless on the floor, his body trapped, his mind trapped too, between two worlds that had made no sense then. They made sense now though. He knew now he'd lived so long in the aftermath of St Albans that he'd never escape it, that his present was riddled with his past, and he was incapable of anything but wallowing helplessly in its snare.

And his future… Last night had shown him that he would never be free, and cruelly so, just at the point when he'd felt he almost was. Perhaps that was how it should be and he must follow his fate, accept his punishment, not try to evade or escape it. Even if he tried, it wouldn't last. He could not allow himself to marry Isolda, because one day she might be in danger again and once more he would be helpless to save her.

Living with St Albans on his conscience was enough. His soul could carry no more.

'Isolda…' he began, then stopped and stared into her eyes. Beautiful eyes, more violet than blue, set in the fairest of faces, framed by hair of gold. An angel's beauty. No, it was too dangerous for Isola if he remained here, even though it would be agony to leave, an agony that matched even that of St Albans. 'I need you to send Simon to me, if you will.'

Her gaze clouded, searched his. 'Of course, if you wish it, but—'

Hal didn't let her finish. 'I have no choice but to remain here for now but there are things that need to be done all the same. A judge must be brought to Ludlow, a date must be set for the trial, witnesses sought and a jury arranged.'

'Surely the constable will arrange all that?'

He nodded, admitting that she spoke the truth. 'He will, but I need to prepare, to submit evidence, compose documents and such like.'

She frowned. 'Yes, I see that, and I too will—'

Again, he cut her off before she could say what he knew she was about to say. 'You won't need to appear in the court, however. Your name can be kept out of it. Only you and I know you wrote those poems.' He paused. 'It might be wiser for you to go and join your mother in Tewkesbury until the trial is over.'

She stared at him incredulously. 'I thought we were working together, Hal. And now we've almost succeeded, why would I go away? Why *should* I?'

'I can proceed better without you, Isolda. There will be no need for you to be involved now, so it would be best that you weren't in Ludlow at this time.'

A flush mounted her cheek, one of indignation as well as disbelief. 'I have been involved from the start, Hal, even before you arrived here. Why do you think I wrote those poems in the first place?'

Hal felt himself flush too. 'I know why you wrote them, but there is no need to bring them up now. They are irrelevant and not necessary as evidence. So it follows that the writer of them can remain anonymous since no more will be written.'

'Irrelevant? Unnecessary? You are forgetting Jac's murder, and why he was murdered. He was doing as I was doing, Hal. He died because of those poems I wrote! Do you think I will not want to be there to see his murderers punished? If so, you do not know me at all.'

He knew her too well, that was the problem. He knew she would stand up in that court, make her voice heard, as she had every right to do. But when the more serious crimes were dealt with, the minor ones might be tried too. She might be judged and punished for penning those poems, the reason for doing so not excusing or condoning the act at all.

And how could he defend her, since what she did was a crime in itself even if it was done for the right reasons?

'Have you considered that you yourself could be put

on trial for writing those verses should you reveal your identity?'

'Of course! And I am ready to answer for that.'

'No, I won't allow it.'

'Not allow it? Surely, you would not keep me from that court—now, after all that we've been through?' She shook her head, her gaze bewildered. 'I don't understand why you are saying this, Hal, but I can't believe you really mean it! Do you, truly?'

'If you stand trial for a triviality, Isolda, other things will come to light. We were found lying together half dressed, albeit in innocence, but that would not be believed by anyone. Shearman's man will relate it to the whole court, you can be sure of that.'

'So I will be judged a whore as well as a writer of poems! As long as justice is done, what does that matter?'

'It matters very much, Isolda! Do you think I will let your name be tarnished?'

'How will you prevent it?' She gave a bitter laugh and pointed to the bed opposite. 'Will you silence that poor wretch even before he can come to trial? Bribe him with gold to say nothing? Lessen his sentence as a reward for his discretion? If so, you are no less corrupt than Ralph Shearman!'

Hal said nothing. Let her think what she liked, if it stopped her from being in that courtroom, for all to hear, to see, to ridicule. She was his heart, his life, but by everyone else in the town she would be judged unfairly, with glee by those who disliked and envied her, and even perhaps condemned for loving him, a Lancastrian in a town largely populated by Yorkists.

A love he didn't deserve.

'That is why I am advising you to go to Tewkesbury before the trial, and to not return until after it is over.'

'Stop!' She leapt to her feet, her hands over her ears, her eyes beginning to shine with tears. 'None of this makes sense, Hal. Have these last weeks that we have been together showed you nothing? Have *I* meant nothing?'

Hal hated himself, but better she thought she meant nothing to him and be safe than to know she meant everything and be in danger. 'You have been most useful, Isolda, but now I need to work alone, as I've always done.'

'*Useful?*' Her face flushed and then paled again and for a long moment she was mute. Then, slowly, like one coming out of a dream, she drew herself taller and her voice when it came was like an icy dagger she plunged deep into his heart.

'I see.' She nodded, her expression and her voice hardening, as if a terrible truth had dawned on her. 'Yes, I see it all very clearly now. I have been foolish—and fooled. I believed...*wanted* to believe...that you were different to Robert. But you are not. You are worse!'

Hal heard the tremor of grief and of fury in her words, saw the fisting of her hands at her sides, the quivering of her body. He said nothing—for he must never refute it—and his silence seemed to enrage her further.

'Robert just lied when he said he wanted my heart and my hand in marriage. You took both my heart and my soul—my very self. You made me forget why I had vowed never to marry. You took everything that I am, Hal, and for that...for that, I will never ever forgive you!'

Then tears sprang to her eyes and her mouth began to tremble. 'Shearman warned me...in the church, right beside Jac's bier...that you would cast me aside when you had no more use for me. Oh, God, his lies might have been the least of his crimes but in that…he spoke true! How I wish I'd believed him!'

With that, she spun away and ran to the door, wrenching it open and flying over the threshold without a backward look. Hal was glad she didn't look back, for she would have seen tears—hot and fast and bitter—had sprung to his eyes too.

The pain of letting her go was far worse than his burns, or the cuts in his flesh, or the wound in his flank where Shearman's sword had struck. The pain was even worse than it had been after St Albans—no, not worse, but different in its awful and inevitable agony.

His tears threatened to spill and swiftly Hal turned his head to the wall and closed his eyes tightly. For long moments he fought for breath, far harder than he'd fought at Halton last night. To his ears, the muttering delirium of the man in the bed opposite, who Simon had dragged out of the flames, was like a refrain, repeating the terrible and inexcusable fact.

If Simon hadn't come when he had—if Hugh hadn't stepped up so bravely—if Shearman had brought more men with him, it would all have been so very different. And he could have done nothing. The dam of tears within him burst and streamed down his face, and desolation swallowed him up, just as it had four years ago at St Albans.

His only consolation, one he must cling to and never forget, was that—unlike his family—Isolda was safe and some day she would be happier too, without him.

Chapter Seventeen

The trial took place on the first day of December in the Guildhall, which was not normally a place for courts but chosen because the accused were mainly members of the Merchants' Guild. Isolda, like many others, closed her shop for the day to attend, even though she had not been summoned. Hal, true to his word, must have seen to that, but she had insisted on attending in view of the fact that Jac had been her apprentice and as such she was the sole representative of his family.

She had not heard from Hal since she'd left his bedside in the infirmary. Someone had told her he was still at the castle, someone else that he'd left Ludlow to rejoin the Earl of Shrewsbury's retinue. She had, however, seen him once, a week after they'd parted, crossing the square as she'd stood in the window of her shop.

The sight of him had shocked her, not just because of the way they'd parted, but because of his appearance. He'd walked with a shuffling gait, leaning heavily upon a staff, all the energy and grace with which he usually moved entirely gone. Instead of boots, he'd worn sacking on his feet, heavily padded, presumably to protect his burns.

His head had been covered by a hood but it had been bowed, as if he stared intently at the ground in front of him, looking neither up nor to the side. His footsteps had faltered just once, right opposite her house, and for a moment Isolda had thought he'd turn and come to her door. But he didn't. He'd walked on, with agonising slowness, and she'd not seen him since.

Now, as she waited on the bench along the left-hand wall with several of the merchants of the town, she realised her seat was exactly where she and Hal had tumbled in through the window above, now repaired, the night they'd broken into the Guildhall. Here was where they'd sat on the floor, so close, and talked, and kissed. A pain shot across her brow and she squeezed her eyes shut, trying to shut out the memory too.

It was no use thinking back to that man who'd held her in his arms, in this room, in the dark. He'd disappeared. He'd never been there in the first place but had, like Robert, acted a role to deceive and ensnare her. The pain in her head travelled down her neck and into her breast, where it hit its target like an arrow bearing a cruel message.

Hal had disappeared, yes, if the Hal she'd loved had ever really been there at all. But somehow the love remained. Whether that would disappear too she didn't know and there was no way she could kill it, no matter how hard she'd tried over the last weeks. Even now, knowing Hal would be here for the trial, had already set her heart into a frantic beating and made her fingers play nervously with the edges of her cloak.

At her side, two merchants were discussing the Parliament at Coventry and to distract herself Isolda cocked an ear to listen. The Parliament had condemned those who had made war against the King at Blore Heath and Ludford, and had listed the Duke of York's treasonable acts, going back a decade. Among them, the battle of St Albans stood out as an execrable and detestable deed caused by diabolical unkindness and envy.

The news of the declaration of York, and his followers as traitors, had travelled the land. All their possessions were seized, their lives condemned and their heirs barred from inheritance for ever. King Henry had granted financial support to the Duchess of York and her young children, and had magnanimously mitigated the act of attainder, saying that he would grant full pardon to those who humbly sought his grace. Now it was a matter of high speculation as to whether Richard of York, his sons, and the Earl of Warwick would return from their exile and do just that.

The men's conversation turned to other matters and, trying to relax in her seat, Isolda looked around the Guildhall. It was full to bursting and there was a big crowd outside too, composed of people not able or eligible to enter, held at bay by some of the castle guards. At the high end of the room, seated on Ralph Shearman's ornate and now forfeited chair, was the judge from Shrewsbury. The coroner and one of the clerks of the town sat on his left and, to his right, sat old Tom Hoke, the former bailiff, hastily reinstated to the vacant office, his honesty and experience making up for his Yorkist sympathies, it seemed.

The accused, nine of them, including the man who'd been wounded at Halton, stood at the lower end of the room. He'd recovered enough to stand trial, and looked as if the noose was already around his neck. For a moment Isolda felt pity, and fury that he was the scapegoat while Ralph Shearman and the murderous Perkin had been granted the reprieve of death.

Opposite where she sat were two long benches where the jury would sit, the floor left open for their speaker, who would present the information they had found and then advise the judge of their verdict. The judge would then decide on the punishment if the accused were found guilty, or... No! Isolda dismissed that possibility before it took root. Surely there was no way a verdict of innocent could be given.

It was then that the jury entered, Hal at its head. Her heart thundered against her ribs as he walked down the room. His gait wasn't as pained as it had been when she'd seen him in the square, and he wore boots now instead of padded sacking. He still used a staff, though he didn't lean upon it as heavily as he had previously, and his head, instead of bowed, was held high.

Isolda watched him and the eleven men behind him greet the judge, then take their seats. He laid the staff he'd carried on the floor in front of him and as he straightened he saw her.

His body jolted and his mouth set into what she could only assume was a grimace of displeasure that she'd disobeyed him and come here today. For a brief moment he stared at her, his gaze unreadable, and then he looked away.

Clasping her hands together in her lap, she turned her head away too, and fastened her gaze upon the judge. From then on, she focused only on the trial—or tried to, but failed miserably.

Hal stood when he needed to. He spoke when he needed to. He questioned when he needed to. He laid all the facts, gathered by the jury over the preceding weeks, before the judge. The enclosures of the common land that robbed farmers of their grazing rights, the increasing of tolls and taxes for no good reason, the numerous other ways in which the poor of Ludlow had suffered at the hands of the rich and powerful, he presented it all. And, foremost, the murder of Jac of Bruges at the Hospital of St John, which he related too, keeping Isolda's part in the discovery of the boy to the barest of mentions.

But all the time, throughout the long hours of the trial, Isolda was at the forefront of his mind. She was at the forefront of his vision too, seated as she was almost opposite, and even when he faced the judge or the accused, he saw only her.

Brother Matthew had finally confessed to Prior Oteley that he'd received a potion for the boy, which had been sent, he was told, by Mistress Breydon. He'd administered it, ignorant that it was poison. As Shearman and Perkin were dead, it could not be ruled whether the boy had died from ingesting this, or from his wound. The man who'd fled had never been found, likely gone to Wales, just over the border, and the man who'd survived the fire swore on the Holy Bible he had no knowledge of the means of Jac's death. So no verdict was given.

All the while, as he spoke and answered, or referred to one or other of the jury, Isolda was right there, in his eyeline, no matter which way he looked. She wore the blue gown he'd first seen her in, that day she'd leaned out of the window, when the King had taken possession of the town. A simple headdress and white veil covered her head, and her golden hair was hidden. Her hands, encased in soft brown gloves, were clasped in her lap and, apart from that first startled look, she'd not glanced at him once. But he knew that her mind, like his, was not wholly on the trial at all.

'And is the jury unanimous in their findings and in their opinions?'

As Judge Watkyns's voice suddenly boomed out, Hal realised he was addressing him, and he cleared his throat. 'They are, my lord, and desire that you see fit to impose punishments suitable to the individual crimes of the accused.'

The judge concurred with no further questions, and the sentences were pronounced. There were to be no hangings, but imprisonment, fines, forfeitures and loss of status were a heavy punishment for men who prided themselves on their wealth and social standing.

The man who'd come to Halton with Shearman was sentenced to gaol for six months, as he'd insisted he was merely obeying orders. The judge, perhaps moved to pity by his wretched state, showed some clemency and ordered him to be sent to Shrewsbury gaol, to avoid any mistreatment by gaolers born and bred here in his native town.

'As to Jac of Bruges,' Watkyns said, shaking his head gravely, 'although I regret his death, the boy was himself breaking the law when he was apprehended.'

There was a gasp opposite him and Isolda was on her feet in a flash, making eyes pop and jaws drop. Up until then, she'd not spoken, nor been asked to speak, but now it seemed she would not be silenced.

'Jac was out that night doing my bidding, my lord judge! I will not have him branded a law-breaker by this court that refuses to bring a just verdict against his murderers, even though they themselves be dead or fled. He is not here to defend himself so I will defend him.'

There was a stunned silence around the room. Hal cursed under his breath and rose to his feet to intervene. But he didn't get a chance, for Isolda walked forward into the centre of the floor and faced Judge Watkyns.

'I am writer of the poems that have appeared in Ludlow these last several months. The night Jac was stabbed, by Ralph Shearman's orders, as he stated quite clearly, he was placing one of those poems upon the church door.'

A ripple of shock ran around the walls, followed by an outburst of shouts. Several of the merchants seated alongside Isolda leapt to their feet, their expression a mix of outrage, astonishment and disbelief.

For a moment, Hal almost smiled. Some of those men were of the very class that she'd criticised in her verses, even if they themselves might not have been named, or even guilty of the transgressions she'd exposed. But he suspected that it was her sex that upset—and unmanned—them most of all. While the men of the town, even those with grievances, merely grumbled and bore it, speculated and condemned, she—a mere woman—outwitted them even as she shamed them.

'And if anyone is to be blamed or punished for that,' she was saying now, her hands gesturing as eloquently as her voice, 'then let it be me, not Jac. I wrote those poems and I told him where to put them, not just on that night, but many others.'

Hal's impulse to smile vanished and quickly he stepped forward, forgetting his staff in his haste, and gritting his teeth as pain shot through his right foot. At Isolda's side, he addressed the judge.

'My lord, I would like to remind you and this court that if it hadn't been for Mistress Breydon's poems, I would never have come to Ludlow, and the crimes investigated and brought to justice here today might well have continued.'

The judge looked from him to Isolda and back again. 'Did you suspect Mistress Breydon was the author of these poems, Sir Henry?'

'He knew nothing,' Isolda replied, answering the question herself. 'Not until he caught me in the act of placing verses upon the door of this very building!'

Hal cursed again, albeit silently, as she attempted to shield him, even now, when he didn't deserve it. 'That is not quite true, my lord. I suspected long before that, but had no proof until the night the boy was attacked. It was as a consequence of that heinous assault that I was persuaded of the truth of the accusations these poems contained.'

'Then you condone them?'

He nodded, aware that Isolda was glowering not at the judge now but at him. 'I do. They spoke what others were too reluctant or too afraid to utter. And alongside crimes of intimidation, oppression, theft, injustice and murder—crimes which their main instigator, Ralph Shearman, is not here to answer for—I consider those verses do not warrant condemnation, less still punishment.'

The judge pursed his mouth and bent his head to speak to the coroner and bailiff seated either side of him. The jury too took up murmuring among themselves, as did the rest of the court, apart from the nine condemned men, who had already been led out.

'I don't need you to advocate for me!'

At his side Isolda's hiss was as deadly as a serpent's. He turned his head and met her eyes, and the discomfort in his feet and in his hands, caused by lingering scars from the night of the fire, faded to nothing as a greater pain drove right into his heart.

'And you had no need to speak out!' he said, harsher than he'd intended. 'I advised against it.'

'I would not have spoken had Jac not been dismissed like that, like a common felon, when he was nothing of the sort.' Her eyes blazed into his. 'The judge was wrong to do so.'

'Wrong or not, he is still the judge.'

'Then I will accept whatever sentence he decides.'

Hal knew Judge Watkyns to be a good man but even the most patient of men wanted to get home to their supper at the end of a long day.

'There will be no sentence, if I can help it.'

'I said I don't need your help.'

'You did once,' he said under his breath. 'On Ludford Bridge.'

'I was under a misapprehension then.' Angry colour flooded her cheeks. 'I had begun to think you an honourable man. I soon learned differently.'

The barb hit and buried deep but Hal didn't blame her. He lowered his voice to an urgent whisper, loud enough for only Isolda to hear. 'That may be—it matters not now. But why must you be so determined to lose on this one point of the poems, after we have won all?'

'*We*?' A bitter little smile twisted her lips. '*We*, Hal? Did you not tell me in the infirmary that there *was* no we? That you didn't need me any more, that I'd served my purpose, that you had no further use for me!'

Beneath the attack, the accusation, the bitterness, Hal heard hurt too, and pride. All at once, every wound he'd sustained at Halton seemed to reopen and tear not just at his body but at his heart and soul.

'I thought it best—'

'Best for *you*, you mean!' she snapped. 'You made that perfectly clear—so clear, in fact, that you didn't consider my feelings at all! The insult of it was bad enough—'

Her scathing yet just retort was interrupted by Judge Watkyns. 'I, and my council, have given this some consideration, and if Mistress Breydon promises that there will be no more poems, then I am content to let this matter drop.'

'Are you addressing me or Sir Henry, my lord?'

Another gasp went around the room and, as the sound of murmuring recommenced, Hal braced himself. It wasn't contempt of court exactly, but Isolda's challenge bordered on it. Moving closer, he touched her arm but she jerked his hand away.

'I will gladly promise there will be no more poems,' she went on, her chin high and her voice quivering with passion, 'not through Sir Henry's mouth but through my own, if the court deigns to listen.'

As the whole room held its breath, a smile creased the judge's face. 'I can tell you are a person of some spirit, Mistress Breydon, and I can also understand why you felt moved to write these verses.'

'Verses I knew about, my lord.' Hal stepped closer to Isolda and, for his pains, got an elbow in the ribs. The outer pain was nothing compared to what he was feeling inside, however. 'A misdemeanour, albeit well intentioned, that I could have stopped but I didn't.'

'I see.' Watkyns's gaze went from him to Isolda and back again. 'Then if I try Mistress Breydon for this, I will have to try you both?'

'Yes,' Hal said.

'No.' Isolda's denial overlapped his. 'Only I am guilty.'

The judge's smile became a frown and it was obvious his patience was wearing thin. He gestured to the clerk of the court, who began to gather his papers together. 'It has been too long a day to argue the point,' he said, 'so I suggest you resolve it between yourselves. But I do not expect to hear about poems on the doors of Ludlow ever again, is that understood?'

'And Jac?' Isolda spread her hands. 'Please, my lord. Don't destroy his good name. He was a fine and upstanding boy, who was cruelly robbed of life long before his time.'

The judge glowered beneath his bushy brows but Hal could have sworn his eyes twinkled. Rising to his feet, Watkyns spoke curtly to the clerk again, who scribbled something on his parchment, and then brought the proceedings to a close.

'Very well. I will accept, as will this court, that Jac of Bruges was done to death without warrant, allegedly, though not proved, on the orders of former bailiff of this town, Ralph Shearman. The boy's name is therefore without stain and this inquiry is now ended.'

Isolda's lungs heaved in relief and then, as tears of other emotions sprang to her eyes, she turned and marched down the length of the room, pushing through the merchants and craftsmen who all began to mill excitedly together. The town would talk of this day for a long time to come but she just wanted it over now. She ignored old Ned, who had managed somehow to squeeze in just by the doorway, ignoring the hand he held out. The farmer's face beamed with gratitude, but she shook her head, resolving to find him later and speak with him. For now she had to get out and far away.

Hal would be caught in the crush behind her, and anyway, he'd never catch her up, not with his injured feet, even if she'd strolled to the door instead of striding like a soldier. A moment later, she was out into the street, the light and her tears blinding her, but there her flight was impeded by the crowd, who still were waiting to hear the verdict, news of which was already being imparted.

Cheers filled her ears as, invisible to them all, she pushed her way through. After all, they didn't know—yet—that she was the poetess of Ludlow. The description brought a lump into her throat. That was what Hal had called her the morning he'd asked her to marry him. When she'd believed in him, trusted him...loved him with all her heart.

And the worst of it all was, even if the first two follies had been shattered, the third remained. She'd loved him more than ever when he'd limped into the courtroom earlier, his face a mask of pain that only she saw through, his mouth set sternly, as it had been the first day she'd seen him. She'd loved him when he'd stood and taken her side yet again...even when she'd told him she didn't need him. The truth was she'd always need him, always want him, always love him, no matter what he'd done. But she would never trust him again.

'Isolda!'

Hal's voice came from behind her. He must have pushed through both the crowd and his pain after all! She quickened her pace and didn't look back. If she did, and saw him limping after her, she would be lost once more. She was at the top of the road now, her house within sight, but suddenly a host of bittersweet memories swamped her.

Of the day she'd first seen him from her window, of market day, the frost as they'd stood on Ludford Bridge, the night of the hue and cry...and there, to her right and most bittersweet of all, the little side alley where Hal had kissed her in the shadows, holding its secret for ever.

'Isolda! Wait!'

Isolda spurred herself forward across the square, forgetting all dignity and lifting her skirts so as not to trip over them. Frantically, she fumbled for the key at her belt and, fingers shaking, turned it in the lock. She all but fell over the threshold and, slamming the door shut, locked it again and leaned against it.

She was only just in time. Against her back, the door trembled as a fist pounded upon it.

'Isolda! Let me in, please. I need to talk to you.'

Closing her eyes, she tried to shut her ears too, and made no response. If she was quiet, he would surely go away, rather than make a fool of himself by beating on her door like a scorned lover. But it seemed he had no shame, for his fist pounded again.

'Isolda! Open the door!'

Isolda pressed her spine harder against the door. It would hold, whether she leaned her weight upon it or not, but somehow, though she knew she should, she couldn't move. A silence fell without, and stretched long. Turning her head, she laid her ear to the wood and listened, but heard nothing. Yet she knew—felt—he was still there, and she was right.

Almost where her ear lay, Hal's voice came again. 'I know you're behind the door, so why don't you open it?'

Her heart leapt and she clasped her hands together to stop them turning the key again. If she opened that door, she'd fall right into his waiting trap. Because that was what love was, wasn't it? A trap of feelings and wants and needs that robbed you of all rational thought and common sense and made you see the world all wrong.

'Isolda, are you going to open this door or not?'

She put her palm to her mouth. There mustn't be any form of converse between them. Better to let him think she didn't care, not even enough to speak civilly to him now. After all, he'd shown her in the infirmary that he didn't care about her, and never had.

There was another silence, and then she could almost swear she heard him draw a breath and sigh it out. The door moved and seemed to sag inwards and with a start of horror she wondered if he was going to force it. But then she realised he must have leaned back against it and his body was aligned with hers.

And as he began to speak, slowly and with solemnity, not even the thick oak could keep his words out of either her ears or her heart.

'I know you hate me now, Isolda. I don't blame you and I don't ask you to forgive me. But I do need to explain to you, even if it makes no difference now, why I said what I said that day in the infirmary.'

Isolda's pulse began to thud so heavily and so loudly that she was sure he must hear it. She turned her head away so that her ear was no longer against the wood but his words came clearly anyway.

'It wasn't true, that thing I said, not wholly true anyway. I pushed you away because I was afraid, not because I didn't need you any more. I've *always* needed you, Isolda. I always will.'

Reluctantly, but unable not to, she turned her head again so that her ear was flat once more against the wood. His voice echoed and seemed to reach right down inside her, tearing her to pieces.

'But when the fire happened and I was helpless to save you, I realised that I loved you too much. And if I married you and we lived together and raised a family I would love you even more, if that were possible, and love our children too.'

Isolda knew she should go into the hall where she

couldn't hear him. She knew she should not listen any more in case what she was hearing was all lies. But she did neither. His voice held her captive, as he himself had done since the moment she'd first seen him.

'When my family died the loss was unbearable, but I did bear it, somehow. I even learned to survive it. But that day at Halton, I realised that if I lost you there could *be* no bearing, no survival. I couldn't live with that loss, that guilt, a second time.'

Tears rose into her eyes and she blinked them back. All the same, one slid down her cheek and bathed her lips with salt.

'Perhaps I am a coward to let you go now rather than risk losing you later. Perhaps I was wrong to fall in love with you in the first place. But I did fall in love with you, the moment I saw you leaning out of the window of this house.'

Isolda turned around and, placing her palms to where his shoulders must be, touched her forehead to the door.

'I will be leaving Ludlow soon, in a day or two. But I didn't want to leave... I *couldn't* leave without explaining why I said what I did.'

Her hand moved down to the key, still in the lock. Her fingers curled around the iron and then stilled.

'And to tell you that I will love you for ever, Isolda, until the day I die. And I hope, even after everything I've done, all the hurt I've caused you, you can, in time, remember me with fondness, if not love.'

Isolda bit back a choke then another, as more tears fell down her cheeks. The urge to open that door, fling herself into his arms, tell him she loved him too and would love him until her dying day was almost too much to master. But he'd said so many words to her—how could she trust these ones?

That day in the infirmary when he'd said he didn't need her, that she was no longer of use to him, had cut her so deeply that it had almost severed her love too. The pain of that was something she'd never forget...nor want to experience ever again. And if she trusted Hal now, if she believed the things he was saying beyond that door, and he hurt her again like that, well, there would be no bearing for her, no, nor survival either.

Best, surely, to let everything lie here, end here, and try to forget.

'Goodbye, Isolda. I wish you a life of happiness and love.' His voice came again, closer, more muffled and, with a jolt, she knew he'd turned to face the door and, like hers, his forehead was pressed to the wood. 'You deserve both, sweeting, and more. For myself, I will always be grateful for the love, fleeting as it was, that you had for me.'

The door moved again, as this time his weight left it, and it was as if the whole world had shifted and heaved. Isolda's fingers tightened around the key and every instinct she possessed screamed at her to turn it, to open that door and run after him. She fought for breath, tried to resist, battled with all her might against her heart, as from without the sudden, empty, echoing silence felt as if all of life had ended in the world.

A silence that was too much to bear or to survive. Quickly, Isolda turned the key and threw the door open, her battle not lost but futile, and not one she wanted to win anyway, for if she did, love would be defeated for ever.

But it was too late. Hal had gone, and although she ran out and looked desperately around the square in all directions, called his name, there was no sight of him. He'd vanished as if he'd never been there at all.

Slowly, with despair dragging like quicksand at her heels, she returned to her house. Locking the door again, she went through the shop and into the empty hall. The fire was out and the room was already darkening as twilight began to fall. There wasn't a sound, not even a mouse scratching in the rafters. She lit a candle and sat before the cold hearth, where the cat came and stared up at her, as if it was complaining she hadn't kindled a fire.

She sat for a long time. The clock chimed the hours of Vespers and then Compline but she hardly heard it. She didn't even go and call the hens in to their hutch for the night. It was as if when Hal had gone he'd taken all her vitality, all the things necessary for movement, for feeling, for life itself, with him.

Not until Matins sounded and a thin chink of moonlight began to peep through the shutters did she rouse herself. Lighting more candles, she kindled a fire and then she took out her pen and a piece of parchment.

Sitting down before the leaping flames, she thought long and hard, searching her heart not her mind for the right lyric. And when it came, Isolda began to compose her poem, the last she would ever pen.

Now Ludlow is free from all tyranny,
Yet here abides one who seeks not liberty.
But yearns for the love that was found and then spurned,
And lives now bereft 'til that love has returned.

Chapter Eighteen

Hal sat before the hearth in the parlour of his manor house. The fire of six weeks previously hadn't spread to the back section, nor the kitchen or outbuildings, the heavy snowfall that day preventing it. Since his return he'd engaged an army of carpenters, masons and labourers to begin to rebuild the destroyed hall and bedchambers above, choosing men who could do with some extra coin to feed their families at this barren time of the year.

Stretching out his legs, he read again the poem that had been delivered in his absence, a few days after the trial. It hadn't been forwarded to him, since he'd resolved to return to Halton before Christmas, and so had only read this for the first time a few days ago.

A smile tugged at his mouth as he looked down at the familiar handwriting, the bold slanting script, the red ink, the wit…and the message set down clearly so that there would be no doubt or misunderstanding. Not a damning tirade about the oppressors of Ludlow now, but a poem from a woman to a man, ending with a challenge that needed response.

If Harry the Cat searches his heart
And finds that he too cannot be apart,

*Will he return and enjoy a good life,
By having the courage to take him a wife...?*

A log shifted in the hearth and broke, sending sparks flying up the chimney. Of old habit, Hal tensed, felt a ripple of alarm and then breathed deep and forced himself to relax again. The iron guard rail was new, thickly forged and sufficient to prevent any logs from rolling out onto the rushes, as the new metal sheath inside the chimney drew sparks upwards, not sending them outwards into the room.

Things had changed here. He had changed too, although it had taken him several weeks since that night he'd slept in Isolda's arms to realise it. And to have the courage—her word—to accept and embrace that change. To go forward, not back.

He read the poem once again and this time his smile broke out. Isolda's pen was so firm, so bold, he could almost hear her voice, daring him, enticing him so that there was only one response he could give. One that had been waiting far too long—all his life, it seemed.

Rising from his chair, he folded the parchment into the pouch at his belt and went through the door into the kitchen. Hugh and Mary were busy filling the piggies, the little clay pots in which gifts of money were given to the poor and needy on this traditional day of bounty after Christmas.

The tinkle of coins as they went in through the slit at the top of each pot echoed around the kitchen like the crotal bells he would soon put on his horse's harness for the journey into Ludlow today.

'Are we nearly ready, Hugh?' he asked of his steward. 'It is gone ten of the clock.'

Hugh nodded and, filling the last of the piggies, placed

them in a sack. 'We've filled forty for the town, Sir Henry, as you requested. And there are the fifteen for the manor families.'

'Good, then I will be away.'

Hugh and Mary would dispense the piggies to the families who lived and worked on his estate. Most were new, as he'd never needed a large workforce before. He'd met them all personally since his recent return here and all of them, men, women and children, had attended the Christmas feast held in the kitchen and in the parlour yesterday, as the hall, though in the process of being rebuilt, was far from complete.

The walls and roof had been destroyed, as had the floor above, but the foundations and stone hearth had survived. Shearman's body had been destroyed too, and only his jewelled rings and some charred bones had been found when the ashes had cooled. It was as if, when finally retribution had fallen upon him, no trace of his evil was to remain.

'It is a good day for riding out, Sir Henry.' Mary wiped her hands on her apron and beamed at him, and the momentary darkening of his mood lifted. 'Sunshine at Christmastide means an early spring, a fruitful summer and a good harvest. Something to look forward to after this long winter.'

Hal couldn't agree more but before spring came he had much to do, and he meant to begin doing it today.

'I may be late back for supper,' he said, bidding his servants farewell. 'But be sure to lay the table in the parlour for two.'

The ride into Ludlow was short and pleasant, the bells on his bridle tinkling merrily, accompanied by the chinking of silver in the piggies he carried behind the saddle.

The sun was in his eyes, making the light overnight frost on the road in front of him sparkle like diamonds. It was cold, to be sure, but the fields and forests all around were free of snow at last, and the river to his left shimmered like silver.

Along the verges, early snowdrops and spear thistle showed their brave colours, and here and there, in more sheltered places, even some sweet violet. His heart sang at the sight of it. Violet—the colour of Isolda's eyes. A good omen, surely!

The trees fell away and Ludlow came into sight. The sunlight had banished most of the frost here, the land being lower than at Halton, so he pushed into a trot, making the bells jingle more merrily than ever.

Crossing the Dinham Bridge, he bade the guards there a joyous season, and rode up Mill Street. He passed the Guildhall and the alley where he'd kissed Isolda and, coming out at the head of the road, saw the market square full to bursting, as it had been on the night of the hue and cry.

But the atmosphere was very different today. Bunting and banners abounded and everywhere was a blaze of colour and gaiety. The whole town seemed to have come out of doors in their hundreds to celebrate this day of St Stephen. In the centre of the square there was a stage with mummers acting out a biblical drama, competing with the singing of songs and carols, and the playing of pipes and lutes.

Near the castle gate a pair of acrobats were turning somersaults, and at the far end, near the beast market, targets had been set up, at which a number of men showed off their shooting skills. Stalls and barrows were laden with food and drink, even though the people would have eaten and drunk to excess the day before, enjoying the feasting after the fasting of Advent.

And amid all the revelry, at the market cross in front of the church, the priest from St Laurence and the various priors, abbots and brethren of the other religious orders in the town, were handing out piggies to the poor—the labourers and servants, the vagabonds and the destitute—filled with the coins that had been placed in the alms boxes during the year.

Oppression and injustice might have ended here in this town, but the world wasn't changed in a day, or even a month. However, this joyful and carefree celebration was a start. The conflict between York and Lancaster was in abeyance, since Earl Richard, his sons, and Warwick too, remained in exile. So peace as well as joy pervaded the land this holy season.

Leaving his horse with the guards at the castle gate, Hal waded into the throng, the sack of piggies over his shoulder and the noise of gaiety swallowing him up. His feet were almost completely healed now and he would have strided quickly but for the masses hemming him in. Once the crush would have irritated him, but not now, and the colours that dazzled him, made more blinding by the sun that crept higher in the sky, lifted his spirits skyward too.

And then he saw Isolda. She was at the cross too, helping with the distribution of the piggies, dressed in a green gown he'd not seen before and a russet-coloured surcoat, with a warm cloak over. Her hood was down, and today no coif or headdress hid the glorious gold of her hair.

Hal thought of the mustard-coloured gown that she'd taken to Halton, which had been burned in the fire too, and his feet faltered for a moment. It had been six weeks since he'd pushed her away from him in the infirmary, a month since he'd spoken to her from beyond the door she'd barred against him. His courage almost faltered too and then he remembered her poem—and her challenge.

She hadn't seen him yet so, making his way through the ranks of the recipients who lined up to get their piggies, Hal handed his sack to Prior Oteley.

'From my manor of Halton, for the poor.'

The Prior smiled at him and shook his hand. 'Thank you, Sir Henry. As you see, we have many who are in need this season.'

'I have heard of the new men appointed to the Twelve and Twenty-Five and hopefully, now Ludlow is in better hands, the need of all who lack will be met,' he responded as, out of the corner of his eye, he saw Isolda's head turn at his voice. 'I have been away since the trial and have not heard what became of Brother Matthew.'

Oteley's smile faded a little. 'The church dealt with his case, not the town, and he has not been punished since he did what he did in ignorance, and in innocence. He has, however, been relocated to our sister house in Bridgenorth.'

'That is wise, not that I think anyone in Ludlow would hold him to account.'

The Prior shook his head. 'No, but it will take a long time for the poor soul to forgive himself, if ever.'

Hal could well believe it. It had taken him four long years to even begin to forgive himself for the death of his family. If he hadn't come to Ludlow, met Isolda, he might *never* have found, nor even sought, forgiveness for himself.

'I wish him well,' he said, 'and you a very merry Christmastide, Thomas.'

'And I you, my son.' The Prior's eyes twinkled. 'Is there not someone else who you wish to greet here today?'

Hal inclined his head. 'There is, and I am just about to do so.'

Turning, he made his way to where Isolda stood. She didn't look up at his coming but the blush that rushed into her pale cheeks told him she knew he was there.

'Merry Christmastide, Isolda.'

Isolda's fingers tightened around the little clay pot she was holding before passing it safely into the waiting hands. She hardly heard the old woman's thanks, nor saw the sheen of gratitude in the faded eyes as she kissed her thin cheek.

'All blessings of the season upon you, Joan, and a year of prosperity and happiness be yours.'

'And upon you, Mistress Breydon.'

Trembling with excitement, Isolda reached into her sack for another pot, then turned to face Hal. 'Merry Christmas to you too.' This time the piggie almost fell to the floor. 'Is that all you have to say, however?'

His smile was wide and bright and beautiful. 'Oh, no, I have much more to say. In fact, I am here on the matter of a certain poem I received lately, and would speak to the author of that poem.'

'Oh, I see...' Hiding a smile of her own, Isolda handed her piggie to the next recipient, bestowing the kiss and the greeting with more haste than was proper. 'And do you know who this person is?'

'I do indeed.' Stepping closer, he reached into the sack, his gloved fingers brushing hers as she reached in too. 'I believe it is the same person who was responsible for the audacious verses that appeared on the doors of Ludlow some months ago,' he said, 'but which have now mysteriously ceased.'

'I wonder why?' she teased in return, a choke in her voice below the humour. When she'd written that poem to Hal and had had no response, she'd begun to believe it was too late. That when she'd bolted her door to him, refused to answer, that he'd really gone and would never return.

'Why they ceased?' He glanced across at her. 'Or why I think it is the same person?'

Isolda held his gaze. 'Both.'

'As to the first, well, now that the poetess has won her victory, there is no need to pen her verses.' The green-gold eyes danced. 'And as to the second...the hand is the same. It is unmistakable, unique, beautiful and unforgettable.'

Her eyes filled at his words, for she knew he was speaking of more than just the way she put words down upon a page. 'It seems the poems have lingered long in your mind, Sir Henry.'

'An eternity.'

They passed more piggies into waiting hands and she sensed that he was as eager to be done and be alone together as she was. Dickon strolled past just then, eating a pie, a piggie in his other hand, so changed now from the frightened boy Hal had released from the pillory. Isolda planned to engage Dickon as her new apprentice when the Christmas feasting was over, if he was willing.

A little moment of sadness fell over her. That morning, she'd put a wreath of bay and holly on Jac's grave, to make it look gay, not solemn, on this of all days, and to let him know that he would never be forgotten.

'Dickon!' Hal's voice stopped the boy in his tracks. 'Will you come and help?'

Dickon did as he was bid, finishing his pie and dusting his fingers on the front of his tunic as he came, his beaming smile and easy charm making the day bright once again.

'Of course, Sir Knight, what do you want me to do?'

'Dispense the rest of these pots for us, will you? They are nearly all gone and Isolda... Mistress Breydon and I need to talk upon a serious matter.'

'Gladly.' He looked from Hal to her and back again. 'I'll never forget what you did for me, Sir Henry. A merry Christmas to you, and to you, Mistress Breydon!'

'And to you, Dickon,' Isolda said, handing him her sack. 'Come and see me next week, will you? I have an offer for you that I hope you will accept.'

Dickon nodded and turned to his task, his expression telling her that her offer might not be a surprise after all. 'I will come, and thank you.'

Hal took her hand and led her away, through the crowd, as he'd done that day the people of Ludlow had thrown missiles at the pillory. The town and its population, its walls and all its houses, were very different, it seemed. New and better men were in power, fear and tyranny had been vanquished, and peace reigned in England.

Isolda followed Hal into the church. At the door, he turned and led her up the narrow spiral stone steps to the Parvis Room, where the clergy and the Palmers' Guild held meetings, but which the townsfolk normally didn't enter. She'd never been in the room and now, as he led her in and closed the little door behind them, she gave a gasp.

The room wasn't round nor square but a combination of both, located as it was in the tower next to the south porch, where she'd once pinned the poem that had brought Hal and her together. The walls were painted with all sorts of images—flowers, leaves, animals, stars, saintly figures—and the beamed ceiling was so low she felt she could have touched it, though of course she couldn't have, not even had she stood on tiptoe.

But it was the sunlight coming in from the arched windows on three sides that took her breath away, illuminating the walls and making the red tiled floor gleam as if a sunset had been spilled over it.

Then, the next moment, she forgot all that awesome beauty as Hal drew her down beside him on a wooden bench at the window where the sun shone brightest.

'I've so much to say to you, Isolda, I don't know where to begin.'

'I think I've heard it already, outside my door, the day of the trial.'

He shook his head. 'I told you then why I let you go, even though it was the hardest thing I've ever done.' His hands closed over hers. 'But you've yet to hear what has happened since I left you, and how that parting changed me. How *you* changed me, Isolda.'

'Then tell me,' she breathed, feeling the warmth of him seep into her veins. 'And quickly, because I've got much to tell you too.'

Hal drew a deep breath and gazed deep into Isolda's beautiful violet eyes. The light coming in through the windows made them almost dazzle him, as she herself had dazzled him, right from the beginning, when she'd leaned out of the window of her house the day the Lancastrians took Ludlow.

When he'd left this town, after the trial, he had ceased to live, only to exist. And in that void he'd greeted every day with a heavy heart and dreaded every sleepless and tormented night—until he'd returned to Halton and to her poem. And he'd known then, as he'd read it, that he could choose to live instead of existing, if he told her the truth. So he began.

'In the infirmary, after the fire, you told me that I wasn't myself. You were right.'

'I should not have said that, but you seemed so distant, so uncaring.'

'I know, and I'm so sorry for that, Isolda. But I'd lived so long with my guilt after St Albans that it had become a part of me, without me realising how it had imprisoned me. Not until I met you did the bars of my prison begin to bend, and then break. I even believed, that night before Shearman came to Halton, that I would never be imprisoned again, that your love—our love—had set me free for ever.'

Hal paused and took a breath. 'But when the fire happened, and I was helpless to save you, all my fears took possession of me again.'

'But, Hal, I wasn't harmed, you knew that. It was alarming and frightening but there was no danger, not really.'

He smiled, squeezed her hands in his. 'It is easy to say that after the event, Isolda. We could all have perished that day.'

'But we didn't!'

'I know, and I thank God for it.' Hal searched her eyes. 'But my fear was so strong, Isolda, I started imagining the next time you might be in danger, or the time after that, and how I might again fail you, as I failed my family.'

'Hal—'

Lifting one hand from hers, he touched her lips with his forefinger. 'Hush, chatterbox!' A smile rose up inside him at the lightness that now filled his heart, the joy and the hope that had waited there for weeks for this moment. 'I haven't finished my story yet.'

'Then hurry!'

He did so. 'After I left the infirmary, when my injuries were healed enough, I spent a fortnight recuperating in the castle, unable to walk very well, not venturing out, only once—'

'I saw you, walking across the square, but you didn't see me.'

'Oh, yes, I did. I saw you, Isolda, in the window of your shop, but was too much of a coward to come and speak to you, after what I'd said. But when I saw you there... I knew how much I regretted saying it so, in hope, I sent a letter to John Talbot, who was at Chester then. A letter asking for a boon.'

Her eyes grew wide. 'What was it?'

Hal brushed his finger along the lovely line of her mouth. 'I requested that I be stationed permanently, in peace time at least, at Halton.'

'Then you are remaining here for ever?'

'If God and you will let me.'

She nodded, her eyes glistening with tears. 'You know you need have no doubts.'

'And neither need you, sweeting, when you hear the end of my story.' Hal took her hands in his again. 'After the trial, when you seemed to hate me so much that you barred the door to me, I thought all was really ended between us.'

'I didn't hate you, Hal—I couldn't.'

'You had good cause, even if you did not. I hated myself for hurting you like that, and knew if I remained in the town I would go on hurting you, even without meaning to. So, the next day, I went to St Albans to see the site of my house.'

'But was it not all burned down?'

'Yes.' He nodded, acknowledging the little ripple of sadness and then letting it go. 'But another had been rebuilt on the site, now the home of another family.'

'That must have been difficult.'

'For a moment, yes, it was. But it was necessary. And it helped me to do what I went there to do. To say goodbye, finally, to my parents, to Beatrice, to Will, to my home.'

'And…how do you feel about that, about them, now?'

'Healed. At peace. And forgiven at last—forgiven by them…and by me myself.' The fact that he could say it, albeit in a voice that trembled, told Hal it was true. 'I want a new home now, Isolda, and a new family, with you.'

The sunlight that slanted into the room turned the walls into a frenzy of colours—blues, greens, golds and, yes, even reds! But now that colour held no nightmares for him and he knew it never would—not if Isolda spoke the words he longed to hear.

'When I returned to Halton, and your poem was waiting me, I knew all was not lost after all, that you still loved me, despite everything. So I too have been waiting for the right moment.'

'The right moment for what?'

'To come and beg your forgiveness, tell you how much I love you, and ask you again to become my wife.' Hal's heart filled his throat but the words came out all the same. 'Will you, Isolda? Will you marry me?'

'Oh, Hal!' This time it was she who squeezed his hands, and so tightly he winced. 'My answer is yes! Yes, and yes, and yes, no matter how many times you ask me… though I hope you will only need to ask it once!'

Hal pulled her to him, kissing the top of her head where the sunlight caught her hair, then her brow, her eyelids, her nose and finally her mouth. She tasted like the honey cakes he'd eaten for breakfast that morning—hastily, as he'd wanted to be away to Ludlow as soon as possible.

But he wasn't in any haste now. He wanted this kiss to last for ever…until the day he would kiss her again before the altar in St Laurence's Church and make her his wife, finally and for ever.

In any event, it was Isolda who broke them apart, lifting her mouth from his and leaning away slightly so that she could look into his eyes. Hers were so beautiful and so full of life and of love that Hal knew himself—once the most wretched and cursed of men—to be the most fortunate and the most blessed.

'But you haven't told me yet if the Earl granted your request. Will you stay at Halton?'

Hal nodded. 'He did indeed. And Halton will be our home, sweeting, for the rest of our lives, and our children's too.'

'Was much of the house lost, Hal?'

'No, only the hall and two bedchambers above.' He touched her cheek. 'I am busy rebuilding and it will be complete before the spring.'

Isolda felt her eyes fill and his face blurred in front of her. In the air, dust motes danced as the sun cast long beams into the room. 'When I didn't open the door to you, and you went away, I thought you were gone for ever, and would never come back,' she said. 'That's why I wrote that poem, that very night.'

'You were very angry with me, weren't you, even if you didn't hate me?'

She nodded. 'I was angry that you forbade me to attend the trial. And you hurt me so much when you said what you said in the infirmary, though I understand it now. But at the time I thought you were just like Robert, and that my usefulness to you was all you wanted from me.'

'I'm sorry. If I could take that back, Isolda, I would. I will never hurt you like that again, ever.'

'I suppose I had convinced myself that when Robert left me it was only my pride that had suffered, but I realised my heart had suffered too. Not because I loved him but because I had betrayed myself, and when you dismissed me I felt that self-betrayal again, even more keenly than what I took for your betrayal.'

'We have both been so hurt and so shaped by what's happened to us in the past, Isolda. But not any longer. We have survived our sorrows, grown stronger, and yet more vulnerable too, and not afraid to show our hearts to each other, because of those experiences.'

'I believe that too, Hal. But do you understand why I needed to speak about the poems in the court? Why I needed to confess to them, to not let Jac's memory be dishonoured? To force the judge to absolve him as he deserved?'

'Yes, I do. I should have understood earlier, but I was so afraid for you, Isolda.' He reached out and touched her hair. 'The jury might not have been impartial, the judge might not have been so honest, and I couldn't take that risk.'

'I was even more furious when you stood up and tried to take the blame too!'

'Did you think I could have sat there and not done so?'

Isolda shook her head. 'No.' A giggle rose up inside her. 'I think we really tried Judge Watkyns's patience though!'

His smile was brighter even than the sunlight that dappled the walls. 'I should say so. The poor man is probably still ruing the day he came to sit on an inquiry in Ludlow.'

She leaned forward, wrapped her arms about his neck, gazed into his beautiful eyes. 'We won, Hal! Ludlow is free, there is no war, the people are happy and, God willing, this year will bring a good harvest and the farmers will prosper again.'

'And by harvest time we will be man and wife.'

Isolda nodded. 'The day cannot come soon enough for me.'

'Nor for me, sweeting.' Lifting a hand, he stroked his fingers down her cheek. 'I think that very first day I saw you I knew nothing could prevent our being together, not even me.'

'Nor me,' she replied. 'No matter how deep my mistrust and my stubborn resolve.' A thought struck her then, one that she needed to think about now she was to be wed! 'But what of my wool business?'

'You will do what you wish with that, my love.' He chuckled. 'Do you think I dare say you nay ever again?'

'I will train Dickon up so I don't have to spend every day…nor night…at work.' Isolda couldn't prevent a little smile of triumph. 'And now the rot has been cut out of it, I will apply to be a member of the Merchants' Guild, and let *them* dare to say me nay!'

'They would not be so brave, nor so foolhardy, my love!' Hal's arms went about her. 'And I will help in your shop too.' His voice sobered, just a little. 'After all, I am the son of a weaver.'

He touched his lips to hers just as the bell in the clock tower began to peal the hour of noon. Their kiss lasted all twelve strokes and when it finally fell silent they parted and were silent too for a moment.

'Do you think we'll hear that bell at Halton?' He was the first to speak. 'For I swear it is the loudest I've ever heard.'

Isolda nodded. 'We may well but I like the sound of bells, don't you?'

'I do...now.' Behind Hal's eyes, she saw that he thought, with sadness but only fleetingly, about the clock tower of St Albans. Then his gaze brightened and filled with love once more. A love for her as strong and as eternal as hers was for him, 'Especially wedding bells.'

* * * * *

*If you enjoyed this story,
be sure to read Lissa Morgan's
The Warriors of Wales duet*

The Warrior's Reluctant Wife
The Warrior's Forbidden Maiden

*And why not pick up
one of her other captivating reads?*

The Welsh Lord's Convenient Bride
An Alliance with His Enemy Princess

Harlequin Reader Service

Enjoyed your book?

Try the perfect subscription for Romance readers and get more great books like this delivered right to your door.

See why over 10+ million readers have tried Harlequin Reader Service.

Start with a Free Welcome Collection with free books and a gift—valued over $20.

Choose any series in print or ebook.
See website for details and order today:

TryReaderService.com/subscriptions